HONOR AMONG THIEVES

A Novel

By

WF Waldrip

WF Waldrip

Honor Among Thieves

WF Waldrip is an attorney, adventurer, and novelist. Since childhood Waldrip dreamed of writing stories that readers would enjoy. He is the author of *The Man With Two Last Names*, *The Guards Themselves, Honor Among Thieves* and *The Float.*

BOOKS BY WF WALDRIP

The Man with Two Last Names

The Float

Honor Among Thieves

The Guards Themselves

Honor Among Thieves

WF Waldrip

FIRST PHARAOH Paperback EDITION

APRIL 2019

Copyright © 2019 by WF Waldrip

All rights reserved. Published in the United States by Pharaoh LLC, Phoenix, Arizona.

The Cataloging-in-Publication Data is on file at Library of Congress.

ISBN: 978-0-9978434-6-0

For my friend, Maurice

Laws are like cobwebs, which may catch small flies,
but let wasps and hornets break through.

  Swift

ONE

Adolph Medina pushed open the glass doors; the refrigerated air of the interior immediately washed over him. He strode inside and stood near the cash register. Removing his tortoise-shell Ray Bans from his sweaty face and tucking them into a shirt pocket, Medina casually surveyed the interior of the busy coffee shop. Noting his arrival, a hostess with orange hair and a nose ring grabbed a laminated menu and began walking toward him; Medina shook his head and the hostess turned indifferently away. Medina could hear dishes rattling as the Mexican cooks jabbered in Spanish from the open kitchen in the front of the restaurant.

The place was packed. The booths were filled with squalling children chowing down on chicken fingers and French fries, beneficiaries of the restaurant's 'Kids Eat Free' policy. Most of the stools at the lunch counter were also occupied, at the far end by an emaciated, scruffy-looking guy wearing a tattered green T-shirt and pants two sizes too big cinched to his waist by a brown leather belt. Near him on the counter was a plate of half-eaten breakfast; he was slurping down a cup of coffee. A dozen torn sugar packets littered the immediate area. That's him.

Medina sauntered down the length of the counter until he stood directly behind the guy. He reached forward, wordlessly grasped the back of the man's head and, with one motion, slammed his face into the countertop. He then drew the bloody head back and slammed it down a second time.

The impact of the man's face striking the counter caused his silverware to bounce onto the tiled floor with a jingle. Medina released the back of his head and stepped away; the guy followed his silverware to the floor, unconscious. What had been his nose was flattened against his face, oozing globs of blood. Blood also streamed from his slack mouth; Medina figured the guy's front teeth were probably lodged in his throat.

Fellow diners at the lunch counter stared down its length in order to ascertain the source of the disturbance that caused their plates to jump and their coffee to slop over the rim of their coffee cups. They looked with a combination of surprise and mild curiosity at the body heaped on the diner floor. Just moments ago, the guy had been minding his own business, dumping multiple packets of sugar into his coffee. Nobody else in the place seemed to notice anything amiss.

Medina turned and walked from the coffee shop, unhurried. Until the orange-haired hostess called 911, it didn't occur to anyone to check on the welfare of the unconscious heap on the floor, although one little kid in an adjacent booth stood, peered over the padded edge of the booth and, his mouth forming a little "o," pointed wordlessly at the supine form lying in an expanding pool of blood.

***

City Manager Earl Welch felt like puking. He knew exactly what happened to Jerry Dawson...maybe not the exact details but, then again, he didn't really *want* to know the exact details. He knew enough to know that Dawson, and maybe others, had been deliberately killed. Although Welch valued, and profited from his association with Sunstone, he had no interest in the sordid aspects of how Sunstone operated. Legally, it was called 'willful ignorance.'

It was all Rosedea's fault. If Rosey hadn't called him and demanded to meet him at lunch, he'd never have been sucked into the whole fucking mess. Ever since then, things had gone from bad to worse. Rosey and Chief Golden bullied him into going along with everything, even though he was opposed to it from the beginning. He wasn't like Rosey or Golden, who were cut from the same cloth; both of them, and much of the Phoenix Police Department, were basically thugs. He wished he'd never got mixed up in the whole ugly business. He was better than that.

Welch hoped he could assuage his conscience by unburdening himself. After all, he'd done nothing wrong...it was all Rosedea's and Golden's idea. He'd vociferously opposed the whole harebrained scheme from the get-go. But even though he'd washed his hands of it, people had gotten hurt. It was now time to put an end to it. He was willing to admit that he may have bent a few laws here and there along the way during his association with Sunstone, but nothing like Golden and some others. His sins were nothing compared to theirs.

As city manager, Welch was entitled to a city vehicle, where he now sat idling as cold air from the refrigeration blasted over him. The digital thermometer on the dashboard told him that the outside temperature was 116 degrees, but he was perfectly comfortable. On the seat beside him was a burner cell phone that he'd purchased earlier that afternoon from one of those independent cell phone stores that had sprung up all over town in the last couple of years. He'd seen the store while driving and impulsively pulled in and purchased the burner for cash. If he called the attorney general's office and left an anonymous tip, he didn't want to risk their tracing the call. Welch picked up the cell phone, took a deep breath, and began to tap out the number.

***

Jim sat in a booth in the empty restaurant, staring at nothing. He wearily looked up when the front door opened and two white guys wearing Dockers and white shirts with narrow ties strode in. Cops. The first customers he'd had in days.

The duo headed for a booth near the front window and sat. Jim resumed staring at nothing.

"Excuse me," one of them finally said, looking directly at him.

With a sigh, Jim stood and hobbled across the room to their booth, where he looked vacantly at the one who'd spoken.

"Are you Mister Thompson?"

"You know'd who I was before you sat down," Jim tiredly responded.

"Are you open?"

"The front door's unlocked, so I guess I'm open."

"I'm Inspector Pruitt and this is Inspector Saturday," the cop said, indicating his partner. "We're from Phoenix Police Internal Investigations."

"I know what you are. The police already been here and talked to me. What do you two want?"

"You already talked to officers from Internal Investigations?" Pruitt was unable to conceal his surprise.

"I didn't say I talked to any 'officers,'" Jim sighed. "I said I already talked to the police." He wasn't entirely surprised to see the two representatives from IA. Since the shooting, Jim let it be known on the streets his suspicion that Jerry's death had been orchestrated. Because the downtown crawled with police informants, Jim had little doubt that his accusation would ultimately make its way to the Phoenix Police Department.

"I see," Pruitt responded, though he really didn't. "We'd like to ask you a few more questions, if that's okay."

"It ain't okay," said Jim. He turned away.

"We understand you were friends with Jerry Dawson and were with him when he was shot by one of our officers," Saturday grunted.

"This is a restaurant, not a quiz show. Are you guys gonna eat, or not? If not, I got work to do." Jim headed toward the kitchen.

"Wait." Pruitt reached out and touched Jim's arm. Jim paused. "We want to clear the air as much as you do."

Jim faced Pruitt. "They'd be no air to clear if you hadn't killed Jerry."

Pruitt turned to Saturday. "What are you eating?" Saturday shrugged. "Two cheese burgers, lots of onions, and two Diet Cokes," Pruit decided.

"What kinda cheese you got?" Saturday interjected, obviously bored.

"Whatever kind comes on your burger," Jim retorted, as he turned away. "This ain't no damned Denny's." He slowly limped to the kitchen to prepare their orders.

In the weeks since Jerry's death, he'd felt like dying, too. The local paper contained a single article on the incident a few days afterward and he'd been briefly interviewed by the police. Once. Beyond that, nothing. No subsequent revelations, no explanation, no additional news stories. Nothing. Jim couldn't bring himself to attend Jerry's funeral. It was simply too sad. He closed the restaurant and sat in the dark, alone, that entire day. He didn't even know where Jerry was buried.

Jim attempted to call the hotel where Jerry and Carol had been staying but, of course, she'd already checked out and the new occupant had no idea what Jim was talking about. He'd not talked to Carol since that day and had no idea where she was. Not surprisingly, Alto Murphy had also disappeared and Jim suspected he'd never lay eyes on Alto again. Now there were two new cops in his dining room for God-only-knew-what-reason. Jim didn't even feel like serving them, but needed the modest income that even two cheese burgers would provide.

Jim assembled the burgers, placed them on plates, are carried them out to the dining room. As he slid the plates in front of the waiting men, Pruitt rubbed his hands together, exclaiming, "That's a good-looking burger." Saturday looked as though he was about to doze off.

"Don't patronize me," Jim told him. "It's just a burger. As soon as you two finish eatin', you can pay and be on your way." He shuffled to a cooler and removed two diet Pepsis. "I don't have Diet Coke," he said, placing the bottles before the two cops.

Pruitt gathered his burger up and took a bite. "Why were you at the train depot with Dawson?"

Jim sighed. "I already told the police."

"You didn't tell me."

"Ain't you the police?"

Pruitt replaced his burger on the plate and wiped his mouth. "Yeah, we're the police. But we're basically independent of the regular police."

"Yeah, I know," Jim sighed. "You're supposed to keep the police honest. Well, you might look for another line of work, 'cause you ain't too good at what you're supposed to be doin'."

"How's that?" Saturday abruptly roused himself from his seeming stupor. He stared at the plate that held his burger.

"Ain't you supposed to be protectin' people?"

"That's part of what we do," Pruitt acknowledged.

"Well, you didn't protect Jerry. You killed him."

Pruitt ignored the accusation. "You were there," he deflected. "Tell me what happened."

Jim dragged a battered chair over from a neighboring table and plopped wearily down.

"Alto said that a couple of cops wanted to meet Jerry about some murder. The cops said it was all a hoax, and were gonna tell Jerry everything about it."

"What murder?"

"I don't know ...just some guy in the paper that got killed."

"Georgio Rosedea?"

"Somethin' like that," Jim acknowledged.

"How was Dawson involved?"

Jim sighed. "He wasn't. Jerry didn't even know him."

"How do you know Jerry didn't know Rosedea?"

Jim shifted positions, wincing from the pain in his joints. "He told me."

"That's good enough for me," intoned Saturday as he drained his Pepsi. "Criminals never lie." He pushed the plate containing his uneaten burger away.

Jim glanced at Saturday. "Mister, ever'body lies. Even the police." He turned his gaze back to Pruitt. "Jerry wasn't no criminal."

"Why would police officers want to talk to Jerry about a murder he had nothing to do with? That doesn't even make sense. Besides, Phoenix PD's investigation established that Jerry *was* involved in the Rosedea murder."

"Yeah, why wouldn't Dawson just go to the police in the first place if he wasn't involved? Why the cloak-and-dagger bullshit?" added Saturday.

Jim leaned back in his chair. "Jerry didn't go to the police because the police gets paid to arrest people, guilty or not. Maybe, instead of talkin' to me, you should be talkin' to Alto Murphy. He's your Judas goat."

Pruitt shook his head. "No, he's not."

Saturday looked evenly at Jim. "You're right, Dawson didn't go to the police because he knew he'd be arrested. He was shot because he was a murder suspect who tried to run one of our officers down. Otherwise, we wouldn't be having this conversation. Why would Phoenix PD want to kill Dawson? He was a nobody."

Jim placed both hands on the table and leaned toward Saturday. "I told you, mister, ask Alto. And tell me something, why would a 'nobody' get involved with murderin' anybody? Jerry didn't even know the guy he was supposed to have killed."

"We checked out Murphy," interjected Pruitt. "He's got a criminal record, but not much of one. How's he involved?"

"Ask him," Jim responded. "He's the only one who knows."

Pruitt reached in his jacket pocket and removed a business card. "Please call me if you want to talk," he said, handing it to Jim.

***

"What's this about?" Ramses demanded. "Bickman and me already made statements to the review board." After all police shootings, the officers involved are automatically suspended with pay, pending a formal investigation of the circumstances. Ramses hated the pricks from IA and their bullshit make-work witch hunts.

"We just wanna confirm some information about the Dawson shooting," Pruitt replied. "We still need to clear up a coupla things.

"Confirm? What's to confirm? And why's IA involved?" Ramses, Pruitt, and Saturday were sitting in a fast food restaurant down the block from police headquarters. Ramses had ignored the several telephone messages Pruitt had left over the past two weeks, finally agreeing to talk with him only after Pruitt showed up, unannounced, at his office. Because Ramses didn't want a couple of assholes from IA hanging around, he told them he'd rendezvous with them at the restaurant. "If you want confirmation, talk to Bickman, Cope, and Hernandez."

Saturday removed a small cassette recorder from his jacket pocket, placed it on the table in front of Ramses, and clicked it on.

"What's that for?" Ramses frowned.

"Just routine," Saturday replied without expression. "Who else was at the depot when Dawson was killed?" he asked.

"I just told you, me and three uniforms."

"Nobody else?"

"Other than the suspect and the guy in the car with him, no."

"By 'suspect' you mean Dawson?" Pruitt asked.

"Yeah, Dawson."

"Who was the other guy in the car?"

Ramses shrugged. "I don't know, his friend. It's all in the report. Read it if you're so interested."

"We did," said Saturday. He paused. "Was Alto Murphy there, too?"

"Who?"

"Alto Murphy."

"Who's he?"

"We were hoping you'd tell us."

"Don't know the man," Ramses grunted.

Pruitt leaned back in his seat. "Hmmmmm, that's funny. We read some of your old reports on unrelated cases and a number of them identified 'Alto Murphy' as your confidential informant."

Silence. Ramses could feel Pruitt's and Saturday's gaze bore into him as the spindle on the cassette recorder slowly rotated.

"Oh, you mean *Alto*," he finally responded, lamely. "Yeah, Alto tipped me off that Dawson was gonna be at the depot. I didn't think of it until just now." Ramses paused. "What's Murphy got to do with anything? He don't know squat."

"That's not what we heard." Saturday remarked.

Ramses forced a laugh. "Alto couldn't find his ass with both hands."

"How'd he know that Dawson would be at the depot?" Pruitt asked.

"Alto's an informant. If you IA guys ever got off your butts and onto the streets, you'd know that's why they call 'em 'informants': they have *information*. I don't know where they get their information and don't care. If ya wanna know, ask Alto."

"We intend to."

"Did you have any history with Dawson before the shooting?" Saturday abruptly changed the subject.

"History? You mean did I know him? No, I didn't have any 'history' with Dawson," Ramses scornfully replied. "All I knew about Dawson was that he was a piece of shit with a long rap sheet who was suspected in the Rosedea murder and tried to run one of our guys down."

"That's something else." Pruitt scratched his head as if perplexed. "Dawson's record. We checked NCIC and Dawson's file goes clear back to the '90's. Like you said, Dawson was into some bad shit. But here's the weird part. We had IT look at the entries and they determined that all of them were entered into the system within the past seven or eight months. They were backdated," he concluded, looking directly at Ramses.

Ramses frowned. "You don't say," he mused. "Who'd do that?"

"I don't know," Pruitt responded. "Weird, huh?"

"I don't know much about computers," Ramses said, with a dismissive wave of his hand. "I don't know how they can tell when stuff was entered."

"I hear ya," Pruitt said. "That's just what the IT guys said. But who really knows, right?"

Ramses glanced at his watch. "On second thought, I'm not sure I want you guys compromising my snitch. If he heads down a rabbit hole because he thinks you're hassling him, I'll never find him again."

Pruitt stood, walked to the soft drink dispenser, and refilled his Diet Coke while Saturday looked at Ramses without expression. Returning to their table, Pruitt slid into his seat. "It doesn't matter what you want," he said, matter-of-factly.

Ramses shrugged. "Well, I haven't seen Murphy in weeks. I don't even know if he's still around."

Saturday drained his Coke, then reached forward and clicked the cassette recorder off. "You might want to find him before we do," he said as he replaced it in his pocket.

***

Ramses flashed his badge at the nurse's station. "Room 314," he grunted.   The nurse staring at a computer monitor, annoyed by the intrusion, wordlessly pointed to the right without looking up.

Ramses received Alto's call on his cell phone two days previously though, at first, he didn't recognize Alto's voice. "You sound like a shit salesman with a mouth full of samples," Ramses said. "What the fuck's wrong with you?"

"I got beat up," mumbled Alto over the phone.

"Gee, what a surprise. Who'd wanna beat you up, Alto?"

"Don't be a dick, Ramses. I can't hardly talk and it hurts like hell."

"Where are you?"

"County hospital. I been here a coupla days while they wire my jaw." Because Alto never carried any ID, the ambulance that retrieved him from the coffee shop automatically carted him to the county hospital, the repository for all homeless people needing medical attention. "It hurts like fuck. I can't even eat."

"So, who'd you piss off this time, Alto?"

"I never saw the guy! Wait a minute while I wipe the slobber...I can't talk without drooling all over myself." Ramses heard Alto drop the receiver onto the bed, then a protracted rustling sound. A moment later Alto returned to the phone. "I was sittin' in Denny's, drinking coffee, when outta nowhere some bastard come up and wallops me. Smashes my fuckin' face into the counter."

"You don't know who did it?"

"Shit, no. Like I said, I'm sittin', mindin' my own business and the next thing I know I'm layin' on the fuckin' floor, bleedin' like a stuck pig."

"What's all this got to do with me? Sounds to me like somebody who doesn't like you very much was just sayin' hello."

"For what? I ain't even talked to nobody since the Dawson thing went down. Been like a fuckin' hermit."

Ramses strode down the hall. A trembling old man with a walker and a physical therapist holding onto him inched his way toward Ramses as he brushed past them to room 314.

The room was dark, illuminated only by the soft glow of the TV. Ramses entered and stepped around the curtain that half-surrounded the bed. Alto looked up.

"Hey," he croaked.

"Jesus, you look like death eating a cracker," Ramses said as he dragged a chair from a corner of the room and plopped down.

Both of Alto's eyes looked like black holes in his face and a large white bandage covered the bridge of his nose. When he spoke, Alto's jaw remained stationary, only his lips moving.

"Believe me, it feels worse than it looks," he said. "They got me on pain pills, Vicodin, but they don't work worth a shit. I can't eat, I can't sleep, and my whole face hurts like a motherfucker."

"Some IA guys have been poking around, asking about you," Ramses abruptly informed him.

"IA? What about me?"

"That's a good question, Alto," Ramses responded. "They're lookin' into the Dawson deal."

"What's to look into?" Alto drooled as he spoke. He wiped his unshaven chin on the damp hem of his sheet.

"Like I said, that's a good question. Who you been talkin' to, Alto?" Ramses leaned back in his chair, crossed his arms, and looked intently at the man in the bed.

Alto wiped his chin again. "I ain't said shit to nobody. You know me better than that."

"Did you give your name to the hospital when they admitted you?"

"I couldn't even talk, Ramses. So, no. Somebody from the hospital came in coupla days ago and I told 'em my name was Joe Smith, that I was homeless, and that somebody jumped me while I was sleepin'."

"How do you know they were from the hospital?"

Alto slurped the string of saliva that dangled from his swollen mouth. "They said so and was carryin' a clipboard."

"Man or woman?"

"Woman."

"You talk to anybody from Phoenix PD?"

"Not since I been in here." Alto looked skeptically at Ramses. "Hey, wait a minute...did you or your goons have anything to do with this?" He pointed to his face.

"Me? Why would I have anything to do with it?" Ramses stood. "It looks to me like somebody just wanted to send you a message. Maybe you better put on your thinking cap and figure out who that might be." He headed for the door. "How 'bout I bring you a big, juicy steak next time I stop by?"

"Fuck you, Ramses. Don't let the door hit you in the ass on the way out."

Ramses paused, his hand on the door frame. Turning to Alto, he said, "If anybody from Phoenix PD tracks you down, make like Sergeant Shultz: you don't see nuthin' and you don't know nuthin'." He furrowed his brow in thought. "In fact, it'd probably be a good idea to put you in a safe house for a day or two...you'll be harder to rough up if nobody knows where you are. Whoever it was may decide to finish the job next time."

Ramses' recent meeting with Pruitt and Saturday had spooked him. He needed to get Alto out of circulation until he could sort things out. If Alto was convinced he was on someone's shit list, Ramses knew he'd be more amenable to staying in a safe house.

"Call me when you're discharged," Rames ordered as he strode from the room.

TWO

The former Georgio Rosedea nursed an anemic bourbon and soda while he waited. He didn't like unfamiliar taverns, not least because they were typically light on the booze. The bars he patronized free-poured with a heavy hand. This place barely waved the cork over the class, then charged through the ass.

"Hey, bring me another drink, and put some booze in it this time," he barked to the bartender rinsing glasses at the other end of the bar.

Mexico was okay, but the language barrier finally got to him. And, although he hated to admit it, he'd grown somewhat homesick. Although his Mexican business enterprises had proved enormously profitable, Rosey finally became creeped out by the Japanese businessmen who constituted the bulk of his customers...they never looked him in the eye and their fastidiousness grated on him. He always felt like taking a shower after dealing with them. Thus, had he initiated contact with Chief Golden about returning to the fold.

"I don't know, Rosey," Golden deferred. "You pissed on a lotta campfires; I'm gonna have to call in some big-time favors to try to get you out of the dog house. There's still a lot of people who don't want you around...all that shit about your blowing the whistle has left a bad taste in a lot of mouths.

"What was I supposed to do, Golden?" Rosey plaintively responded. "I knock my brains out for everybody and get shipped off to Mexico for my trouble. 'Fuck you very much, Rosey'. Maybe I *did* say some stuff I shouldn't have...what would you have done in my shoes?"

"So, where's all the records?"

"I ain't got no records, just some odds and ends I kept around thinkin' I might need one day. Everything's in my head, Golden, and it ain't goin' nowhere."

After two months of such conciliatory telephone conversations, Chief Golden finally suggested that Rosey fly to Los Angeles to further discuss the matter with an emissary. Rosey dutifully complied and now found himself seated at an upscale bar on Los Feliz, not far from Griffith Park. As the bartender placed another drink in front of him, Rosey looked toward the door and saw Chief of Detectives Oren Ramses stride in. Ramses rapidly glanced around the mostly empty interior and spied the object of his rendezvous sitting at the bar.

"Long time no see," Ramses grunted as he approached Rosey. "Let's take that booth over there." He nodded his head toward the back of the room. Rosey grabbed his drink from the bar and followed Ramses. "So, what's your name these days?" he asked as they sat down.

"My passport says 'Adolph Medina,'" replied Rosey. "You guys made me a fuckin' Spik," he groused.

"You kinda look like a Spik," Ramses observed, "but I didn't have anything to do with it. Sunstone did all that."

"Well, I got two eyes, just like Spiks, if that's what you mean," Rosey scowled. "Otherwise, I don't see the fuckin' resemblance."

"It's nuthin' to me. I was just makin' conversation," Ramses indifferently responded. From behind the bar, the bartender looked expectantly at Ramses, who peremptorily shook his head. "Have any trouble getting through immigration?"

"Nope. Although I got a Mexican name, my passport's American. It worked like a champ," Rosey replied as he drained his glass. "As far as everybody knows, I'm Adolph Medina from the good old USA."

"Good, 'cause I've got a job for you, Adolph."

Rosey was taken aback. "A job? Golden didn't say nuthin' about a job. I thought we were here to talk about me comin' back." He paused as the bartender wordlessly arrived with another bourbon, which he deposited on the table in front of Rosey.

Ramses shrugged after the bartender's departure. "It's the price of admission. How bad ya wanna come back?"

"Bad enough, I guess. What's the job?"

"Nuthin' much. I just want you to deliver a message to a guy."

"What's the message?"

Ramses smiled thinly.   "That the world is a dangerous place, and that he should stick close to the people who can protect him."

"That's easy enough. Just like the good old days, huh? Where?"

"Phoenix."

"Done," Rosey smiled expansively.   "Consider it a good faith gesture on my part."

"I'll make sure the right people hear that you've found religion, Adolph," Ramses coolly responded.

"Yeah, you do that, Ramses. Make sure you tell Sunstone that I'm back in the saddle."

Ramses removed a twenty-dollar bill from his pocket and dropped it on the table before standing. "I don't know about that. Just call me when you get to Phoenix." Ramses headed for the door.

***

"What's with those two pricks from IA?" Ramses posed the question as he and Golden sat in the Chief's office.

"What about 'em?"

"They been hanging around, wantin' to talk to one of my snitches."

"About what?"

Ramses sighed. "The Dawson deal."

Golden leaned forward and fixed his gaze on Ramses.

"Tell me you're kidding, Oren. I thought Dawson was yesterday's news. Now you're telling me that IA is involved? How the hell did that happen?"

"I'm guessing they're just going through the motions," Ramses opined. "You know how IA works; they don't say nuthin' to nobody."

"It isn't unheard of for IA to look into departmental shootings," Golden acknowledged. He leaned back in his chair. "Due diligence before putting the whole thing to bed. Let's hope that's all it is." He paused and frowned at Ramses. "Unless somebody's been talkin' out of school. Your snitch maybe?"

Ramses shifted in his seat. "Maybe, but I don't think so. He'd have no reason to. Besides, IA told me they can't find him, so they obviously haven't talked to him."

"You may want to keep in mind Stalin's advice, 'Death is the solution to all problems. No man, no problem.'"

"There isn't a problem, Bob," Ramses testily responded. "Besides, my snitch is reliable and has been helpful in the past. I'll reel him in before IA has a chance to talk to him. "If they can't find him, they'll have no choice but to go bug somebody else."

Golden couldn't conceal his skepticism. "Yeah, maybe. Just so you know, Rosedea may be coming back. Use him if you have to."

"I thought he was dead!" Ramses snorted.

"Well, I'm putting you in charge of resurrecting him. Like I said, use him if you need to. I want this Dawson business put to bed, here and now. Don't give those IA pricks any excuse to keep hanging around."

***

Ramses pulled his unmarked Caprice into the loading zone and pushed the transmission lever into 'Park.' Because Alto wasn't expecting him, he would probably decamp the hospital out the main doors directly in front of him, rather than try to sneak out by using another exit. Flipping the car's air conditioner on full blast, he sat back in his seat to survey the stream of humanity that streamed through the sliding door.

After about twenty minutes of waiting, Ramses feared that Alto had somehow eluded him. He sighed, turned the ignition off, and swung open the Caprice's door, intending to check with somebody inside who might know what the hell happened to patient Joe Smith, who was supposed to be discharged today. A wave of scorching heat assaulted him as he slammed the car door and headed for the hospital entrance.

A nurse pushing a wheelchair occupied by an emaciated guy wearing sun glasses and a bandage over the bridge of his nose emerged as the glass doors slid open. Ramses immediately glided over.

"I'll take it from here," he smiled, gently nudging the nurse out of the way and grabbing the wheelchair handles.

"Great!" The nurse gladly yielded her shabby cargo to Ramses, who guided the wheelchair toward the Caprice.

"Christ o' mighty, Ramses," muttered Alto as Ramses pushed him along. "Can't I ever get away from you?" Alto sounded peculiar when he talked because of his missing front teeth, and he repeatedly thrust his tongue through the resulting gap, as if to confirm the teeth had not grown back.

"How'd you expect to get home, genius? Walk?"

"The nurse called a cab. In fact, that's probably it." Alto nodded toward a taxi gliding up to the entrance. The nurse had already disappeared into the cool interior of the hospital. He started to rise from the wheelchair.

Ramses clamped a hand on Alto's bony shoulder and roughly shoved him down. "Not so fast." They drew up to the Caprice. "No sense paying a cab when I'm here to help you for free. Your tax dollars at work."

Not finding his fare waiting as expected, the driver left his cab idling while he went inside the hospital to make enquiries. Emerging from the building, he got into his cab and pulled away from the curb, riderless. Alto wistfully watched the taxi depart as Ramses unlocked and opened the passenger door.

"Get in," he ordered.

Grimacing, Alto rose unsteadily to his feet and stepped into the Caprice. Ramses shoved the wheelchair away, walked to the driver's side, and slid in.

"How'd you know when I was getting' out?"

"Believe it or not, there's such a thing as a telephone," said Ramses as he cranked the engine and flipped on the air conditioner. "I thought you were gonna call me when you were discharged." He depressed the accelerator and pulled from the loading zone.

"Oh yeah, I musta forgot," replied Alto. "Where we goin'?" he asked, apprehensively.

"I told you. I'm taking you to a safe house before whoever beat you up can finish the job."

"I don't wanna go to a safe house. I wanna go to my house."

"Good thinking, Alto. Here, lemme pull over so you can hike home." Ramses steered the Caprice to the curb and stopped. He leaned back in the seat and looked at Alto. "But if the guy who roughed you up knows where you eat, don't you figure he knows where you live, too? What's to keep him from goin' over to the Deuce to finish the job?"

"Since when do you care what happens to me? Why the sudden concern?"

Ramses smiled coldly. "I don't give a crap what happens to you. I'm just lookin' to protect my snitch. I figured that, with you tucked away in a safe house, I could poke around to see who has a hard-on for you. But, if you don't wanna take me up on my hospitality," Ramses punched the button on his armrest to unlock Alto's door, "that's fine with me." He looked expectantly at Alto.

Alto was silent for a moment. "Well, I guess crashin' at a safe house 'till I get back on my feet wouldn't hurt," he finally said. "Where's it at?"

"Not far, just up the road." Ramses cranked the Caprice away from the curb, accelerated from the hospital parking lot, and headed north.

***

The safe house was a deteriorating single-story building with four individual apartments, built in the late 1950's, near 27th Avenue and Indian School Road. Ramses wheeled into the trash-strewn parking lot. Tall weeds grew through cracks in the asphalt.

Alto immediately saw that heavy wire mesh covered the windows of each unit.

"Hey, what's with the windows?" he asked, warily.

Ramses pulled in front of an end unit and slipped the car into 'Park.' "This is a shitty neighborhood. Remember, this is a *safe* house. The windows are like that to keep you safe." He switched the engine off and unlocked the Caprice's doors. "Come on."

Ramses exited the car, strode to the steel front door of the apartment, and slipped a key into its deadbolt. Alto hobbled after him. The deadbolt snapped open and Ramses stood aside as Alto lurched inside the apartment.

"There's food in the cupboard," Ramses said, pointing to a tiny kitchen. Alto stood in the middle of the room, peering around.

"It's hot as fuck in here," he announced.

Ramses walked to a thermostat on the wall and flipped it on. "Nobody's been in here for a while," he said. "I guess everybody but you must feel safe." He pushed the front door shut with his foot. Alto noticed there was no interior knob, only a round steel plated welded to the inside of the door where the knob should have been.

"How long do I hafta be here?"

"You don't hafta be here at all, Alto," Ramses replied. "Like I said, you can go back to the Deuce right now if you want to. Just say the word. Just don't come bawlin' to me when that prick shows up again and decides to finish educating you."

Alto sighed then shuffled over to a threadbare couch and flopped down. "Is there cable, at least?"

"All the comforts of home." Ramses gestured to the remote control of the clunky television sitting on a table along the opposite wall. "Gimme your cell phone," he ordered.

"What for?"

"They have GPS in 'em and we don't want the guy finding this place."

Alto looked at Ramses skeptically. "Yeah, right. I ain't got a cell phone, anyway."

"No problem. If you need to get hold of me, use this." Ramses reached into his shirt pocket and removed a beeper. "You can leave a message."

"Fuck, they still have those things? There's no phone in this dump?"

"No, but I'll get your message when you beep me." Alto took the beeper from Ramses' outstretched hand. Ramses turned to the door. "I'll be back in a day or two. Remember, beep me if you need anything." Then he was gone.

Alto heard the deadbolt thrust home, Ramses' retreating footsteps, the slam of a car door, then the crunch of gravel as the Caprice pulled from the parking lot. After a moment, he stood and walked to the front window of the apartment, where he pulled the curtain aside and looked out. Between the accumulated filth on the glass and the wire grate, he could scarcely see anything. But he couldn't leave even if he wanted to. There wasn't even a door knob.

THREE

Jim looked up from his newspaper when the front door opened. Carol was framed in the doorway.

"Oh, my God," he blurted.

Carol walked to the old man and sat beside him in the booth. Wordlessly, she placed her arm around Jim's shoulders and pulled him close as his body wracked with sobs.

"Oh, Carol, I wondered where'd you went. I didn't know how to contact you. I'm so happy to see you. I'm so sorry, so sorry..." The words tumbled helter-skelter from Jim's lips.

"I know, I know," she softly cooed as she stroked the old man's face. "It's okay," she whispered.

Carol held Jim and gently rocked him as he cried. "I was afraid you'd never come here again. I'm so sorry."

"It wasn't your fault, Jim. Don't blame yourself. You loved Jerry and Jerry loved you. He knew you'd never do anything to hurt him...he knows it now."

Jim lifted his ancient head from Carol's shoulder. "I didn't know what to do, Carol. I just wanted to help Jerry," he said, imploringly.

"I know that, Jim, and so did Jerry. None of us knew what to do." She began crying. "It just didn't work out like we'd hoped, and now Jerry's gone."

"I'm so sorry, so sorry. I wished it was me instead of Jerry. I'm just an old man with nuthin' to live for anymore, but I guess the Lord already got too many old men and don't want any more."

Carol smiled and, using a napkin on the table, blotted her tears. "Well, I'm thinking the Lord must have other plans for you here, Jim. He couldn't spare you right now."

"Carol, I ain't never intentionally done a violent thing in my life but, if the Lord hisself was here right now, I'd tell Him to his face that, if I knew who was behind killin' Jerry, I swear I'd do the same to them. I don't care if I went to hell for it; I'd do it."

"I know you would, Jim, and I'd help you. We'd both be in hell, selling ice water," Carol smiled ruefully.

"Are you hungry, Carol?" Jim abruptly asked. "Lemme make you somethin'. You're as poor as a snake. I'll bet you ain't eaten nuthin' since Jerry's passin'."

"I actually am kinda hungry," Carol admitted. "I wasn't until I got here, but am now."

"That's a good sign," asserted Jim as he slid from the booth. "You sit right there and don't move. I'll be right back." Jim felt as though a tremendous weight had just been lifted from his shoulders as he headed for the kitchen.

He returned to the dining room a few minutes later, carrying a plate with a sandwich sliced in half and a pitcher of iced tea. "Here ya go, Carol. I hope you like egg salad."

"It's my favorite," smiled Carol as Jim set the plate before her. "But I can't eat it all; you're gonna have to split it with me."

"I reckon I'm about the only guy in town who ain't afraid to eat his own cookin'," Jim chuckled as he filled two glasses with tea and sat down. He grasped Carol's hand. "You been doin' okay?"

Tears welled in Carol's eyes. "Not really. I still can't believe what happened, Jim. I can't believe Jerry's not here anymore."

"Are you workin' again?"

Carol blew her nose on a napkin, then nibbled a bit of sandwich. "I went back to work last week, but still can't concentrate on anything."

"Two cops was in here the other day, askin' about Jerry."

"Can't they leave us alone?" Carol burst out, sobbing.

Jim reached over, placed his arm around Carol's shoulders, and pulled her to him. "It's okay, it's okay," he murmured as she wept.

"There's gotta be something we can do, Jim. Something..." she said, plaintively.

"Well, for right now, about all we can do is eat this sandwich before it dries out," Jim said, gently. "I'm startin' to think you don't like my cookin', Carol."

She wiped her nose, then sat upright, straightening herself out. "You know better than that," she said, almost apologetically.

Jim took a bite of his sandwich. "Do you want me to talk to them police that was in here? I think they're different from the main police...one of 'em, anyway," he said, referring to Pruitt.

"About what, Jim? The police killed Jerry."

"I know, Carol, but what else can we do besides sit here and wring our hands? Jerry would want us to do something."

A slight frown crossed Carol's brow. "What about the attorney general? He's all over TV and seems like a go-getter. Do you think he'd do anything?"

"I sure don't know, but somebody's gotta be able to do something. Murderin' innocent people is what they do in Russia, not here. We just gotta find the right people to talk to, Carol.

***

"Those guys from IA buttonholed me." The chief sipped coffee in the police cafeteria and watched Ramses over the rim of his cup. "They wanted to talk about you, Oren."

"Me? I already talked to them." Ramses feigned nonchalance.

"Yeah, that's what they said. They also said that your memory wasn't too good."

Ramses scowled. "Big fuckin' deal. They asked me about my snitch and I told 'em what I remembered. Hey, I'm human, right? Besides, what difference does it make?" He smiled lamely.

Golden set his empty cup on the table. "Your snitch is becoming problematical. Where is he at this moment, Oren? Do you even know?"

Ramses smiled craftily. "I got him locked away like Rapunzel. He's incommunicado."

The chief leaned forward and lowered his voice. "Sunstone's tired of this whole fucking thing, Oren, so here's how it's gonna work. We're gonna do things one step at a time. "

Ramses looked at Golden without expression, almost dumbly.

"First, you're gonna take care of your snitch. I don't want him talkin' to anyone, especially those guys from IA. Do we understand one another, Oren?"

Ramses remained stoical. Golden ignored him and continued. "Use Rosedea, or whatever he calls himself these days. He's accustomed to dealing with shit like this. Put him on it and do it now. I want your snitch completely out of the picture. After that, we'll deal with the rest of it, including IA." The chief stood. Looking down at Ramses, he continued, "I want to hear from you by the end of the week."

Two plainclothes officers drifted over to their table and, after acknowledging the chief of detectives, engaged Chief Golden in animated conversation. Ramses got to his feet and wordlessly departed the cafeteria.

***

Pruitt and Saturday returned to Jim's. Pruitt held two fingers aloft. "Two burgers," he said as they slid into a booth.

Jim carried a basket of condiments to their table before turning toward the kitchen. "Why are you back?" he asked.

"We like the food," responded Saturday, dryly.

"I told you the police lie," Jim said. "You seem determined to prove it."

"We're here to see whether Alto Murphy happened by," interjected Pruitt. "We're having a hard time locating him."

"Why would he come here? Alto ain't welcome."

"Why?"

"Because he was part of killin' my friend."

"How's that?" Saturday couldn't mask his skepticism.

"Alto told Jerry that two police was out to get him. We was supposed to meet when you shot Jerry, so I guess Alto was right."

"We didn't shoot anybody," Pruitt corrected him. "That aside, why would anybody from the police department want to kill your friend? That doesn't even make sense."

Saturday concurred. "Like I told you when we came here the first time, Dawson was a nobody. Nobody from Phoenix PD, or anywhere else, even knew he existed."

"Then why are you back?" Jim looked intently at Saturday. "You two are interested in Jerry, even if nobody else is."

Pruitt steered the conversation in another direction. "Did Alto say who the two officers supposedly were, or why they had it in for Jerry?"

Jim shook his head. "Jerry never found out. That's why we was meetin' Alto." He paused. "But I know there's bad apples in the police department."

"There's bad apples everywhere. Welcome to reality," Saturday retorted. "The bad apples keep us in business."

Jim thoughtfully rubbed his chin. "Yep, I reckon that's true. If there wasn't bad apples in the police department, you two wouldn't have no job." He looked directly at Pruitt. "But I know a bad apple."

"Alto, you mean?"

Jim shook his head. "Alto's a bad apple, but I mean somebody in the police department."

"What makes you think he's bad?" Saturday skeptically asked.

"Because he hurt somebody I know."

"That makes 'em bad? What was your friend doin' that a cop hurt him?" Saturday couldn't conceal his disdain.

"*She* wasn't doing anything." Jim angrily retorted.

Pruitt leaned forward in his seat. "Wait," he softly interjected. "Did this have anything do to with Jerry?"

Tears pooled in the old man's eyes. "Yeah. A policeman hurt me and Jerry's friend," he murmured.

"What happened?" Pruitt asked.

"He raped her." Jim slumped into the unoccupied booth across from Pruitt and started crying.

"Bullshit," Saturday snorted.

"You can say whatever you want, mister, but I think you're bullshit," Jim wearily responded. "Why don't you two get out of my restaurant now?" He wiped his eyes on a napkin, then stood and looked at them expectantly.

"Wait a minute." Pruitt placed a hand on Jim's sleeve. "My partner's just a little cynical. We hear bad stuff about cops all the time just because people are angry. But if what you say is true, we want to hear about it."

Jim looked directly at Saturday. "Do I look angry to you?"

"Tell me about your friend," Pruitt interjected.

Jim turned his gaze back to Pruitt. "A policeman who said he was workin' on Jerry's case raped her."

"Who is she? Why would a cop want to rape her?" demanded Saturday.

"Ask him. Ain't that your job?" Jim directed his reply specifically at Saturday.

"Does she know his name? His badge number? His department?"

"I don't think she knows none of them things," Jim sighed.

"Would she recognize him if she saw him again?" Pruitt asked.

"I don't know," Jim replied. "But she don't ever want to see him again."

"Will she talk to us?" Pruitt persisted.

"She's not too keen on the police anymore."

"So why are you telling us all this, then?" Saturday blurted. "You apparently don't want to identify this mystery person who claims to have been raped by a police officer, and she won't meet with us. What's the point?"

Jim met Saturday's gaze. "If you two are serious about the bad apples, she might look at some pictures."

"Lemme get this straight," Saturday caustically responded. "You want us to bring you a bunch of random pictures of police officers, so your phantom friend can pick through them to find the picture of the cop that she claims raped her? Did I get that right? Not a problem." He turned to Pruitt. "How many sworn police officers do you suppose there are in Arizona? Three thousand? Four thousand? More?"

"It don't matter how many police there are in Arizona.   You two been in my place twice now, askin' questions 'bout Alto Murphy, so it seems to me that you already got your eye on a bad apple or two," Jim asserted. "And if that apple had anything to do with Alto we probably lookin' at the same apple."

Saturday looked disgusted, but Pruitt leaned back in his seat as he pondered Jim's words. "Tell ya what," he finally said. "We'll bring you some photos to show to your friend." Saturday shook his head in disbelief.

"Fair enough. If you do that, I'll show 'em to her. Not promisin' anything though."

"I don't expect you to," affirmed Pruitt. "We'll just play it by ear. All we expect for now is two burgers."

***

Alto stood on the rim of the toilet, slid the tiny bathroom window open, and peered out into the blinding afternoon sun. The bathroom window was the only one in the safe house that lacked a wire grille, but was far too small to permit ingress or egress of a human body.

An alley overgrown with weeds and bordered by a chain-link fence ran parallel to the rear of the apartment complex. Twenty yards from Alto's bathroom window a bum had erected a makeshift shelter by stretching an old blanket between the fence, an adjacent telephone pole, and an abandoned shopping cart, creating a semblance of shade. Within the resulting oasis Alto could see piles of trash and what appeared to be a sleeping human form.

"Hey, buddy!" Alto yelled. The form didn't stir. "Hey! Hey! Over here!"

The figure slowly sat up and looked around. "Hey, man! Over here!" Alto hollered with increasing fervor.

The human slowly turned toward the apartment complex and stared at it dumbly. Alto thrust a scrawny arm out the bathroom window and waved it around. "Here!" The figure didn't budge, but simply sat and stared.

Ramses hadn't returned to the safe house since depositing Alto five days previously. Alto hadn't beeped him, either. What would be the point? He was sick of eating soup, canned tamales, and stale Pop Tarts, which comprised the only food in the cupboards. No cars had entered the parking lot and the building was dark and quiet at night, so Alto suspected he was the sole occupant of the complex. And, despite Ramses' assurances, the place didn't even have cable TV...just local channels, half of which were in Spanish. Alto concluded that, irrespective of the program, everybody on Spanish-language TV talked too loud and a recurring motif invariably involved a big-titted model with lots of cleavage and a clown. He'd finally had enough "safety." He had to get out of here.

"Hey, dude, come over here," Alto called to the homeless man, beckoning with his outstretched arm.

The figure slowly rose to its feet and stumbled toward the tiny window with the flailing, disembodied arm. He stood beneath it, mouth agape. Alto's face was framed in the bathroom window with the guy's face only about six feet away.

"Hey, man," Alto called. "I'm trapped in here." The homeless man didn't blink. He just stared. "Will ya get me out?"

"What are you doing in there?" The guy finally asked in a thin, reedy voice. He was skinny and dirty and had a patchy beard. His teeth were brown.

"I'm trapped. I lost my key and can't get out," Alto responded.

"Out?" It was clear the homeless man didn't understand.

Alto was becoming impatient. "Yeah, I need to get out. I'm stuck in here."

The guy looked perplexed.   "You're stuck in the window?"

"No, goddammit! I'm stuck inside this apartment! I need to get out!"

"How?" He asked, uncomprehendingly.

"Go around to the front and see if you can open the front door," Alto ordered him.

The guy shrugged and began shambling around the corner of the complex, toward the front.   Alto jumped off the toilet and hastened to the front door. "Hey! Can you hear me?" He shouted through the steel door. He pounded on the door.

"Yeah, I hear you," the homeless man responded after a few moments. "You in there?"

"Fuck yes I'm in here," Alto hollered.   "Can you open the door?" Alto could hear the guy fiddling with the exterior knob.

"Hey, it's locked," he announced.

"I know it's locked," Alto yelled.   "If it wasn't locked, I wouldn't be in here!"

"What?"

"Can you open the fucking door?" Alto screamed.

"The door's locked," the guy said again.

"Can you break it down?" Alto shouted through the door.

"Wait a minute...lemme see," said the homeless man. Alto could hear him feebly pushing against the door. "No," he said after fifteen seconds of struggling. "It's locked."

"Go back to the window!" Alto bellowed in exasperation. He returned to the bathroom and clambered onto the toilet. Seconds later, the homeless man rounded the corner and approached the window.

"Now what do you want me to do?" he asked, looking up at Alto.

"Listen, I gotta friend who's a locksmith. Can you call him?"

"I ain't gotta phone," he affirmed.

"Use a pay phone. I'll pay ya back. Wait here." Alto stepped from the toilet, returned to the living room, and wrote the locksmith's number on a scrap of paper. Returning to the bathroom, he tossed the scrap to the homeless man. "Tell him that Alto needs him right away. Can you remember that?"

"Yeah, no problem." He glanced at the paper and began shuffling away.

"Don't forget, okay? And hurry it up." The homeless guy didn't acknowledge Alto's command. Instead, he headed back to his camp, where he promptly flopped down and fell asleep.

***

"Jesus, it looks like the moon out here," marveled Rosey, looking around through his Ray-Bans. He and Ramses were sitting on the deck of a houseboat in the middle of Lake Pleasant. "I ain't never seen such desolation." He was referring to the terrain surrounding the lake: desert scrub and rocks scorched white by the unrelenting sun. "Who the fuck would come out here?" He mopped his brow with a cloth and took another sip of beer. "I can piss colder than this. Gimme another one." Rosey tossed his can of warm beer over the railing into the tepid water.

"Fishermen mostly," replied Ramses, handing Rosey a cold beer from the ice chest. "Water skiers, too."

"Why don't they just buy fish from the store, like normal people? Why come out here and sweat like fuckin' pigs?" Rosey rhetorically asked.

Ramses rented the houseboat for the day so he and Rosey could meet, away from downtown. Because it was mid-week, they appeared to be the only boat on the shimmering lake.

Rosey took a sip of his fresh beer. "Is this what the old lady owned?"

"I don't know if old lady Collier actually owned the lake itself," Ramses replied. "But it's all part of Linda Verde now."`

"Well, I'm glad I could do my part." Rosey held his can of beer aloft in a mock salute.

"Funny you should bring that up, Rosey, 'cause we got another job for you." Rosey looked at Ramses expectantly. "You know the guy you roughed up at Denny's a coupla weeks ago?"

"The dirt-bag lookin' one? Yeah, I remember. How's his face?"

Ramses laughed. "Not too good."

"So, what about him?"

"We need you to finish the job."

Rosey shrugged. "Okay. Where is he?"

"I got him tucked away in a safe house."

"How soon?"

Ramses drained his beer and flung the empty into the lake. "Yesterday."

"I can do that," Rosey acknowledged. "But I want off probation."

"Probation? What are you talkin' about?"

Rosey tossed his nearly full can of beer over the railing and held his hand out for another. "Fuckin' beer gets hot in about two seconds," he explained. He popped the tab on a new beer, leaned back, and said, "I thumped the guy like you wanted. Now you want me to finish him. I'm cool with that but, then, I wanna 'come outta the shadows,' like the Spiks say."

Ramses nodded. "I don't think anybody will have a problem with that. But, like the Spiks, you're still gonna have to be 'Adolph Medina.' Georgio Rosedea's dead, remember? Some prick murdered him."

"I never liked that guy, anyway," Rosey indifferently responded, gulping his beer before it grew warm.

FOUR

Carol was angry. "Why did you tell them about me? Who gave you permission?" They sat in the pizza parlor that she and Jerry previously frequented.

"Nobody, Carol. Nobody," Jim said, softly. "I didn't mean to hurt you. I only wanted what's best for Jerry and you." Tears welled up in his eyes. "I didn't tell 'em your name...I only told 'em that a policeman raped my friend. That's all, Carol."

"How will that help Jerry? What's that got to do with anything, Jim? Don't you know how embarrassing that is? How humiliating?" she sobbed.

Jim grasped her hand. "I'm sorry, Carol. It was the wrong thing for me to do. I didn't think..." His voice trailed off as Carol continued to cry. "I thought maybe there is good police, that they can't all be wicked."

Carol removed a napkin from the dispenser on the table and dabbed her eyes. "I don't know. I don't know anything anymore. It probably doesn't make any difference one way or the other. We're all just grist for the mill, Jim."

"They gave me some pictures," Jim tentatively volunteered.

"Pictures? Of what?"

"Bad police."

Pruitt and Saturday had returned to Jim's with a manila envelope containing the photos of ten unidentified officers, half in uniform, half in mufti. In fact, they were pictures of random Phoenix Police officers arbitrarily taken from their personnel files; none was under investigation by IA.

"Let's see if he fingers one of these virgins," Pruitt remarked to Saturday.

"What are you supposed to do with them?" Carol asked.

"I was hopin' you'd look at 'em, Carol."

"Why would I want to look at their stupid pictures?" Carol scoffed. "I've seen enough cops to last me a lifetime."

Jim grasped Carol's other hand in his own and look at her intently. "Will you look at them, just to cater to an old man? You don't even have to talk to the police...just look at the pictures, Carol. Maybe the two police who came by my place are good men. Maybe, just maybe, there's some justice in the world."

Carol looked at Jim silently, searching his lined face. Finally, she said, "If it's that important to you, Jim, I'll look at the pictures. Not for them. For you." She smiled wanly and squeezed his gnarled hand.

Jim, too, smiled, an expansive, genuine smile. "Thank you, Carol. If push came to shove, I was gonna try to bribe you with an egg salad sandwich."

Her smile broadened. "You owe me an egg salad sandwich."

**

Rosey proceeded slowly down the overgrown ally behind the safe house. He was driving an unmarked police cruiser that Ramses requisitioned from the police fleet. Although the sun dropped below the horizon an hour ago, it remained blistering hot and it remained light enough for Rosey to easily see. He eased the car past the improvised shelter of a homeless person, who stared at him sullenly. At the end of the ally, Rosey put the vehicle in 'Park' and surveyed the rear of the last apartment.

Like most small apartment complexes dating from the 1950's, this one was framed with two-by-fours interspersed with plywood, its roof comprised of tar paper and asphalt shingles. Flimsy wooden sheds attached to the exterior housed a gas hot water heater for each individual unit. Perfect.

A rap on the driver's window startled him. Rosey's head snapped around. Standing next to the car was the bum he'd driven past moments ago. He pushed a button and the window glided down.

"What the fuck do you want?" Rosey demanded.

"Got any change?" the guy mumbled.

"Yeah, lots of it, but not for you, shitbag. Fuck off." Rosey punched the button again and the window slid closed. Although their exchange had occupied the space of five seconds, the heat that rolled through the open car window was brutal.

Rosey stomped on the accelerator and shot away from the safe house. The bum had to leap away from the car to prevent it from running over his feet.

***

Jim spread the police officers' pictures on a table at the restaurant.   Carol nursed an iced tea as she examined them. After a few minutes, she said, "No, it wasn't any of them."

He was disappointed. "I know it's hard, Carol. Look again."

She sighed and once again directed her attention to the photos. "Nope."

"You sure?" Jim persisted.

"I'm sure."

Jim looked thoughtful for a moment. "Would you recognize him?"

Carol's face grew hard. "I'll never forget what that bastard looks like. I think your new buddies on the police department may be playing you, Jim."

"Maybe," Jim conceded. "But I still believe there's still some good people." He looked sadly at Carol. "Maybe it's just 'cause that's the way Lorraine wanted me to think. The whole police department can't be crooked, can it?"

Carol didn't answer.

***

It was 2:30 a.m. and, because of the absence of traffic, Bickman beat the fire engines to the scene. He could hear their sirens screaming in the distance as he turned down the street leading to the four-unit apartment complex.

It was an old structure, probably from the '50's or '60's and one entire end was already engulfed in flames. Back then, building codes were pretty lax and such modest apartment complexes were popular because they could be constructed in less than a month using cheap materials. Phoenix's mild climate rendered it unnecessary for contractors to pay much attention to the quality of their work; who cared if the walls weren't completely plumb or there was any insulation behind the clapboard walls? The hordes of people flooding into the Promised Land in the post-war years were delighted simply to find a cheap apartment to rent.

Bickman exited his car as a fire truck pulled into the parking lot. Fire fighters spilled from the first unit when a second fire truck lurched up.

As the fire crews scurried about unrolling hoses, one of them approached Bickman. "Anybody inside? The place looks more or less abandoned."

"I don't know; I just got here," Bickman replied.

"Well, if there were, they're probably toast. At least at that end." The fire fighter pointed to the end of the complex that was completely aflame. As he did so, the roof of the end unit collapsed with a roar and a shower of sparks. "These old apartments go up like tinder," he continued, "they didn't use any fireproofing and the roofs were tarred. Might as well live in a box of kindling." He wandered off as other fire fighters frantically attempted to breach the steel front doors of the remaining units, before the fire reached them, too.

A homeless man emerged from the darkness beyond the conflagration and stared silently at Bickman from twenty feet away. Bickman could see the fire reflected in his eyes. "Go away, man," Bickman told him.

"There was somebody in there."

Because of the surrounding tumult, Bickman wasn't sure he understood the man.

"What?"

"There was a dude in there. In there." The guy pointed toward the end unit, now roofless and obliterated by flame.

Bickman immediately raced toward the complex, but was driven back by the heat.

"Hey!" he shrieked to one of the fire fighters. "There's somebody in there!" He grabbed him and spun him toward the end apartment. "In there!" he shouted, pointing.

The fire fighter placed his mouth near Bickman's ear. "We can't get in there! It's too far gone! We've gotta try to save what's left of the building!" He pulled from Bickman's grasp to return to his crew. Bickman walked back to the bum, who stood unmoving, seemingly mesmerized by the spectacle.

"Hey, how do you know there was somebody in there?"

"I talked to him."

"When?"

"Coupla days ago. Maybe one." He looked blankly at Bickman. "I forget."

"How did you talk to him?"

The homeless man looked confused. "How? Like other people talk...we just talked."

"Where?"

"Out back, where I live."

"Show me."

The bum turned and began ambling toward the back of the complex, seeming oblivious to the clamor around him. Bickman followed. Half of the building was now a collapsed, smoldering ruin and the smell of wet, charred wood filled the air. Although two remaining units appeared to be largely intact, they were badly damaged by the combined effects of smoke and water and, despite their efforts, the firemen were unable to secure entry to them. The formidable steel doors and the wire cages covering their windows would not yield to their axes.

As they rounded the corner into the alley behind the structure, Bickman spotted the homeless guy's temporary shelter. "This is where you live?"

Even in the half-light, Bickman could see the guy grin. "Yeah, that's my place." Notwithstanding the fire that had raged only yards away, the guy's camp miraculously escaped damage.

"So, tell me again where you talked to the guy in the apartment."

"I was sleepin' and the guy yelled at me," the bum explained. "He was in there and said that he was locked in." He pointed to the heap of wet, smoking debris that had previously been an apartment.

"If he was locked inside, how did you manage to talk to him?"

"Through a window. I think it was the bathroom."

"And this was a coupla days ago?"

"Yeah, I think," the guy said. "Thereabouts."

"What did he look like?"

The homeless man shrugged. "I don't know. I only saw his face and arm."

"Well, was he young? Old? Thin? Fat? Black? White?"

"He was a white guy." The bum shrugged again. "I don't remember stuff too good," he concluded, vaguely.

Bickman stared at the pile of charred wood as a fire fighter approached them. "What's up back here?"

"This guy says that somebody was in this apartment," Bickman told him, pointing to the blackened ruins. He turned back to the bum. "Do you think he was in there?"

"I don't know...I didn't see him leave." He paused, then continued, almost apologetically. "But I sleep a lot and the door is on the other side. He may have, I guess, but I think maybe not...I heard somebody yellin' while the fire was goin' on."

"Yellin'?"

"Yeah, screamin' really. I think he was maybe trapped inside and tryin' to get out."

"Well, if there was somebody inside, he's dead," interjected the fireman. "The place went up like fireworks and we couldn't have gotten inside if we wanted to. All the doors are steel and the windows have grates on 'em. If somebody was in there, he couldn't have gotten out. We'll tape it off and send an investigator and the ME over when it gets light."

"Any idea what caused it?" Bickman asked.

"Not a clue. These old buildings weren't built to code and if they have gas water heaters on the outside, like this one, they're really vulnerable. Homeless people sometimes store stuff in the shed that houses the hot water tank, to keep it from getting stolen. They rat-hole the damnest shit in there: newspapers, old blankets, boxes of oily rags, bottles of booze, even cans of gas they use to light campfires. If they put stuff too close to the pilot light, poof!" The fire fighter flung both hands outward to mimic an explosion. "Who knows what kinda stuff this guy hoarded in there," he concluded, nodding toward the homeless guy.

"Well, let me know what you find," Bickman told him. "I just hope somebody wasn't inside."

"Will do," responded the fireman as he headed toward the corner of the complex. "I hope nobody was inside, too, but the fact is, the city's a lot better off without these firetraps."

Bickman turned to the homeless guy, who stood to one side, silently gazing at the charred ruin. "Did you store anything in or near these apartments? Something that might burn?"

"Hey, man, I didn't have nuthin' to do with this shit," the guy defensively responded. "I keep all my stuff over there." He indicated his camp.

"Relax," Bickman smiled. "I wasn't accusing you of anything. I'm just tryin' to figure out what might have caused the fire. Did you see anyone around here earlier tonight?"

The man nodded slowly. "There was a guy here earlier. I seen him here before, too."

"A guy? What was he doing?"

"I dunno. He got out of his car and put something in the shed where the hot water tank was. He didn't think anybody seen him, but I did."

"The hot water tank? Which apartment?"

The homeless guy pointed to the smoldering remnants of the end unit of the complex. "That one. "

"Could you see what he put there?"

"Not too good. It was kinda dark. Something in a box."

Bickman look thoughtful. "And you said you saw him before? When?"

"When he was here before," the man responded, as if the answer was obvious.

"When was that?" Bickman patiently asked.

The guy furrowed his brow. "Not too long, a day or two." He looked at vacantly at Bickman. "I can't remember stuff too good."

"Did you talk to him?"

"That time, yeah. Not tonight." He paused. "He was an asshole."

"How come?"

"I asked him for some change and he almost ran over me," he said matter-of-factly.

"Did he say anything?"

"He called me a 'shitbag,'" he replied without emotion.

"Remember what he looked like?"

"Mmm, middle-aged, not as tall as you, but heavier. He kinda looked Mexican."

"Do you remember what kind of car was he driving?"

"A white Caprice both times. Real plain. Kinda looked like an unmarked cop car." He looked intently at Bickman. "I wasn't always a bum. I usta be the service manager at Imperial Chevy," he proudly declared, referring to a venerable Chevrolet dealership on Camelback Road. "I always hated Caprices, though..." his voice trailed off.

"I don't guess you got the license plate," Bickman wistfully said, more to himself than to the homeless guy.

"Hell no! I didn't want him to run over me again."

Bickman pulled his wallet from his pocket, opened it, and withdrew a twenty-dollar bill. "Here, man. Go buy yourself a hamburger. Thanks for your help." He handed the money to the bum and turned to walk back to his patrol car.

"That's cool, brother. Anytime." The homeless man stuffed the bill into his tattered pants then wandered back to his improvised camp, eager for some shut-eye.

***

"My friend didn't recognize any of 'em," Jim informed Pruitt. He slid the manila envelope of photos across the table. Saturday feigned surprise.

"Do you think she'd be willing to look at some more photos?" Pruitt asked. "It would be a tremendous help."

"I can ask," Jim replied. "How many more?" The three were drinking coffee in Malcolm's.

"Just a few. It'll help eliminate some possibilities."

"You seen Alto Murphy?" Saturday abruptly grunted as Pruitt returned the photos to his briefcase.

Jim looked at him. "I told you before. Alto ain't welcome here. I don't expect to see him. You two seem to spend a lot of time drinkin' coffee and eatin' burgers, instead of findin' Alto. Tell ya what, gimme your salary and I'll find Alto. "

"Well, he's not been to his apartment for a couple of weeks," replied Pruitt. "Got any ideas where else he might be?"

Jim turned to Pruitt. "You know that bad apple we been talkin' about? I reckon he knows."

"Maybe, but we gotta find the right apple. That's where your friend comes in." He removed his wallet from his suit jacket and placed a ten-dollar bill on the table. "We'll bring you a few more photos."

Jim stood and gathered the men's cups. He turned toward the kitchen wordlessly as Pruitt and Saturday departed the restaurant, into the suffocating heat.

***

"That's the bastard," spat Carol, placing her finger on Ramses' photo.

"You sure?" Jim adjusted his glasses and hunched over the picture.

"Absolutely. That's him." The black-and-white picture before them on the table was a full-face shot of an unsmiling Ramses, taken from his official police file. Carol was sitting in the kitchen of the restaurant, having just finished eating a piece of chocolate cake that Jim baked that afternoon. Ramses' picture was fourth in a stack of photographs that Pruitt had dropped off two days previously.

Jim flipped the picture over and squinted at the back, hoping it would contain some identifying information. Nothing.

"He looks mean as snakes." Jim scrutinized the photo again. "I seed him, too," He said after a moment. "He was one of the police at Jerry's shooting...I think he was in charge." Jim carefully surveyed the remaining photographs in the bundle, then pulled out three pictures of uniformed officers: Bickman, Cope, and Hernandez. "These cops was there, too."

Carol stared at all four photos. "The only one I recognize is the first guy." She looked imploringly at Jim. "Who are they? Do you think Jerry knew any of them? Why would they want to kill him?"

Jim leaned back in his rickety chair and frowned. "Carol, I surely don't know. But I'm fixin' to find out."

FIVE

Ramses, Pruitt, and Saturday sat in Ramses' office on the fourth floor of the police department on Washington Street, across from the federal courthouse. It pissed Ramses off to meet them there, but Pruitt insisted.

"What have you heard from Alto Murphy?" Pruitt asked.

Ramses shook his head. "Nuthin'. You haven't found him yet? I'm thinkin' you two must've run him off...thanks for nuthin'." Ramses adopted a thoughtful expression. "On the other hand, Alto has a habit of dropping out of sight periodically."

"Actually, we think we *did* find him, though he wasn't too talkative," Saturday causally remarked.

"Oh yeah?" responded Ramses, apathetically. "Where'd he turn up?"

"We found him a week and a half ago in a burned-out apartment over off Indian School," said Saturday. "Fried."

"No kidding? How do you know it was Alto?"

Pruitt made a show of removing a small notebook from his jacket pocket and flipping through it. "According to the ME, it was a Caucasian male, five feet five to five feet eight, thirty-five to fifty-five years old, buck twenty-five to a buck fifty pounds." He closed the notebook, tucked it back into his pocket, and looked expectantly at Ramses.

"Yep, that's definitely Alto," Ramses concurred. "Along with about seventy-five percent of the Anglo population in the Phoenix metropolitan area. Have you confirmed that it isn't Martin Bormann? I heard they're still lookin' for him, too."

"You're a real funny guy," Pruitt said. "All the brothers in the joint will be laughing like crazy while they're corn-holing you."

"Screw you," was all Ramses could respond.

"According to the fire marshal, an accelerant was used to set the fire," Saturday added, unperturbed. "It started in an exterior shed, next to the hot water heater. Oh yeah, we also have a witness," he concluded, almost as an afterthought.

Ramses didn't take the bait. Rosey was far too careful for witnesses.

"What's all this got to do with me?" he asked Pruitt. "I don't know why you two were so hot to talk to Alto in the first place. Sounds like you're gonna have to take your ball and bat and go home now."

"The whole case is getting curiouser and curiouser," said Pruitt, ignoring Ramses' invitation. "For one thing, there doesn't appear to be a record owner of the apartment that Alto, or whoever it was, burned up in. We did a title search and came back empty. An apartment complex with no legal owner. Have you ever heard of such a thing?" he asked Ramses, rhetorically. Without pausing, he continued. "And get this, there was only one door to the apartment, and it didn't even have a knob on the inside! And all the windows were barred. According to the fire marshal, somebody locked the guy inside the apartment, then set it on fire, knowing that the poor sumbitch couldn't get out. Can you believe it?"

"If something happens it must be possible," Ramses shrugged. "But, like I said, what's this got to do with me?"

"Our witness said that the guy who probably set the fire was drivin' a white Chevrolet Caprice," Saturday informed him. "He said it looked like a police car."

"Yeah? So what?" Ramses shifted in his chair and gazed out the window, down onto Washington Street.

"We looked into it and discovered that you checked a white Caprice out of the police lot twice during the past three weeks. Both times corresponded to the dates when our witness said he saw an identical car in the vicinity of the apartment complex that was torched."

"What the fuck are you two fucks saying?" Ramses snapped. "Are you accusing me of arson, or murder, or both? Get the hell outta here." He rose to his feet and glared at the two IA officers. Neither of them budged.

"Relax, detective," Pruitt said, evenly. "We're just doing our job...nobody's accusing anybody of anything."

"Get the hell out of here," Ramses repeated. "Why don't you ladies try solving some actual crimes sometime, instead of harassing dedicated police officers?"

Pruitt sighed, then he and Saturday slowly stood.

"We'll see you around," he said as they headed for the door. "Call us if you hear anything from Alto."

"From what you two assholes just told me, the only way I'll hear from Alto is if I use a Ouija board."

Pruitt paused and turned toward Ramses. "Maybe, but you know what today is, right?"

"Wednesday," Ramses grunted.

"Anything Can Happen Day," smiled Pruitt on his way out the door.

Ramses realized he was shaking, though he hoped Pruitt and Saturday failed to notice. Snatching the phone from his desk, he hurriedly dialed Golden's extension. The chief wasn't in, so Ramses left a terse message. He didn't know whether to call the police union rep, the union lawyer, or somebody else. He was fed up with the IA's fishing trip and wanted them off his ass. Maybe the chief could help. He turned the overhead light off, then sat at his desk staring out the window at the traffic below. Thinking.

***

The interior of Katrina's was dark and cramped and stale. It had been a long time since Jim had been there. No one was behind the bar and the place appeared empty. Jim waited for his eyes to adjust to the dimness, then peered into the gloom for some sign of life.

"Hey, Jim, long time no see," floated a mellifluous voice from the void.

Jim squinted into the dim interior. "Katrina?"

"Big as life," responded the disembodied voice. "Don't be a stranger. C'mon in."

Jim stepped from the doorway into the unlit interior.   After about five steps, Katrina's bulk materialized; she was sitting in her customary booth at the back of the room.

"What brings you here?" she inquired.

Katrina appeared to be wearing the same yellowed slip she characteristically wore. Her hair was darker than Jim remembered though, in the darkness, it was hard to tell for certain.

"Jerry," he answered as he sat opposite her and placed on the table between them a manila envelope.

Katrina slowly shook her massive head. "That was a damned shame. Between you and me, I could take or leave the guy, but it's too bad he got waxed. Far as I knew, he was as straight as a string."

"That he was," Jim said, softly.

Katrina shifted slightly. "So, what's the late Jerry got to do with me?"

"A lot of police come in here, don't they?"

"Lotsa people come in here," Katrina suspiciously responded. "I don't ask their occupation."

Jim slid the manila envelope toward her. "Do you know them?"

Katrina glanced down at the envelope but didn't touch it. "I don't want to get involved," she said.

"You ain't involved. You're just looking at some pictures." Jim nudged the envelope a little closer.

"Why should I care? It ain't my problem and I don't want it to be my problem."

Jim leaned back and folded his arms. "You're right, Katrina, it ain't your problem. And I ain't gonna make it your problem." He paused. "Now I don't know whether you got a conscience or not, but all I want is for you to look at some pictures. Nuthin' more. Ain't nobody gonna get hurt by it."

Katrina sat motionless several seconds, contemplating, before extending a tentative, pudgy hand and pulling the envelope across the table.

"I suppose I could look," she acknowledged. "I'm pretty sure I won't know the guy...there's more cops in Phoenix than you can shake a stick at and only a few of 'em come in here."

Opening the envelope, Katrina removed four photographs. She flipped through them, surveying them in the dimness. After a minute, she said, "I don't know these guys," indicating Bickman, Cope, and Hernandez. "Him, I know." Katrina slid Ramses' picture back across the table to Jim, the flab on her arm jiggling.

Jim took the photo and held it up. "Who is he?"

Katrina was noncommittal. "Just a guy that comes in here now and again. He likes my girls, but I'm not sure how much they like him."

"Do you know his name?"

"Yeah, I know him. He's a bigwig in the Phoenix PD."

"Well," Jim sighed, "are we just gonna dance with each other, or are you gonna tell me?"

Katrina lowered her voice. "Look, I liked Jerry okay, but his shit isn't my problem. He fucked with the bull and got the horns. Okay?"

Jim couldn't conceal his anger. "No, Katrina, it ain't okay. This guy," he shook Ramses' photo, "is supposed to be protectin' people, not killin' 'em. What he does in your place is between you and him. I don't care what your customers do while they're here. But when they leave here and start hurtin' other people, I get mad, especially when them other people are my friends." Jim rose from his seat, placed his palms flat on the table, and leaned menacingly toward Katrina. "Now you're gonna tell me this man's name without any more of your nonsense."

"You're a good guy, Jim, and I don't mind helpin' ya out. I just don't want it comin' around and biting me in the ass," she said.

Jim eased back into his seat. "Ain't nuthin' gonna bite you, Katrina. You got my word on that. Like you said, this ain't got nuthin' do to with you." Jim could feel Katrina's pig-like eyes searching his face in the dimness.

Katrina sighed. "His name is Oren Ramses." She spoke so softly that her voice was scarcely audible. "He's a piece of work."

"How do you spell it?"

"I dunno. R-A-M-S-E-S, I guess."

Jim gathered up the photos, then grasped the edge of the table and eased himself to his feet with a grimace. "Thank you, Katrina. You're a good woman," he said.

"No, I'm not," she responded matter-of-factly. "I'm an old, use-up broad that runs a shitty bar." Katrina smiled, almost imperceptibly. "But maybe even an old used-up broad can do something right once in a while."

Jim leaned down and kissed Katrina's clammy forehead. "You just did, Katrina."

"Yeah, I guess," she replied. "Just remember that you didn't hear it here."

Jim slowly headed for the door, into the blistering afternoon heat.

***

Jim and Carol sat in the restaurant, drinking iced tea. Although it was past sunset, the antiquated air conditioner mounted on the roof struggled to cool the stifling interior. It made periodic groaning sounds as it ran non-stop, feebly blowing semi-cool air into the dining area.

"Gangs been goin' up and down the block, stealin' and resellin' the copper coils from all the AC units," Jim told Carol. "They ain't stole mine yet but I hope they do...maybe my landlord will replace it with an air conditioner that actually blows cold air...I heard that's what they's supposed to do," he smiled.

"Yeah, it's pretty warm in here," Carol acknowledged, draining her iced tea and pouring each of them another glass from a plastic pitcher. "Do your customers complain?"

"'Bout the only customers I been getting lately is them two cops." Jim dumped two packets of sugar into his glass of tea and stirred it with his finger. "They's getting' to be real regulars. I'm thinkin' about raisin' my prices," he winked. "One of 'em complains all the time, but the other one seems okay."

"They're the ones who gave you the pictures?"

"Yeah. As a matter of fact, I got some news for you, Carol." She raised an eyebrow and looked expectantly at the old man. "I know his name."

"The cop?"

"The cop." Jim couldn't conceal his satisfaction.

Carol leaned back in the booth. "Really," she said, skeptically. "How did you find him?"

"I know somebody who knows him," Jim explained. "When you're in the restaurant business, you meet lots of people."

Carol's face assumed an expression of ineffable pain. "What is it?" she asked, almost as if she was afraid to hear it.

"Ramses," Jim told her. "Oren Ramses. He's somebody important in the Phoenix Police Department.

Carol stared vacantly across the room, then she began to softly cry. "It's so unfair," she murmured, wiping her eyes with a napkin. "That bastard is alive and living his life without a care and Jerry's gone. Forever. It's so unfair..." He voice trailed off into nothing.

Jim reached over and grasped both of Carol's hands in his own. "It ain't fair, and I don't know why the Lord does what He does. But I know that He's got a reason for everything He does, Carol. I know it." He squeezed her hands.

Carol wiped her eyes and blew her nose on a napkin. "So now what? We know who he is, but what good is that? How does that help Jerry?"

"Jerry don't need no help, Carol. He's with the Lord. It's you and me, and ever'body else, that needs help." Jim smiled, mysteriously. "And, pretty soon, Mr. Oren Ramses is gonna need some help."

Carol looked perplexed. "Help? What are you talking about?"

Another smile illuminated Jim's weathered face. "I got some ideas, Carol."

***

"Mexico agreed with you," Golden remarked to Rosey. They were eating lunch at a nondescript diner across town from the police annex.

"I don't know about that," Rosey said. "It was okay, but weird. Mexicans talk too much." He shrugged and looked expectantly at Golden, as if seeking confirmation. When none came, he continued, "Besides, I missed regular food. The fuckin' Mexicans put mayonnaise on pretty much everything, French fries with mayonnaise, hot dogs with mayonnaise, cottage cheese with mayonnaise, mayonnaise with fuckin' mayonnaise. And do ya think I could find ziti in fuckin' Mexico? Forget it! I don't think the Mexicans even know what pasta is! It's unbelievable!" he marveled.

Golden sipped his iced tea. "Like I said, a lot of people weren't too happy to hear that you're back in town. They're still bugged because you got your nose out of joint and threatened to burn the whole goddamned house down around everybody."

"Yeah, I probably shoudda kept my big mouth shut," Rosey conceded. "But I'm ready to mend fences."

"Yeah, you did okay with the job you did for Ramses," Golden acknowledged. "But now we got a bigger problem."

"What kinda problem?" A look of genuine concern clouded Rosey's face. He knew that, if Golden thought he'd botched the apartment fire, his chances of returning to the Sunstone fold would be imperiled. "The guy Ramses wanted outta the way is outta the way. What problem?"

Golden took another sip of tea, then fixed his gaze on Rosey. "This is completely between you and me, understand?"

"For fuck's sake, what do you think?"

"I just want to make sure whose side you're on," Golden said, evenly.

"I do what needs to be done. You already know that. Steady Freddy, that's me," Rosey smiled coldly.

"Maybe," Golden said without conviction. He leaned forward and looked intently at Rosey. "A couple of IA turds are looking at Ramses, and it's becoming a problem."

"What are they lookin' at Ramses for? What's their beef?"

The chief shook his head. "Nobody knows. I checked with some of my contacts in IA and they don't know anything, either. All I know is that IA is interested in Ramses."

"Do you suppose somebody ratted him out?"

"It could be that, or it could just be that IA is doing a random inquiry...they do that periodically."

Rosey leaned back in his chair. "So, what's the big deal? They poke around, find nuthin', then go to lunch. End of discussion."

"Yeah, maybe," Golden replied, "but maybe not. If they actually find something there's gonna be a lot of tits in the wringer."

Rosey looked contemplative. "So, what do ya wanna do about it?"

SIX

Over the past three weeks, Jim learned quite a lot about Chief of Detectives Oren Ramses. He knew, for example, that Ramses had been with the Phoenix Police Department for twenty-six years, working his way up the ladder from simple patrolman, to detective, to Chief of Detectives. He also learned that Ramses was widely considered a thug and bully by the downtown habitués, and was universally disliked and feared. He knew, too, not only the Ramses' home address, but the name, address and phone number of his mistress, and even the small restaurant where Ramses typically ate lunch every day. The restaurant where he and Carol now sat.

It had taken Jim several days to convince Carol to accompany him. For one thing, he wanted her to positively identify Ramses, rather than simply rely on Pruitt's and Saturday's photograph. Jim also wanted to confirm that Ramses was the police officer in plainclothes who peered into Carol's Buick moments after Jerry was shot. Both he and Carol looked up when the glass door opened and Ramses strode in. He glanced over at Carol, whose face immediately paled. Jim gently placed his gnarled hand over hers.

"That's him!" She urgently whispered.

Ramses walked confidently to a booth at the rear of the restaurant, oblivious to Jim and Carol. He slid into the booth and pulled a menu from the chrome holder on the table and began scrutinizing it.

"You two doin' okay?" A waitress materialized before Jim and Carol's table.

"Yeah, we're fine," Carol answered, without taking her eyes off Ramses. Two more customers entered the restaurant, seated themselves two tables away, and looked at the waitress expectantly.

Ignoring them, she turned on her heel and approached Ramses' booth. "Hey, Sugar," she greeted him with easy familiarity. "What are we havin' today?"

Ramses slid his menu back into its chrome holder. "What's the soup today?"

"Bean with bacon, but I wouldn't eat it. It looks like the cook just cleaned out the sink trap and dumped everything into a pot," she replied, matter-of-factly. "It looks bad and smells worse."

"In that case, I'll have a taco salad," Ramses said.

"Good choice," the waitress assured him as she headed toward the kitchen. The two new arrivals watched with dismay as she disappeared into the back.

"What should we do?" Carol whispered to Jim.

"Me and him are gonna have a little sit-down," Jim responded with a gleam in his eye. "You wait right here and don't worry." He slowly rose to his feet, his joints groaning audibly.

Carol grabbed his hand as he began to move away from their table. "Don't, Jim. Please. You don't know what he'll do."

Jim smiled gently and patted Carol's hand. "Ain't nobody gonna hurt me, Carol." He pulled away and ambled toward Ramses' booth.

Ramses looked up as Jim approached. "You must be detective Ramses," said Jim as plopped down.

Initially startled, Ramses quickly recovered his sangfroid. "Do I know you?" he suspiciously asked.

"In a way. I was there when you killed my friend, Jerry Dawson."

Ramses' face instantly grew hard. "I don't know what you're talking about."

"Sure you do. You may not have pulled the trigger, but you killed him."

"Get the hell out of my booth before I arrest you, old man."

Jim feigned alarm. "Arrest me? For what, Detective? This is a public restaurant and I just wanted to say hello. Why would you arrest me?"

"Threatening and intimidating, for one, "Ramses glowered.

The waitress materialized at Ramses' table. "Hun, I forgot to ask what you're drinkin'." She glanced at Jim, "Is your friend eatin', too?"

"He's leaving," Ramses said.

"I'll have what he's havin'," Jim beamed at her.

"Young lady?" One of the two other diners called to the waitress, who ignored them.

"Fair enough," said the waitress, nodding toward Ramses, "he's havin' the taco salad." "Now what are we drinkin'?" She looked expectantly at Ramses.

Ramses swiftly withdrew his wallet from the pocket of his slacks. Flipping it open to display his Phoenix Police identification, he thrust it toward the waitress. "I'm a police officer. This man is a dangerous fugitive that I'm placing under arrest. Call 911 and request a patrol car."

"Huh?" The waitress looked skeptically at Jim, who continued to smile, apparently unconcerned at the prospect of his imminent arrest. "He doesn't look like a dangerous fugitive. He's an old man."

"Young lady!" called the other diner, more imperiously. "We've been waiting for five minutes!"

Ramses glared at the waitress. "Goddamn it, call 911!" he barked.

"Yes, just make sure that the cop car they send is big enough to hold both of us," Jim instructed the waitress. He turned in his seat and happily waved to Carol, who watched in disbelief from her table.

Ramses had not, until that moment, paid any attention to Carol. When he saw her, his face blanched.

"Wait!" he blurted. "Check that...don't call 911."

"Young lady!" shouted the peeved diner from across the room. "We're leaving unless we get some service."

The waitress continued to ignore the duo, though she was becoming annoyed by their impatience. "So, which is it?" she asked Ramses. "Call or don't call?"

"Don't call yet," Ramses told her as he returned his ID to his pocket.

"I'll have what he's having," Jim reminded her as she headed toward the other table just in time to see the two disgruntled diners exit the restaurant. "And two ice teas, please." He turned toward Ramses. "Ice tea okay with you?" he asked, innocently. Ramses looked as though he was about to punch Jim.

"What do you want?" Ramses muttered after the waitress departed. "And am I supposed to know your friend, too?" He indicated Carol, who continued to watch them with growing fascination.

"Who you think you're foolin'?" Jim asked him. "You know her. Besides killin' Jerry, you raped her. We just wanted to get a look at you, make sure you were the guy."

Ramses glared at Jim defiantly. "Screw you. I never laid eyes on either one of you and I sure as hell never raped anyone. Who do you think you're talkin' to?"

"I'm talkin' to you, son. Or should I talk to your boss at the police department?"

Ramses forced a laugh. "You can talk to anybody you want. It's nothing to me. Everybody will just write you off as a couple of crack pots. You think you're the first asshole to claim that he was mistreated by a cop?"

Jim looked thoughtful. "Yeah, you're probably right. You can't fight city hall...ain't that what they say?" Their waitress returned and placed two glasses of ice tea on the table.

"So fuck off," Ramses grunted after she departed.

"I ain't leavin' until I've had my say," Jim said, defiantly. "If you want to arrest me, have at it." He held his wrists out before him, above the table. "Might as well cuff me now, since I'm such a dangerous fugitive." Ramses didn't avail himself of the offer.

"Nobody will believe anything you say because it isn't true. The city's full of nut-cases and publicity whores like you." Ramses had regained his composure.

"Maybe. But there's one way to prove it."

"Fuck you, old man. There's nothing to prove. You and your friend are full of shit. There's nothing to connect me to either one of you."

Jim took a sip of tea. "Man, there ain't nuthin' to cool ya down like a glass of ice tea on a hot day!" he exclaimed. "Ya know, though, my friend is hungry, too. Mind if I order something for her?" Ramses glared at Jim without responding.

Jim signaled to the waitress and she sauntered over. "Your taco salads are almost ready," she said, listlessly, anticipating a complaint.

"Great!" Jim said. "My friend over there would like one, too." He pointed to Carol. "And an ice tea."

"Sure," responded the waitress, somewhat confused by the unorthodox seating arrangement. "It'll be right out." She walked away.

Jim turned his attention back to Ramses. "Like I was sayin', there's one way of proving me wrong." Ramses stared at him impassively, refusing to take the bait, so Jim continued. "Nobody's gotta take our word for anything. Lemme ask you something, Detective Ramses, do you remember what my friend was wearin' the night you raped her?"

"Since I never saw your friend before today, I have no idea what you're talking about," Ramses replied.

"I guess it don't matter," Jim shrugged. "But it was a real pretty sun dress..." he paused as the waitress returned with their taco salads.

"Two taco salads," she announced, placing them on the table before them. "Your friend's will be out in a minute. You guys want anything else for now?"

"I'll take a refill on my tea," Jim smiled.

"How 'bout you, hun?" she asked Ramses, who shook his head. "Be right back," she told Jim.

"Like I was sayin', "Jim resumed after she'd walked away, "Carol was wearing a real nice sun dress, blue and orange. Least it was nice before you ruined it by leavin' a big semen stain. Ya know what? I seen on them TV crime shows that you can identify people just by analyzing things like semen stains." He slowly took another sip of ice tea and watched Ramses over the rim of the glass. "Man, that's good tea!"

Ramses' eyes grew wide and his face flushed. His pulse raced and he could feel his heart thump in his chest. Beads of sweat erupted on his forehead; he grabbed a napkin and attempted to wipe them away. Still, he remained impassive.

"Yep, you can tell who people was, how old they are, and all kinda stuff...just from analyzing semen stains and such." Jim chuckled. "Man, I wouldn't be surprised if you could even tell what size shoes they wear and what kinda car they drive! It's amazing what they can do with semen stains." He took a bite of taco salad. "Hey, this is pretty good!" How's yours?"

The waitress returned with a pitcher to refill Jim's tea. "You okay, hun?" she asked, looking at Ramses' untouched meal. He nodded. She left the pitcher on the table and left to retrieve Carol's salad from the kitchen.

"But I reckon, bein' a police officer, you already know about all that DNA stuff, huh?"

Ramses finally managed to speak.

"You're threatening me with some bullshit about a dress that you claim has my DNA on it?"

"Nope. Just tellin' ya that Carol has a dress with your semen on it. No threat."

"Since I never met 'Carol,' you're lying."

"Easy enough to find out," shrugged Jim as he continued to eat his salad. "And if you never met Carol, you got nothin' to worry about."

"I'm not worried," Ramses said, unconvincingly. "What's your point?" He wiped his face again with a napkin.

Jim took another sip of tea, then placed his glass on the table. He fixed his dark eyes on Ramses, who could see the spark of anger in them. "I was just wonderin' how a man like you could get to be a police officer. You ain't nothing but an animal."

Ramses smiled coldly. "Yeah, an animal who protects even lying pricks like you from bad guys. In my business, you sometimes gotta get your hands dirty."

Jim looked startled. "Your *hands*? Son, you dirty all over!"

Ramses looked away and signaled for the waitress, who was carrying Carol's taco salad to her table.

"The check," he grunted when she returned.

The waitress glanced at Ramses' untouched salad. "Wanna box?"

"Just the check."

"My friend and me would like some dessert, too," Jim interjected. "Might as well add that to the tab."

The waitress looked at Ramses, who simply pushed his plate away with neither acknowledgement nor protest. "We've got apple, cherry, and pecan pie, and ice cream," she mechanically informed Jim.

"We'll each have a slice of pecan pie with ice cream," he smiled.

"Right. Be right back with the check," the waitress clipped as she walked away.

When they were once again alone, Ramses hissed, "I don't know what the fuck you think you're up to, old man, but don't try blackmailing me. Understand? I'll throw your black ass in jail so fast it'll make your head spin."

Jim frowned. "Jail? Puttin' me in jail don't make much sense 'cause people tend to talk in jail. But I'm just an old man who runs a greasy spoon and you're a police officer, so I guess you know best."

"You're right, old man, but there are places even worse than jail," Ramses said as their waitress returned with the check and Jim's pie and ice cream. Ramses glanced at the bill, tossed a twenty and a five on the table, and rose to his feet. "Think about what I said."

"Thanks for lunch," Jim responded. "Maybe I'll see ya again."

"You better hope not," Ramses growled as he turned and headed for the door, deliberately avoiding making eye contact with Carol as she watched with astonishment. She waited until the door shut behind him, then gathered up her taco salad and walked to Jim's booth.

"I can't believe what I just saw," she marveled.

Jim chuckled. "I think I did pretty good. He surely didn't know *what* to do when he saw you, Carol!"

"So, what did he say?" Carol eagerly asked.

"He said that you and me are liars, and that he was gonna arrest me."

Carol took a tentative bite of taco salad. "So why didn't he?"

"'Cause he knows we ain't liars," Jim said. He only now realized that he was trembling.

"Now what do we do?"

"Honestly, I don't exactly know, Carol," Jim conceded. "What I do know is that things have a way of working themselves out. For now," he continued, "I'm gonna enjoy this lunch, courtesy of the Phoenix Police Department."

***

Outside, in his unmarked Caprice, Ramses couldn't stop sweating, and not simply because of the stultifying heat. He flicked the air conditioning to max, closed his eyes, and tried to force his pounding heart to slow down.

Ramses couldn't believe the balls on that old man. Didn't he know who was dealing with? The stupid bastard was lucky that Ramses didn't just haul his ass off to jail. Where the hell do people get off, talking to a police officer like that? Ramses already had enough problems with those two IA fuckers hanging around. The last thing he needed were more potential flies in the ointment. He couldn't be sure whether the old man was bullshitting about the semen-stained dress, but he had to make damned sure that, if it existed, it never saw the light of day.

Ramses shoved the transmission lever into 'R' and backed out of his parking spot in front of the restaurant. He was gonna have to talk to Rosey about taking care of this new problem. This time, though, it would be entirely between the two of them. No need to involve Golden, especially since the chief was getting pissy.   Just as well as take care of matters himself this time.   Ramses shoved the transmission into 'D' and spun out of the parking lot.

SEVEN

Bickman fidgeted in Pruitt's small office on the second floor of the Phoenix Police Department. He'd received Pruitt's call earlier that week, requesting an informal meeting about an unspecified matter. In the intervening days he'd wracked his brain in an effort to figure out what he'd done wrong, why IA wanted to talk to him, but couldn't think of a single thing. He'd talked to Pam about it, who reassured him that it was probably nothing. Still, Bickman was so nervous that he almost felt sick. He'd never had any dealings with IA but had heard plenty of stories, all of them bad. The prevailing opinion among the uniforms was that IA was the proverbial 'Isle of Misfit Toys,' where cops who couldn't cut it on the streets ended up, pursuing make-work investigations of "real" police officers and making their lives miserable. On a good day, the esteem in which IA was held among the rank-and-file approached zero. Making matters worse was the fact that today was supposed to be Bickman's day off.

The door opened and Bickman quickly stood as Pruitt and Saturday entered the room.

"Officer Bickman," Pruitt smiled as he extended his hand. "I'm Pruitt and this is my partner," he said, indicating Saturday. Saturday also shook Bickman's hand, but without introducing himself. "Sit, please."

Bickman resumed his seat as Pruitt sat behind a plain metal desk in front of him. Saturday sat wordlessly on an ordinary couch along one wall. Pruitt pulled a small cassette recorder from a drawer, turned it on, and placed it atop his desk.

"At the threshold, I'd like to thank you for coming here today, Officer Bickman. I realize that today is supposed to be your day off."

Bickman forced a tense smile but did not respond. The tape recorder made him nervous. After all he'd heard about IA, he was afraid to say anything.

"We want you to know," Pruitt continued, "that you're not in any kind of trouble, so put yourself at your ease." Bickman didn't know whether to believe him or not. Bickman used the same line on suspects in order to instill in them a false sense of security, thereby inducing them to betray themselves. "My partner and I just want to talk to you about a recent police shooting that you were involved in."

Bickman's mind raced. The only shooting he'd ever been involved in had been Dawson's, and he'd previously given his sworn statement to the board of inquiry. Had he said something wrong? Was IA out to hang him?

"I already testified about that before the board of inquiry," he managed to say. Bickman's mouth was as dry as paper and his heart had begun to pound.

"Yes, we're aware of that," Pruitt acknowledged. "We also interviewed the two other uniformed officers who were present at the Dawson shooting, Cope and Hernandez."

"I'm not sure how much more I can add to what they said," Bickman said, wanting more than anything to get the hell out of Pruitt's office as quickly as possible.

"Maybe nothing," Pruitt conceded, "but there's still a couple of things that remain unclear."

"Well, I'll help anyway I can," responded Bickman, though he wasn't sure he meant it.

Pruitt nodded slightly. "How is it that you were even on site when Dawson was shot?"

Bickman looked genuinely perplexed. "I don't understand your question."

"Well, were you simply driving by and happened upon the scene?"

"No, an officer called in to dispatch and requested assistance. Since I was already on patrol in the area, I responded. Everything's in my report," he concluded.

"So, you were dispatched to the scene?"

"Well, not me exclusively. Immediate assistance was requested from any units in the vicinity. As it turned out, Officer Cope was also in the area and showed up with his trainee."

"Hernandez?"

"Yeah, Hernandez. I didn't know his name at the time, but learned it later."

Pruitt looked intently at Bickman. "Do you know who called the dispatcher?"

"I didn't at the time, but when I got there I learned that Detective Ramses was the one who called it in."

"Did you know Detective Ramses? Were you friends?"

Again, Bickman looked puzzled. "Friends?   The detective and I had crossed paths a coupla times in the field...I wouldn't say we were friends, though."

"Who was there when you first arrived at the scene?"

Bickman furrowed his brow. "Cope's vehicle was already there...I pulled up behind him. "

"Did you see Detective Ramses?"

"I saw his vehicle when I pulled behind Cope, though I didn't actually see him at that moment."

"What did you see?"

Bickman had begun to relax a bit under Pruitt's questioning; it was basically the same thing he'd previously testified to before the board of inquiry.

"I already told the board of inquiry all this. Why are you asking it again?"

Saturday spoke for the first time. "We just want to make sure that you didn't remember something new between then and now," he said without emotion.

Bickman shifted position. "You already talked to Cope and Hernandez?"

"Yeah," Saturday grunted.

"Okay," Bickman shrugged and resumed. "When I got there, Cope's vehicle was already in front of mine, along the curb. I could see Detective Ramses' vehicle parked less than a block away but couldn't see who was in it because the sun was too bright."

"Who else did you see?"

"About block away I could see a pedestrian. Otherwise, just Cope and Ramses' vehicles."

Both Pruitt and Saturday perked up. "Could you recognize the pedestrian?" Pruitt asked.

"Not then...he was too far away. But he was there when Dawson was killed."

"Did you know who he was? Had you ever seen him before?"

"He looked kinda familiar, but I couldn't be sure. Detective Ramses apparently knew him."

Pruitt's curiosity was piqued. "How do you know that?"

"Because he told us over the radio not to accidentally shoot him."

"So, Detective Ramses expected shots to be exchanged?"

Bickman was becoming slightly exasperated. "I guess. Why don't you ask him? All I know is that I received a call asking for backup. I responded to it and Detective Ramses advised us not to shoot some pedestrian. I actually didn't give it much thought at the time because we were focusing on a guy in another car. Other than that, you'll just have to ask him."

"Did you have any idea why Ramses called for assistance?"

"Not at that moment. "

"Later?" Pruitt asked.

"Yeah. Just a few seconds after I'd pulled in behind Officer Cope, Detective Ramses radioed us that he was surveiling a murder suspect and that he needed our assistance to apprehend him."

"What happened to the pedestrian? Did you see where he went?"

"I saw him approach the car that the suspect was sitting in. After that, things got so chaotic that I couldn't tell you what became of him."

"Where was Detective Ramses?"

Bickman furrowed his brow in thought. "Everything happened so fast that I don't remember where exactly he was. All I remember is that he was there after the suspect'd been shot...after he tried to run me over. I never physically saw Detective Ramses until after everything happened," he added. "I just talked to him over the radio for a few seconds when I first got to the scene, like I told you. Cope and Hernandez may have seen him, but I didn't." He paused and looked at Pruitt. "Like I said, everything happened so fast."

"Have you talked to Detective Ramses since the shooting?" Saturday asked.

"Yeah, briefly, at the board of inquiry. Other than that, no."

Pruitt nodded his head slightly and looked thoughtful. Saturday looked bored. "Other than what you've told us today, do you have anything else you'd like to add about that day?" Pruitt finally asked, reaching for the cassette recorder.

Bickman was relieved the ordeal was apparently about over. "Nothing that I haven't already testified to before the board or put in my report."

Pruitt nodded again. "We appreciate your cooperation today, Officer Bickman. I want to reiterate that you are in no way in any sort of trouble. Officers like you are a credit to the Phoenix Police Department and a credit to the community as a whole. Thank you for coming in today." Pruitt clicked the recorder off, stood, and extended his hand to Bickman, who shook it perfunctorily. Saturday remained seated on the couch.

A tiny smile crossed Bickman's face. "I wish I could say that I was glad to be here."

Pruitt shrugged and made a wry face. "Yeah, I know. We get that a lot. IA guys are about as popular as morticians."

Bickman turned and headed for the door. He wasn't sure whether he should be relieved or worried. Maybe a little of both.

***

"Why isn't this the city's problem? Why should I get involved?" Attorney General Booth Butler leaned back and placed his feet atop his desk. He was in his third-floor office on Jefferson Street, having just finished reading a staffer's report on the Dawson shooting and the resulting, ongoing IA investigation by the Phoenix Police Department.

"I can think of at least two reasons," responded his chief of staff. "First, it may not just be the city's problem because it may involve malfeasance at the state level. Second, and more to the point, how bad do you want to be governor? The state lottery investigation ended weeks ago and, since then, you've vaporized in the public's mind. If the attorney general's office takes the lead on this, your reputation as a tireless take-no-prisoners crime fighter will resonate with the voters. You'll be right back in the thick of things. I'll schedule a press conference and you'll be back in the papers, above the fold, before the end of the week." The chief of staff looked directly at the attorney general. "That's why."

Butler laughed and took a sip of coffee. "You know, people told me that I shouldn't have hired you because you're an ambitious son of a bitch. But you're my ambitious son of a bitch and, like Lyndon Johnson said, I'd rather have you inside pissin' out, than outside pissin' in." He handed the report to the chief. "Do it."

***

Rosey shoved opened the door to the cafe and stepped inside. Behind him, the mid-day sun sizzled overhead like a disc of molten lead. The interior of the restaurant was scarcely cooler than the scorching air outside. A noisy oscillating electric fan on the lunch counter made a feeble attempt to blow the hot interior air around.

He was clearly overdressed for the place, which was nothing more than a downtown, long-in-the-tooth, greasy spoon. He'd waited until lunchtime to pay a visit, thinking it would be filled with diners from the surrounding office buildings, as well as with the staff of the superior court just down the block. Instead, there were only two other customers sitting in a booth along the far wall. Rosey ambled to a wobbly table as far from the two other diners as possible and sat down. He was wearing a pale linen suit but sweat had already soaked through the fabric, leaving large, wet stains at his armpits. Under ordinary circumstances, Rosey would have removed his jacket but, because he had his Glock tucked into his waistband, that option did not present itself.

An old black guy wearing a white apron emerged from what was presumably the kitchen and slowly made his way toward Rosey's table, carrying a glass of ice water.

"Good afternoon," the old man smiled as he placed the water on his table. Medina couldn't help but notice the man's beautiful, white teeth.

"Yeah, how ya doin'," Rosey grunted, absently, as he examined the menu that had been leaning against the salt shaker on the table.

"I'm fine," said the old man. "It's a hot one today."

"You ain't fuckin' kiddin'," Rosey concurred, still looking at the menu. He looked up. "You own this dump?"

"Guilty as charged, but it ain't a dump," the old man affirmed. "If it ain't up to your standards, you already know where the door is."

"Fair enough. Bring me a BLT and a beer if ya got it." Rosey propped his menu against the salt shaker again. He liked the old man's spunk.

"No beer. I'm not licensed to sell alcohol. How 'bout a Pepsi instead?"

"Well, if that's all ya got, I guess I ain't gotta choice." Rosey dabbed a sausage-like finger against the condensation on the side of his water glass. "I sure as hell don't want fuckin' water. I'm thirsty, not dirty." Jim responded with a weary look, then limped back to the kitchen.

Rosey already suspected he had the right guy; Ramses told him about his encounter with Jim and Carol, which is what prompted this afternoon's visit. He just wanted to confirm, since lots of blacks and

Mexicans work in restaurants and they all look the same. Don't wanna get the wrong guy. Rosey indifferently turned his attention to the two other customers as he waited for his sandwich.

Both men in the booth across the room were wearing slacks and, notwithstanding the stifling heat, white shirts with narrow ties. Too old to be Mormon missionaries, they could only be cops. It was as plain as day. Rosey wasn't too keen on eating in the same place as two cops but, since he was supposed to be dead anyway, guessed it didn't matter. Who'd suspect the guy sitting across the room was a corpse? Besides, Rosey knew that virtually no one in law enforcement knew what he looked like when he was alive. Even so, their unwelcome presence was going to force Rosey to rethink his plan.

Jim returned with a cold can of Pepsi and a glass of ice. He placed them on Rosey's table and fished a drinking straw out of his apron pocket.

"Where's all the business?" Rosey asked, absently, after pouring the Pepsi into the glass and spearing it with the straw.

"I keep askin' that question myself," Jim replied.

"I don't imagine the fucking heat helps much," Rosey suggested.

"No, I reckon you're right. I'm thinkin' about raisin' my prices on BLT's to $300 so I can have the air conditioning fixed."

Rosey nodded toward the other diners. "The heat don't seem to bother those two." He took a sip of Pepsi. "They look like cops," he idly remarked.

"That's 'cause they are."

"Lotta cops eat in here?"

"If by 'lotta' you mean two, lotta cops eat here."

"They come here a lot?"

Jim looked quizzically at Rosey. "You sure are interested in my customers. Why don't you walk over and ask them?"

Rosey shrugged. "I was just wonderin' how cops can afford to eat $300 BLT's."

"I give cops a break and only charge 'em $250." Jim turned and headed back to the kitchen to assemble Rosey's sandwich. The two cops continued talking in low voices for a few minutes, then stood. One of them placed some money on their table before they headed for the door. Rosey lowered his head and pretended to read the menu, though they didn't even glance at him as they exited the café.

A few minutes after their departure, Jim returned with Rosey's BLT.

"How late you open here?" Rosey asked as Jim placed the sandwich before him.

"Usually 'till five, but business been so poor that I been leavin' early lately," Jim replied.

"Ya know, I ain't too hungry after all," Rosey announced. "Have a BLT on me." He stood. "What's the damage?

"Six bucks for the sandwich and Pepsi," Jim said, apparently unsurprised by Rosey's abrupt change of heart.

Rosey withdrew a thick wallet from his jacket pocket and removed a $10-dollar bill.

"Seems kinda pricey for a dump with no air conditioning, but I'm a generous guy." He stood and tossed the money onto the table. "Keep it." He donned his tortoise shell Ray-Bans and headed for the door without another word.

Jim sighed and sat down at Rosey's table. He picked up the BLT and took a bite before the sandwich grew cold. He knew Rosey would be back.

***

Jim was in the kitchen when he heard the bell on the front door jingle. It was just after five and he'd deliberately waited to close up, though he'd not had a single customer since the light lunch crowd. Jim's joints hurt all the time now and all he wanted to do is go home, soak his feet, and watch television. It had been three days since he'd seen Rosey and he was getting tired of waiting for him to return.

Leaning against the refrigerator was an old break-open twelve-gauge shotgun he brought from home. Jim used to hunt birds with it when he was a kid in Texas. He picked it up and eased himself into his rickety chair near the open back door.

"I'm in the back!" he hollered. "Come back here!"

After he'd scoped the place out a few days previously, Rosey figured the old man would be an easy mark. He'd make it look like a robbery by killing Jim in the back of the restaurant, then cleaning out the till. The downtown area around the café was a ghost town after five, so there would be nobody to intrude. Besides, he'd flipped the lock on the front door as soon as he'd entered the restaurant, so nobody could enter even if they'd wanted to. Rosey would worry about Carol later; Ramses told him the old man was the immediate threat.

Jim heard footsteps approach the kitchen doorway and raised his shotgun. The muzzle of a pistol slowly appeared at the doorway, followed by a gloved hand and wrist.

"C'mon in," he invited. "It's nice and cool back here."

Rosey emerged fully into the kitchen and swiveled his head around. Jim's 12-guage shotgun was pointed directly at his face. He was stunned.

"What the fuck?" is all he could say before his voice trailed off.

Jim continued sitting and motioned with the shotgun. "I said come in."

"What the fuck do you think you're doing, old man?" Rosey barked as lowered his pistol as a precaution. He was afraid Jim would panic and blast him.

"I got a rat problem," replied Jim. "They usually come in from the alley, but sometimes they come in through the front door." He shifted in his chair but the muzzle of the shotgun didn't waver from Rosey's face. "Drop your gun." Rosey appeared stupefied that an old black guy who could barely walk managed to get the drop on him. Maybe he'd underestimated Jim.

"I said drop your gun. Now." Jim repeated with a discernable edge in his voice. With a slight smile, Rosey complied and his Glock clattered to the floor. "Kick it this way," Jim ordered. Rosey complied. "Now get on the floor, on your belly, with your feet towards me. Move real slow, like you're froze." Jim motioned with his head and, after hesitating, Rosey began to kneel. He considered, just for a moment, leaping across the room and wresting the shotgun away from the old man, but quickly thought the better of it. Jim might freak and blow his head off. Better to reason with the old man. Besides, he had back-up gun hidden in an ankle holster.

"What's this all about?" Rosey growled as he leaned forward on his palms until he was flat on his stomach. "You better not shoot me, old man."

Without taking his eyes off Rosey, Jim reached down with the dish towel from his apron pocket and retrieved Rosey's Glock from the floor near his chair.

"Man, how many people you plan on killin' tonight?" he asked. "This thing weighs a ton. How many bullets does it hold?"

"Fuck you. I don't know what you're talking about. I use that for self-protection."

"Well, it don't look like it's working too good tonight," Jim said. "You may want to get a refund."

"What the fuck do you want with me?" Rosey spat, his cheek pressed against the floor. "I come in here to get somethin' to eat and you pull a gun on me. What kinda bullshit is that?"

"You came here to eat with a pistol in your hand? I'm thinkin' that you came here for mischief." Jim shifted positions again...it made his joints hurt to sit too long in one position. His shotgun remained pointed at the back of Rosey's head.

"Can I sit up?" Rosey mumbled. "We can talk better that way."

"Nope. I like you the way you are and we're talkin' just fine." Jim knew it was no coincidence that Rosey appeared at the restaurant only days after his confrontation with Ramses. Rosey dressed too flashy and had never set foot in the place before. He was also inordinately interested in Pruitt and Saturday, the other two diners in the restaurant at the time. The longer you live, the more you learn.

"What do you want with me?" Rosey asked. "You're makin' a big mistake."

"I made one or two mistakes in my time," Jim replied. "I reckon I'll make one or two more before it's over."

"So, what do you want?"

"What's your name?"

"Adolph." It almost pained Rosey to say it.

"You don't look like 'Adolph'."

"My ID's out in my car...lemme go get it."

Jim ignored the taunting suggestion. "Who killed Jerry?"

"Who?" Rosey was genuinely perplexed by the question.

"Jerry Dawson."

"I don't know who that is. You got the wrong guy, old man. I wanna sit up."

"You can sit up in a minute. Why did you come here before?"

"I was hungry."

"So, why'd you leave without eating?"

"I wasn't as hungry as I thought."

Jim clucked his tongue. "Ya know, my wife, Lorraine, liked to dance but, between you and me, I never cared much for it. I'd go dancin' with her just 'cause it pleased her. I'm thinkin' that, when I get to heaven, the first thing Lorraine's gonna wanna do is go dancin'."

"You ain't goin' to heaven."

Jim looked thoughtful. "You may be right, especially after tonight. If you are, you can have my bed turned down for me in the other place. But what I know for sure is that I ain't gonna dance with you." Jim leaned forward and jabbed the prostrate Rosey with his shotgun. "Do you know Detective Ramses?"

"Never heard of him. I just came by to get something to eat."

"Kitchen's closed, but here's what I'm thinkin', I'm thinkin' that Detective Ramses sent you here to kill me. Ain't that somethin'? You came here to kill me but you're the one layin' on the floor with a shotgun stuck in your back. Ain't nobody woulda predicted that."

"I don't know what you're talking about, old man."

Jim labored to his feet. "I think you know exactly what I'm talkin' about, Adolph. He pushed his chair away with his foot and stepped back against the wall. Get up," he said, coldly. "Don't turn around, just stand up."

Rosey got to his knees. His ankle holster was now within easy reach but figured that, if he tried to grab it, Jim would wig out and shoot him. Rosey stood and slowly brushed the dust from his linen jacket and trousers.

"Walk to that wall in front of you, then turn around and face me."

Rosey complied. When he turned, he saw Jim's shotgun aimed directly at his chest. It would take at least three strides for him to reach Jim and, from a standing position, he couldn't quickly access the emergency pistol still in his ankle holster.

"I don't know how many folks you killed in your life, but there's gonna be one less tonight," Jim said as, without a flinch, he squeezed the trigger.

***

It wasn't like on TV, where a blast from a shotgun lifts the bad guy completely off his feet and flings him across the room. Rosey just slid down the wall and collapsed onto the floor. His head flopped forward and blood immediately began seeping onto the fabric of his pastel shirt.

Jim's ears were ringing from the discharge of the shotgun and smoke filled the enclosed kitchen. He propped the shotgun against the refrigerator and returned to his chair where, using the dish towel, he picked up Rosey's Glock. He returned to Rosey's body and placed the pistol in Rosey's lap. He then walked to the kitchen wall-phone and punched in Pruitt's cell number.

"This is Jim," he spoke calmly into the recorder, "a guy just tried to rob my place and I shot him." Hanging up the phone, he then called 911 and, providing a minimum of details, asked that an ambulance be dispatched to the restaurant. Assuming that Rosey took the precaution of locking the front door after he entered, Jim placed the receiver back on the hook and hobbled into the dining area to unlock it. He then opened a Pepsi, sat down in a booth, and waited. His feet hurt and he could already hear the wail of an ambulance far away.

***

Jim didn't bother to get to his feet when the police car, roof lights ablaze, pulled up in front of the café. Two uniformed cops burst into the dining room.

"You're the one who reported a robbery?" one of them accused.

"Yep, I reckon that would be me," Jim acknowledged, taking a sip of Pepsi. "He's in the kitchen." Jim pointed toward the back.

One of the cops withdrew his service weapon from its holster and headed for the kitchen. The other cop stood over Jim as the ambulance slid to a stop behind the police car. The first cop emerged from the back as two EMT's bustled into the restaurant through the front door.

"No hurry," he informed the foremost EMT. "The guy's as dead as a doornail." He turned toward his partner. "Some guy dead in back. Looks like a shotgun to the chest."

"Call the ME," instructed the other cop. "And tell the EMT's to cool it for now." He turned and looked down at Jim, who watched the commotion with interest. "What happened here?"

"I was closin' for the night when some cat busted in on me and tried to rob the place."

"So, you shot him?" the cop asked, skeptically.

"Well, he's dead, ain't he?" Jim replied.

"You just happened to have a shotgun at hand?"

Jim finished his Pepsi. "You know, I think I'll wait until Inspector Pruitt gets here before I say anything else."

"Who's 'Inspector Pruitt'?"

Jim didn't respond, apparently determined to disclose nothing further.

"Got any weapons on you?" the cop probed.

"No," Jim responded.

Stand up," the cop ordered. Jim grasped the edge of the table and pulled himself to his feet, joints groaning.

"Turn around and put your hands behind your back." Jim complied and the cop gave him a perfunctory pat-down before snapping handcuffs on him. By this time, the room was full of people milling around and chatting.

"Ain't you gonna read me my rights?" Jim asked.

The cop removed a small printed card from the pocket of his uniform and mechanically recited the standard Miranda warnings. Slipping the card back into his pocket, he grasped Jim's arm and guided him through the throng out the front door, to his police cruiser parked at the curb. Opening the rear door, he held the back of Jim's head as Jim eased himself into the vehicle. Slamming the door shut, the cop returned to the commotion in the dining room.

Even though it was past sundown, the interior of the police car was suffocating. Jim hoped that Pruitt would arrive quickly even as a plain Crown Vic angled to the curb in front of the police cruiser. Jim watched through the scratched Plexiglas screen as Pruitt and Saturday exited the Ford. Neither of them glanced into the police car where Jim was imprisoned, but hustled directly into the building. Jim watched through the vehicle's side window as they made a beeline to one of the uniformed cops.

"Where's the old man?" barked Pruitt. Jim saw the cop point to his police car parked outside, in front of the café. "Get him the hell out of there," Pruitt ordered.

Saturday continued talking to other officers as Pruitt and the uniformed cop made their way across the increasingly crowded dining room to the front exit. Moments later, Pruitt swung open the cruiser door and assisted Jim to his feet. Using the handcuff key on his key ring, he removed Jim's fetters.

"You can go now," Pruitt said to the cop. "Sorry about that," he apologized after he'd departed. "Uniforms are trained to consider everyone guilty until proven innocent."

"Yeah, I already figured that out," Jim remarked. "I'm glad you got here so quick...I was roastin' in there."

"They're supposed to keep the engine running with the a/c on," Pruitt said. "But with the price of gas, the city's more-or-less lookin' the other way if they don't. Let's go back inside so you can show me what happened."

Jim and Pruitt reentered the restaurant and Jim led him back to the kitchen. Several people were standing around the small room and there was a collapsible gurney crowded in the middle of the floor. Rosey was still slumped along the wall, though somebody had thrown a sheet over him. Pruitt squatted down, pulled the sheet aside, and silently gazed at the body.

"Any ID on him?" he asked no one in particular.

"Nuthin'," responded somebody from the coroner's office.

Pruitt flipped the sheet back then steered Jim into a corner; Saturday remained out in the dining room, talking to the responding officers.

"So, what happened, Jim?" Pruitt quietly asked.

"I was in the back here, getting ready to close, when I heard the front door open. I yelled for 'em to come back here and that dude," he pointed to the lump beneath the sheet, "came back with a gun. He told me to open the till, that it was a robbery."

"A robbery?" Pruitt echoed, quizzically. "How much cash do you have in the register right now, Jim?"

"I don't know. Maybe forty or fifty dollars."

"Why would a guy whose wristwatch cost more than this entire restaurant bother to rob you of fifty dollars?"

Jim raised his eyebrows. "I don't know why. If he wasn't dead, you could ask him."

Pruitt looked dubious. "Yeah, speakin' of that, how'd he end up dead?"

"Like I said, he had a pistol and was robbin' me, so I shot him to protect myself."

"You just happened to have a shotgun in the kitchen?"

"This neighborhood ain't too good," Jim noted.

Pruitt sighed. Under Arizona's 'Stand Your Ground' law, Jim had every right under the circumstances to protect himself.

"Did you know the guy?"

"I didn't know him, but I seen him once before."

"Oh? Where?" Pruitt's curiosity was piqued.

"Remember last time you and Saturday was in here, three or four days ago? He came in and ordered a sandwich, but left right after you two. He didn't even eat his sandwich."

Pruitt furrowed his brow, trying to recall the day. "Other than that, had you ever seen him before?"

"Nope, never." Jim glanced over at Rosey's body. "Don't reckon I'll be seein' him again, neither."

"Do you know how he got here? I mean, did he drive?" Pruitt asked.

"Don't know," Jim responded. "He said something about a car, but all I know is that I was here in the back and he came in with a gun, threatenin' to rob me."

Pruitt was clearly finding it a strain to believe Jim's account of what happened.

"Jim, you're an old man. If he already had his gun out, how'd you manage to shoot him before he shot you?"

Jim smiled. "I may be an old man, but I'm still pretty spry. There's the proof of the puddin'." He pointed at Rosey's body beneath the sheet.

Somebody materialized with a zippered, opaque plastic body bag and placed in on the floor next to Rosey's body. After multiple photographs in situ, the body would be driven in the ambulance outside to the Medical Examiner's office only a few blocks away, where it would be fingerprinted, identified, and autopsied. Not that cause of death was a mystery.

"Why do you think that guy was really here?" Pruitt finally asked, softly. "You and I both know that he wasn't here to rob you."

Jim turned squarely toward Pruitt. "He was here to kill me."

"Who'd want to kill you, Jim? Why?"

"You know that bad apple we talked about? He knows him."

EIGHT

Pruitt and Saturday returned to Ramses' office a week later. Ramses was not happy to see them.

"Now what the fuck do you two clowns want?" he growled when they entered. "Don't get comfortable 'cause I'm on my way out." He wasn't.

Pruitt and Saturday sat down and got comfortable. Pruitt removed the portable tape recorder from his pocket, flipped it on, and placed it on Ramses' desk.

"This thing keeps gettin' weirder and weirder," he announced.

Ramses looked at them blandly, refusing to take the bait, which prompted Pruitt to continue. "Weren't you the lead investigator on the Rosedea murder?"

"We already established that. Everything's in the report. Read it," Ramses said.

"I told you before, I did," Prutt told him. "But I can't tell which Rosedea you're talkin' about in there."

"What do you mean 'which Rosedea'? How many Rosedeas do you need?" Ramses skeptically responded.

"Well, that's the deal," Saturday volunteered. "Ya see, Pruitt and me just got back from an autopsy over at the ME's office."

"Congratulations."

"Get this," Saturday continued. "The dead guy was a zombie! I thought zombies only existed in monster movies, but the ME's got a died-in-the-wool zombie layin' on the slab right now!"

"What are you talkin' about?" Ramses asked, feigning boredom. "Why are you wasting my time? Don't you girls have a cat to get out of a tree or something?"

"We did that earlier today," Saturday affirmed. "After that we went to a fashion show at a kindergarten, then to the flower show."

"Wait, it gets better," Pruitt interrupted. "That's what Saturday's tryin' to tell you. When the ME fingerprinted the stiff and we ran 'em through NCIC, there were no records of the stiff's prints. "

"The dead guy didn't have any ID on him?" Ramses asked.

Saturday looked at him in indulgently. "What do you think? If he had ID do you think we'd be havin' this conversation?"

"The fact that the John Doe's prints aren't on record means nothing," Ramses said. "Either he was never arrested or never worked for the government. Most peoples' fingerprints aren't on record. If you girls were real cops, you'd know that."

"I guess that's why you're Chief of Detectives and we're marooned in Internal Affairs." Pruitt looked at his partner. "See, why didn't you think of that, Saturday?" Saturday looked at him impassively.

"But that's not the weird part," Pruitt resumed. "We located the John Doe's car, an Escalade, parked a coupla blocks from where he was killed; the keys were in his pocket, so we know it was his car. There was no registration in it but we lifted a bunch of prints off it, which matched the prints the ME pulled from the stiff. When we ran the plates, it turns out that the Escalade's owned by a Nevada Corporation."

"Big deal. That's not exactly unusual, genius. Lots of people register their cars through Nevada corporations so nobody can trace 'em to a specific owner."

"True enough, but then we ran the VIN through the manufacturer. GM's records show that the Escalade was wholesaled to a local Cadillac dealer. When we contacted the dealer, they checked their sales records and, lo and behold, the Escalade was sold two years ago to 'Georgio Rosedea.' So, what we got is a dead guy driving an Escalade owned by another dead guy. Who'd a thunk it?" Pruitt paused and focused a penetrating stare on Ramses. "Who do you think the John Doe might be, Detective? We thought that, since you were the lead detective on the Rosedea investigation, you might be able to shed some light on it."

"It's a puzzler," added Saturday. Both men gazed at Ramses, who stared out the window onto Washington Street, four floors below, because he didn't know what else to do.

"Well, I know who it ain't. It ain't Rosedea because Dawson blew Rosedea's head off months ago."

"Yeah, that's what your report said. We were as surprised as you are to find the John Doe was drivin'

Rosedea's car." Saturday assured him. "You are surprised, aren't you?"

"Well, whoever he was, he isn't Rosedea," Ramses reiterated. "Rosedea's been dead for months, so he obviously can't be out drivin' an Escalade. I outta know."

"That's exactly what we were thinkin'," Saturday agreed. "Trouble is, Rosedea Number One was cremated, so we can't get an exhumation order to dig him up and straighten the whole thing out."

Ramses changed the subject. "What's the guy at the ME's look like?"

"You mean aside from lookin' dead?" Pruitt was toying with Ramses. "He looks kinda Mexican."

"Or Italian," Saturday volunteered.

Ramses scowled. "You know what I mean...how'd he end up dead?"

"He found himself on the wrong end of a shotgun."

"Who was on the right end?"

"Somebody you know."

Ramses continued to stare out the window, wondering how this could have happened. "I know lots of people," he said, vaguely.

"Remember the old guy who was in the car with Dawson when he was killed?"

Ramses furrowed his brow as if thinking. "Not really. The old black guy? I wouldn't say I know him. You're tellin' me that he killed somebody? You're shittin' me!" Ramses found it inconceivable that a feeble old man killed Rosey. Pruitt and Saturday were fucking with him, hoping to goad him into betraying himself. "Where'd it happen?" he asked.

"In the old guy's restaurant, not ten blocks from here.   But get this, the old man said the John Doe was trying to rob the place!   Now, why would a guy who wears a $2,000 suit and drives an Escalade try to rob some shitty greasy spoon?"

"No idea." Ramses stretched his arms luxuriantly and spread his fingers. "But it looks like it turned out to be a bad idea. I guess he never heard that crime doesn't pay." Ramses was pissed. He couldn't believe that dumb bastard Rosey had managed to get himself killed if, in fact, he had. Pruitt and Saturday clearly had a hard-on for him, and Ramses still wasn't entirely convinced they weren't simply fucking with him.   He needed to get on the phone and make some calls, starting with Larry McKeever. "But I'm sure you girls will be able to figure it out between all the 'workshops' and seminars you attend."

"Well, we got this idea," Pruitt resumed.   He noticed that Ramses' face had become flushed and sweat beaded his forehead. "Remember that we told you we had a witness who says he saw the guy who burned up your snitch, Alto?   The guy drivin' the Caprice?"

"I thought you said you couldn't identify the body," Ramses responded. "So how do you know it was Alto?"

"Oh, we gotta a pretty good idea it was him," Pruitt said. "Why, have you heard from him?

Ramses shook his head. "He'll pop up sooner or later."

"Ain't that the damndest thing!" exclaimed Saturday. "Two zombies in one day! One laying on the slab down at the ME's office, and another zombie walkin' around after bein' killed in a fire! What are the fuckin' odds?"

"You're a real funny guy, asshole," Ramses spat.

"Well, as I was saying," Pruitt resumed, "we're gonna show our witness the photos of the John Doe the ME just took during the autopsy. We're thinking that he may have been the guy who set the fire."

"One, you don't know that the fire was deliberately set. And, two, you don't know who the guy was who was killed in the fire. Anyway, what does any of this have to do with me?" Ramses tried to look disinterested. He wished they'd leave, so he could get on the phone to McKeever.

"In your investigation of Rosedea's murder, who identified the body?"

"How the hell would I know? The ME, I guess."

"How could the ME identify a body he'd never seen before?"

"Then it must've been Rosedea's family. Ask the ME."

"We looked at the pictures the ME took when he autopsied *that* body and they don't look anything like the John Doe down at the morgue."

"Why would they? They're two different people!" Ramses replied. "They wouldn't resemble one another unless Rosedea had a double. Or a twin." He swung around in his chair and faced Pruitt. "What's your point?"

"We're just trying to figure out why the John Doe down at the ME's office was tryin' to rob a shitty greasy spoon, driving a high-end car belonging to a guy who was supposedly killed nearly a year ago."

"What do you mean 'supposedly'?" Ramses warily asked. Without waiting for an answer, he continued. "Besides, I don't understand why you two find any of this so remarkable. People do all kinds of weird, inexplicable shit. How would I know? My job was to investigate Rosedea's murder, which I did."

"Yeah, that's what your report says." Pruitt reached forward and switched off the tape recorder. "Well, we gotta go. We just thought you'd like to know what's going on, since you're the Chief of Detectives, and all..." His voice trailed off.

Ramses flicked his gaze between Pruitt and Saturday. "Here's what I know," he said, curtly. "Georgio Rosedea was murdered months ago by some bastard who subsequently tried to run over a uniformed police officer who was attempting to arrest him for that murder. The uniform shot and killed the bastard in order to save his own skin. Case closed. Now, according to you guys, some other guy shows up driving Rosedea's car, tries to rob a restaurant, and gets killed in the process. Again, case closed. What the fuck is so hard for you two dumbasses to comprehend? You remind me of the crop-circle crowd. Even after the guys who created the damned things went public and said that crop-circles are a complete hoax, people refuse to believe them. They keep insisting that Martians make 'em, even though there isn't an ounce of evidence that Martians, or anybody else, have anything to do with crop-circles. That's like you guys, always lookin' for alternative, idiotic, explanations for shit."

"Occam's Razor," murmured Saturday.

"What?" Ramses glared at him.

"Occam's Razor," Saturday repeated. "You know."

"I have no idea what you're talking about," Ramses snorted. Now beat it; I have work to do." Ramses motioned with his head toward the door.

Pruitt stood and slipped his tape recorder back into his pocket. "I thought you were on your way out."

"You're right, I am. As soon as you two idiots leave, I'm gonna go take a shit," Ramses told him.

***

Butler liked press conferences. The attorney general enjoyed basking in the uncritical adulation of the compliant local news outlets, even if the pressers frequently turned into quasi-social events for the reporters themselves. Press conferences too often deteriorated into opportunities for reporters to interview one another, rather than him; Butler preferred, of course, that all the attention be focused exclusively on him. Oh well, one had to take the good with the bad.

Butler was seated behind, and slightly to the left of, the polished wooden podium, at which stood his chief of staff. Lined up in seats on either side of him were various staffers from his office, all trying to look crisp and professional for the six o'clock news. His chief of staff had nearly concluded his introductory remarks, priming the audience for Butler's imminent address regarding the purpose of the press conference. Butler rose as his chief of staff stepped aside and invited the Attorney General forward with an officious sweep of his arm. Butler approached the podium and gravely surveyed the audience of reporters before beginning his rehearsed presentation.

"Good afternoon, ladies and gentlemen," Butler began in the most somber tone he could muster. "I'm certain that all of you remember that, less than one year ago, my office called a press conference in order to acquaint the media and the community with the details arising out of the murder of, frankly, an unsavory member of our community, Georgio Rosedea. Mr. Rosedea's murder was important because it called attention to the criminal element that had, until my election as your attorney general, insinuated itself into the fabric of our community. Thanks to the diligent efforts of my office, working hand-in-glove with law enforcement, however, that web has now been broken and the lawless element is now on the run, frantically seeking environs more congenial to their criminal enterprises."

Behind him, Butler's chief of staff fretted that the attorney general would turn the reporters off by using the word "community" too much.

Oblivious, Butler continued. "My office recently received intelligence that Mr. Rosedea's murder may have been merely the tip of the ice burg, however. We are informed that corruption may have seeped into the very bones of the body politic. I called you here today to reaffirm my office's unrelenting commitment to the elimination from our midst of those persons and organizations who seek to undermine public confidence in the fidelity of our public institutions." Butler paused dramatically. "Be warned," he intoned, "no matter who you are or how you may attempt to conceal your misdeeds, you will be found out and, as your attorney general, I will personally see to your indictment and prosecution to the fullest extent mandated by law. Those who would do us evil, no matter their station in the public or private sphere, have no place in our community." Butler paused again but found it impossible to gauge the press's immediate reaction to his manifesto. So, he took a drink of water.

Thankfully, somebody in the crowd raised a hand. "Mr. Attorney General, you just said that your office 'recently received intelligence' about corruption in 'the body politic.' What, exactly, are you referring to? What 'corruption?' What do you mean by 'the body politic?' And how did you receive this intelligence?"

Butler was delighted at the opportunity to respond, thereby assuring a larger sound-bite on the evening news.

"An anonymous tipster recently called my 'Crime Busters' hotline," the attorney general mysteriously confided. "In it, he suggested that I train my sights on certain governmental departments and agencies for evidence of wrongdoing. Now," Butler smiled knowingly, "it is not unknown for cranks to utilize my hotline for personal, nefarious reasons, venal people who are motivated by nothing more than the substantial rewards that are offered through the Crime Buster's hotline for the arrest and conviction of legitimate criminals. In this case, however, we have no reason for believing that our tipster was anything less than an honest, concerned citizen. Irrespective, my office takes all Crime Busters calls very seriously and if my investigation, which is ongoing, reveals malfeasance, you can expect an immediate and vigorous response from the attorney general's office."

"What kind of corruption?" the reporter asked again. "What 'departments and agencies' are involved?"

"Given the ongoing nature of my investigation, I regret that I cannot at this time reveal the agencies involved. The public may rest assured, however, that my office is diligently proceeding with its investigation, without fear or favor."

Another hand went up in the audience. "Have you determined whether there is any factual basis for the allegations of corruption?"

"My investigation has so far failed to reveal any evidence of malfeasance or illegality on the part of any public official or department," Butler assured the questioner. "But the investigation, as I said, is ongoing. Naturally, we will keep the media apprised of our labors on behalf of the people of Arizona. They deserve nothing less."

"The attorney general's office has a staff of investigators," someone else in the crowd remarked. "Is it adequate to conduct the apparently wholesale investigation you're currently engaged in?"

"I wouldn't characterize our investigation as 'wholesale,'" Butler corrected the reporter. "The allegations of malfeasance were specific and my ongoing investigation is, therefore, highly targeted. However, in order to preclude any suggestions of factionalism, my office is prepared to create an independent, blue-ribbon, task force." Butler simply invented, spontaneously, the idea of a blue-ribbon task force because it seemed appealing. He glanced toward his chief of staff for a confirming nod, but received only a perplexed stare.

"Who would comprise this proposed task force?" a reporter asked. "And wouldn't that create potential conflicts of interest?"

"Not at all," Butler dismissively responded. "My office will insure the absolute fidelity of each member of the team. They will be above reproach." His chief of staff noted with dismay that Butler's proposed blue-ribbon investigative task force, a mere hypothetical concept only moments ago, had suddenly turned into a fait accompli. He had to shut Butler up before the attorney general made additional off-the-cuff promises that he couldn't keep. He discretely leaned forward and tugged gently at Butler's trouser leg.

After responding to a few more nebulous questions, Butler thanked the media for their attention, then stepped away from the podium as an underling from his office traded places and switched the presentation to the attorney general's recent investigation of the state lottery.

"How'd I sound?" Butler leaned over and whispered to his chief of staff. "I think we hit it out of the park!"

"What the fuck were you talking about a 'blue-ribbon task force'?" hissed his chief. "Where the hell did that come from?" He was clearly displeased.

Butler was taken aback. "I just thought of it while I was talking," he confessed in a whisper, "but I think it's a good idea. It'll show the voters that we're all over this thing."

"What 'thing'? There is no 'thing.' All you were supposed to say is that you'd received uncorroborated reports of political wrongdoing and were looking into it. The whole purpose of the press conference was just to get you some face time! I didn't want you to promise the moon and the stars, for Christ's sake!"

Butler attempted to respond, but his chief of staff waved him off in disgust. "We'll talk later...everybody's watching."

***

McKeever telephoned Chief Golden as quickly as he reasonably could after finishing Rosey's autopsy. The two of them now sat in the chief's office, drinking coffee.

"I knew this thing would blow up in our faces," McKeever said for the umpteenth time.

"Relax, Larry." The last thing the chief needed was for McKeever to melt down. "All you've got laying back at your office is a John Doe killed in a botched attempted robbery. It happens all the time. You know that. Everything is exactly what it was before. Absolutely nothing has changed. Nobody knows nuthin', so why the panic?" Golden hoped he sounded reassuring.

"If it's no big deal, why did two guys from your office show up at my office, asking questions about an unidentified body?" McKeever skeptically retorted.

"The two cops who came to see you aren't technically from my office. Yeah, they're cops but they're IA, which I have no direct control over. They're basically independent."

"Well who does have control over 'em, and what do they want from me?" As McKeever took a sip of coffee Golden noticed that his hand was trembling.

"IA answers directly to the city council and, in some cases, the attorney general. It's supposed to keep everything on the up-and-up that way."

"So, like I said, what do they want from me?"

Golden finished his coffee and placed his cup on the polished edge of his desk. He removed from the pocket of his uniform the white business card that McKeever handed him when he arrived a half-hour ago. He absently flicked a corner of it with his thumb as he studied it.

> Insp. Andrew Pruitt
> Internal Investigations
> Phoenix Police Department

"That I don't know," muttered the chief, sliding the card back into his pocket. "I don't know if it's related or not, but Pruitt and his partner have been down at my office, asking about Oren Ramses."

McKeever set his cup down with a bang.

"Bob, how could it *not* be related? The common denominator in all this shit is Ramses!" He leaned his head back and closed his eyes. "Fuck, fuck, fuck, fuck. Ramses is goin' down in flames and takin' us with him." He sighed and opened his eyes. Looking directly at the chief, he asked, "So what are you gonna do?"

"What am I gonna do?" Golden removed his cup from his desk. "Right now, I'm gonna have another cup of coffee. You want one?" McKeever shook his head.   The chief rose to his feet.   "And while I'm drinkin' it, we're gonna brainstorm about what we're gonna do to protect everybody's ass." He headed for the coffee maker in the adjacent antechamber.   "Like I said, Larry, not a damned thing has changed.   The situation is exactly the same as it was six months ago. The only thing that's changed is your panicked overreaction, which is exactly what IA is counting on." Golden stepped into the vestibule, refilled his cup, then returned to the office where he resumed his seat behind his desk.

"We can't keep killing people," McKeever murmured, more to himself than to the chief.

"Nobody's killing nobody," Golden replied.   "All this crap is just gonna blow over and it'll back to business as usual."   He watched McKeever over the rim of his cup as he took a sip of coffee.   "Have you talked to Ramses?"

"He called but I didn't call him back. I wanted to talk to you first."

"That was the right thing do to," the chief acknowledged.   "What are ya gonna do with Rosey's body?"

"The IA guys told me to hang onto it until they finish their investigation. What 'investigation' are they talking about, Bob? Who are they investigation? Me?"

Golden shook his head.   "Why would IA investigate you?   In the first place, they have no jurisdiction over you. And, in the second place, what possible reason would they have?   You're just the medical examiner, doing your job."   He took another sip of coffee.   "It's pretty obvious, though, that somebody must've dropped the dime. I don't know who or why, but that's the only possible explanation."

"Ramses?"

Golden frowned unconsciously and slowly shook his head. "Maybe, but I don't think so. Why would he? In fact, Ramses's been bitchin' to me that IA has been hounding him about the Dawson shooting. If he's the snitch, why would IA be buggin' him?"

"Who, then?"

"I was thinking about it and at first I thought the most likely candidate was probably Ramses' snitch. But it can't have been him because Rosey fried him, so he's out of the picture."

"Maybe he said something before Rosey got to him," McKeever suggested.

Golden sighed. "Yeah, maybe. I considered that." He drained his coffee cup and placed it back on the desk, then folded his arms. "Here's what I *do* know, IA has a wild hair up its butt about Dawson and is pestering everybody in sight about him. I don't know what whoever it was told 'em, but they have absolutely no evidence of anything, Larry. If we look at the situation objectively, all they've got is a dead guy with no ID. That's it." He paused, trying to assess McKeever's reaction. "The worse part about the whole thing," continued the chief, "is that, with Rosey dead, we'll have to get a replacement from the Coast."

"We can't just keep killing people," sighed McKeever again.

"Agreed, but Rosey was useful for a lot of things," Golden responded. "He was a regular jack-of-all-trades," he ruefully smiled.

"So, what am I supposed to do now?"

"There's nothing *to* do, Larry. IA will eventually run out of steam and move on to something else. When that happens, you can plant Rosey's body in Twin Buttes." Golden was referring to the potter's field located on the border of Phoenix and neighboring Tempe. "No fuss, no muss."

"But what if they actually find something?" asked McKeever, plaintively.

"They've already found something: some asshole killed in an attempted robbery with no ID. So what? Everything else is just a circle-jerk. As soon as they realize they're drivin' on a bridge to nowhere, they'll pack it in. Relax."

"Rosey can be identified by his dental records," said McKeever.

Golden shook his head. "Rosey always had his teeth worked on in Algodones, or somewhere else in Mexico. There *are* no dental records."

Both men were silent for a few moments. Finally, McKeever asked, "Are you gonna talk to Ramses? I'm not sure what I'm supposed to say if I call him back."

"Yeah, I'll talk to him," said Golden as he rose to escort McKeever to the door. "Don't worry about it. In fact, don't worry about anything. This will all blow over. You'll see."

NINE

IA wanted to see him again. Now what? Bickman fidgeted nervously in the hall outside Pruitt's second floor office. He'd not heard squat from IA since originally meeting with Pruitt and Saturday. What could they possibly want with him again? Was he going to be made the scapegoat for something? Bickman wracked his brain in an effort to come up with any transgression he may have committed, but could think of nothing.

The elevator down the hall dinged and, after a pause, the door slid open and Pruitt and Saturday stepped out into the hall. Both of them were laughing. By contrast, Bickman felt like vomiting.

"Officer Bickman," called Pruitt as the duo rapidly approached. "Thanks for coming."

"I didn't exactly have a choice," Bickman responded, matter-of-factly.

"Yeah, true enough," concurred Pruitt as he unlocked his office door. "C'mon in...you remember my partner, don't you?" Bickman nodded at the stoical Saturday. Tossing his keys on his battered desk, Pruitt pointed to a chair, "Sit." Bickman did as he was ordered. Pruitt sat at his desk while Saturday slumped against an adjacent filing cabinet.

"Did you ever meet Georgio Rosedea?" Pruitt abruptly began.

"Where's your tape recorder?" asked Bickman, suspiciously.

"We don't need it," Pruitt responded. "We just want to pick your brain about something."

"My brain? Why my brain? I'm sure there are lots of better brains in the Phoenix PD."

"Maybe," interjected Saturday, "but yours is the one we're interested in."

Bickman was suspicious, and perplexed, in equal measure. "I guess," is all he could say.

"Did you ever meet Georgio Rosedea?" Pruitt asked again.

"Not that I remember. Why?"

Pruitt ignored the question. "So, you wouldn't recognize Rosedea's picture if you saw it?"

"No, I don't think so. Like I say, I don't think I ever met him."

Pruitt opened his desk drawer, took out a manila envelope, and removed from it an eight-by-ten photograph. Reaching across the desk, he handed it to Bickman. "Know him?"

Bickman scrutinized the photo. It was a head shot of a man, obviously dead and obviously lying on a stainless-steel mortician's table. "Nope." He handed the photo back to Pruitt.

"That's Georgio Rosedea," said Saturday.

"Okay," Bickman shrugged. "So?"

Pruitt slid the photo back into the manila envelope and placed it atop his desk. "That photo was taken two days ago at the ME's office."

"Huh?" Bickman was confused. "Rosedea's been dead for months, shot in the head. Why's his body's still down at the ME's office?"

Pruitt smiled cryptically. "Rosedea was shot, all right, but not in the head and not months ago. He was killed a week ago in a dumpy restaurant a few blocks from here."

Bickman slid forward in his seat. "What are you talking about? Rosedea was killed last summer. I don't know who that guy is, but he isn't Rosedea."

"How do you know?" Saturday asked. "Did you guys go to school together or something?"

Bickman swiveled to face Pruitt's partner. "Everybody knows it. Hell, I shot the guy who killed him."

"Yeah, you shot a guy, all right," Pruitt responded. "But it wasn't the guy who killed Rosedea. The guy who killed Rosedea is still flipping burgers. In fact, Saturday and I just had lunch there today."

"Unfortunately," Saturday added.

Bickman felt almost overwhelmed. "Are you guys screwing with me?"

"Not a bit," Pruitt assured him. "You see, Officer Bickman, we don't think that Georgio Rosedea was killed months ago. We can't prove it yet, but we think that he was killed just a few days ago."

"So, who *was* killed? And how do you know the guy you just showed me is Georgio Rosedea?"

"That's where you come in," Saturday said.

Bickman couldn't conceal his skepticism. "What are you talking about? I told you, I never met Georgio Rosedea. I know nothing about the guy, other than he's dead. If you brought me here to talk about Georgio Rosedea I can't help you."

Pruitt remained unperturbed. "Remember that apartment fire off Indian School about six weeks ago? You talked to a bum who said that someone was in the apartments when they burned?" Without waiting for Bickman's response, he continued. "Turns out that there was somebody in the apartments, and he died in the fire."

"Okay..." Bickman couldn't figure out where this was going.

"Your report said that the bum told you that he saw somebody who he thought might have set the fire. Remember?"

Bickman tried to think back. "Yeah, I remember."

"Well, we think the guy who set the fire is this guy," Pruitt tapped the manila envelope resting on his desk. "We want you to track the bum down and show him this photo."

Bickman grimaced. "Why me? And how am I supposed to find him if he's no longer hangin' around the apartments? Homeless people tend to move around a lot. By definition, they're 'homeless'."

"Because you're the officer who initially responded to the fire and talked to him. You're the only guy who'll be able to recognize him," said Saturday. "How you find him is your problem. Check soup kitchens, ask other bums."

"I'm not sure I'd recognize him even if I fell down over him," declared Bickman. "I only talked to him for a few minutes, and it was dark."

"I guess you'd better get crackin', then," Saturday replied. "Oh, by the way, we already talked to your SO and made arrangements for you to help us on our little project."

Bickman was silent as he attempted to grasp the significance of Pruitt's revelations. "So, what about the guy I shot?" he finally asked.

"He was just some schlub," said Saturday. "Wrong place, wrong time."

Bickman wasn't sure he'd heard correctly. "What? Say again?"

"The guy you shot was set up," Pruitt softly responded. "He panicked when he realized what was comin' down and tried to get away. No one holds you responsible for what happened."

Bickman couldn't believe what he was hearing. Sweat broke out on his face and his heart began hammering. He feared he was about pass out. "What?" he again asked, almost in a daze.

"Officer Bickman, this isn't about you," Pruitt continued. "We're determined to find the people behind all of this, and you're gonna help." He reached across his desk and handed Bickman the manila envelope containing Rosey's photo. "Go."

***

"So, was it Rosey?" Ramses and Golden were sitting in the chief's office. "Did you actually see the body?"

"Yeah, it was Rosey," Golden replied. "He was shot in the chest, so his face wasn't messed up. It was him."

Ramses couldn't believe his ears. Until this moment, he was convinced that Pruitt and Saturday were just yanking his chain when they told him that Rosey'd been killed. How was this possible?

"I figured those two IA bastards were fucking with me when they were in here," Ramses grunted. "I tried to call McKeever, but the prick didn't call me back. He's probably scrambling to cover his own ass."

"I talked to him," Golden replied. "He's freaked, just like everybody else. I called the Coast, too."

"What did they say?"

"Nuthin'. What could they say?"

Ramses shook his head. "This thing is turning into a royal cluster fuck."

"Look, Oren," said the chief, turning squarely in his chair to face Ramses, "I'll tell you the same thing I told McKeever: absolutely nothing has changed. The situation is exactly the same as it was six months ago. All IA, the attorney general, or God himself, have is an unidentified body layin' on a slab down at Larry's office. That's it. Even if somebody manages to identify the body, it'll come back as 'Adolph Medina.' So, what? That's exactly why we gave Rosey a new identity in the first place. Rosey was stupid to get himself killed, but what is, is. Let everybody chase their tails until they get tired, then they'll go away. Like I said, nothing's changed."

"I can't figure out how that old man managed to kill Rosey," Ramses stated in disbelief. "That's what makes it so weird."

"I have no idea, Oren, but if something happens it must be possible. The fact is, he *did* kill Rosey. The how doesn't make a hill of beans difference."

Most worrisome to Ramses was not Rosey's inconvenient death, but the fact that he was unable to silence Jim, or locate Carol's supposedly semen-stained dress, before checking out. Ramses had to promptly devise a 'Plan B.' "IA was hectoring me even before Rosey croaked," he said. "Who do you suppose threw me under the bus?"

"I'm not convinced that anyone threw you under the bus, Oren. IA has to justify its existence, so it creates make-work investigations. For all we know, they pulled Dawson out of a hat. Rosey's death does nothing to change that. Everybody knows IA is a bunch of pussies and, like I said, the only physical evidence they have of anything is Adolph Medina's body, killed during a robbery attempt. Big deal. Hell, they don't even know whose body it is!"

"Did you hear the AG's press conference?" Ramses asked. "He said that he received a tip that he's investigating. Do you think it had anything to do with Rosey?"

Golden shrugged. "Who knows? Who knows whether Butler even received a tip? Don't forget that he also said that his 'investigation,' whatever that means, has uncovered nothing. Butler's just playin' to the crowd, positioning himself for a run at the governor's office." He paused and smiled, coldly. "The one thing I know for sure is that Butler hasn't grown any new smarts since being elected AG."

Notwithstanding the chief's reassurances, Ramses felt only slightly more relieved. He still had to figure out a way to take care of Jim, and maybe Carol, too.

"Should I keep talkin' to the pricks from IA?"

"Talk to the union if you're worried about it, Oren. One of the reps will know whether you should cooperate with 'em or tell 'em to pound sand. That's why we pay dues. You got nuthin' to worry about."

Ramses didn't look convinced.

"But I've got a question for you, Oren," Golden continued. "Why was Rosey at the old man's in the first place? What was he doing there? If he hadn't been there, he'd still be breathin' and we wouldn't have this problem. I didn't send him there, the Coast didn't send him, and everybody I talked to said they didn't know anything about it. Do you?"

If that idiot Rosey hadn't managed to get killed, Ramses' plan to eliminate Jim would never have seen the light of day. Now he felt like an errant schoolboy, having to explain to his father how he'd accidently thrown a rock through the front window. "I asked Rosey to check on something for me," he vaguely responded.

Golden looked perplexed. "'Check on something' for you? What the hell does that mean, Oren?"

"I just wanted to make sure the old man wasn't gonna cause any trouble."

"What are you talking about? Why would the old man cause trouble? Until a week ago, when he shot Rosey, the old man was a complete nonentity. What made you think he was going to cause trouble?" The chief was attempting to make sense of what Ramses was saying.

"The old man threatened to blackmail us," Ramses finally confessed. "I asked Rosey to nip it in the bud."

"Blackmail us? *Now* you tell me this shit?" Golden was incredulous. "How could he possibly blackmail us? With what? Why didn't you talk to me about this before going off half-cocked?"

"I didn't think it was a big deal," Ramses lamely responded. "I didn't think Rosey would fuck it up."

Golden was astonished by Ramses' insouciance. "You're telling me that Rosey's dead because you unilaterally decided to send him on your own private wild goose chase? Is that what I'm hearing? If that's what happened, Rosey didn't fuck it up. *You* fucked it up."

Ramses bristled at the chief's imperious attitude. "No, that isn't what you're hearing. I said that the old man threatened to blackmail us and I sent Rosey to make sure that didn't happen. I don't know how it happened, but he ended up dead. I can't be blamed because Rosey was a dumb fuck."

"For Christ's sake, when did this happen?" Golden exploded. "And why did you take it upon yourself to deal with it? Do you have any idea of the can of worms you've opened up?"

"The old man was apparently stalkin' me and accosted me while I was eatin' lunch. He threatened to blackmail us, but I don't know with what," Ramses lied. "I knew he was talkin' out his ass, but figured that everybody would be a lot happier if he was out of the picture, so I talked to Rosey. It was no big deal, which is why I didn't run it past you or Sunstone first." He hoped his facile explanation would mollify Golden.

"So, you decided, on your own, just to kill the old man, without consulting anyone? Because of your stupidity, Rosey's dead and we've got IA and idiot Butler engaged in a witch hunt. And, to top it all off, the old man is still alive. What the hell is wrong with you, Oren? Could you have screwed this up any worse?"

Ramses could barely restrain himself from telling Golden to go fuck himself, and storming out, but prudence dictated that he endure the chief's tirade. He held his tongue.

"Do you know whether those assholes from IA talked to the old man?" Golden managed to ask in a reasonably calm voice.

"I don't know. They never said," Ramses responded. "But why would they? IA wouldn't get involved just because the old man wasted somebody who, as far as everybody knows, was trying to rob him. Why would IA get involved?"

Golden sighed. "So how did the old man intend to blackmail us?"

"I don't know. He never said," Ramses flatly lied.

"It never occurred to you that he may have been just rattling your cage?"

"Yeah, I considered that," Ramses replied. "Maybe he was. I just figured it was better not to take the chance. Like you said, 'no man, no problem.'"

Golden had to admit there was nothing inherently blameworthy in Ramses' decision to permanently silence the potentially troublesome Jim. His beef was that Ramses decided to forge ahead without consulting anyone.

"Well, we can't unring a bell," the chief said, resignedly, attempting to put the best face on it. "Like I told Larry McKeever, hopefully, it'll all blow over, sooner rather than later." He looked intently at Ramses. "Do me a favor, Oren. Talk to me before you decide to do something like this in the future. I don't want any more damned surprises. Rosey's gonna be hard to replace."

"Yeah, ok," Ramses said without conviction. He frowned. "I still can't figure out how he managed to kill Rosey. It's amazing."

"Rosey obviously just got careless. Maybe livin' in Mexico rubbed off on him. You know, the *mañana* attitude. Who the hell knows?"

Ramses rubbed his eyes, as if tired. "So, what are we gonna do about the old man?"

"I don't know," Golden slowly shook his head. "I don't know." More to the point, Golden didn't know what he was going to do about Ramses.

***

"You painted us into a corner with your idiotic 'blue-ribbon task force'," scoffed the chief of staff. He and Butler were sitting in the attorney general's office on Jefferson Street. "Everybody's gonna be expecting you to make good on it."

"So, what?" countered Butler. "I have every intention of making good on it. It'll be good public relations...show that we take allegations of corruption seriously."

"Well, since it's basically going to be window dressing, who do you want on it? It should be names the public will recognize. Otherwise, what's the point?"

"I've been thinking about that," replied Butler. "Do a Google search for law enforcement figures who've been in the local news over, say, the past year or so. They'll still be fresh in the publics' mind so we'll appoint them to the team. We shouldn't have any trouble rounding up volunteers because it'll be kind of prestigious. And it isn't like they're actually gonna be doing anything. We'll give 'em a plaque or something."

The chief of staff laughed. "Napoleon said that 'men will die for baubles.'"

"I don't know about that," Butler said, "but I don't anticipate they'll be much dying involved. Just get me the names of some candidates before the public loses interest and forgets about the whole damned thing."

***

"My God, I can't believe you actually killed someone," Carol marveled. "You must've been terrified, Jim." She took a sip of Pepsi.

The old man smiled, the wrinkles on his face creating a map of his life. "I really wasn't, Carol, 'cause I expected to see him. Besides, I was the one holdin' the gun!" It was late afternoon and they sat in the empty restaurant. Thankfully, the sun had dropped behind the building across the street, cloaking the dining room in shade.

She shook her head in disbelief. "Even so, I would've peed myself."

"I was more worried about the cops than about him. They treated me like I was the bad guy until Pruitt and Saturday showed up."

"Did you break any laws? Did they arrest you?"

"Self-defense is the oldest law of nature, Carol, and that's just what I did. If the law won't let you defend yourself, something's wrong with the law."

She nodded in affirmation and took another sip. "Why did you expect to see him, Jim? Did you know him?"

"I didn't know him, but I saw him once before. He came in a few days before, actin' strange. I could tell he was up to no good."

"How? What was he doing?"

"He was dressed like one of them uptown cats. Stuck out like a sore thumb. He ordered a sandwich, then left without even touchin' it."

"So, what made you think he'd come back that night?"

Jim shifted his position in their booth because his knees were beginning to ache. "I didn't know he'd be back that night, just that he'd be back."

"Yeah, but how did you know that?"

He smiled again, his beautiful teeth gleaming. "'Cause Ramses sent him, Carol. He was here to kill me." Jim's voice was strangely devoid of emotion. "He came here because he thinks I've got your dress, the one I told him about when he was eatin' lunch. That's why he was here."

"But there is no dress, Jim," Carol sighed.

Jim chuckled. "Yeah, but he don't know that. Now he ain't got the dress *or* the guy he sent to get it."

Jim looked thoughtful. "I guess he got it all right, just not what he expected to get!"

Carol finished her Pepsi and both of them were silent for a minute. "Hey, isn't this a restaurant?" she finally asked. "Don't you have any food around here?"

"Well, it used to be a restaurant when I had customers," Jim acknowledged. "But I could probably scare something up for you. Wanna burger?"

"Only if you'll eat one with me," she smiled.

"Done." Jim began to slide out of the booth.

"Wait a minute." Carol reached out and grasped the old man's gnarled hand. "Aren't you afraid somebody will come back?"

"What's the sense in being afraid of what's certain to happen, Carol? The only thing that scares people is what they don't know. I know Ramses ain't finished with us, but I ain't finished with him, neither. We just gotta be ready for 'em when they come."

***

Golden was bugged. His latest conversation with Ramses had simply reinforced his conviction that his chief of detectives was losing it. If that happened, it wasn't impossible that Ramses would pull the whole fucking house down with him. With Rosey *hors de combat* he had to come up with an alternative method of dealing with the situation. Golden tried calling the Coast with his concerns, but they were unmoved. They simply ordered him to deal with it. Deal with it how? Golden thought of Mother Theresa, who remarked that she knew God would never burden her with more challenges than she could handle, but that she wished

God didn't have so much confidence in her. Golden was beginning to appreciate how she felt.

He thought about forcing Ramses into early retirement then spiriting him out of the country, as they had Rosey, beyond the reach of those IA fuckers. With Ramses out of the picture, they'd surely turn their attention elsewhere. Trouble was, Ramses wasn't likely to prove as malleable as Rosey. Further complicating matters, Ramses had a wife who would undoubtedly pitch a bitch about being forcibly relocated to some third-world shithole. And, aside from the Ramses problem, there was the matter of who ratted them out the attorney general in the first place? Although Golden was pretty confident that Butler was too preoccupied running for governor to actually investigate anything, it was none-the-less a niggling worry. Finally, what about the threatened blackmailer that Ramses talked about? Golden sighed. Ramses was right, it was turning into a royal cluster fuck.

***

Earl Welch watched the attorney general's press conference with eager anticipation. He'd called Butler's Crime Busters hotline over a month ago but hadn't heard shit since. Although his message had been terse, it contained enough detail to establish its bona fides. Welch also recently heard through the grapevine that Rosedea was dead, though he had no idea of the particulars and had no desire to telephone Golden about it. All he wanted was for the AG to do his job and to leave him out of it. As he watched, however, it became increasingly apparent that Butler's press conference was nothing more than an opportunity for some face-time. Welch realized the AG's call for a blue-ribbon investigative task force echoed JFK's definition of a committee, five people doing the work of one where, either because of or despite this, absolutely nothing ultimately gets accomplished. Disgusted, Welch turned off his television.

It was a waste of time to have contacted the attorney general, who was obviously more interested in advancing his political fortunes than in draining the swamp. That aside, if Golden, or anybody else from Sunstone, discovered that it was Welch who contacted Butler's office, it was a virtual certainty that he'd end up like Rosey. Now he was really screwed.

***

As he fully expected, the homeless guy who previously lived behind the burned-out apartment complex had decamped; there remained no trace of him. Bickman wandered over to the shell of the building and surveyed the remains. Roughly a quarter of the building still stood, although it was charred and largely collapsed. The rest of the structure had been reduced to a heap of blackened debris. Weeds had already begun sprouting through the concrete foundation cracked by flames. Forlorn toilets still sat in situ in what had previously been bathrooms, surrounded by ruin.

Bickman flipped a fragment of scorched wood with the toe of his shoe. Aside from what Pruitt told him about finding a body in the rubble, he'd heard nothing about its identity. It must've been a helluva way to die. He turned and walked back to his police car.

TEN

"I pulled five candidates for you," said Butler's chief of staff, handing the attorney general a sheet of paper. "The two most recent 'Officers of the Year' from Phoenix PD and a couple of deputies from the Pima County Sheriff's Office." He thought it politically judicious to choose token law enforcement officers from Arizona's two most populated counties, rather from the state's thinly-populated rural counties where comparatively few voters resided. "I also managed to find a female. They're as good as anybody."

Butler surveyed the list of names. "I never heard of any of 'em," he announced, "but I'm glad you put a woman on it, gotta keep the feminists happy."

"Believe me, anybody who follows this kind of stuff has heard of 'em. The media certainly has. Besides, unless we can get Tom Cruise or Brad Pitt to volunteer for your hair-brained task force, these are about the most appealing candidates we can get when it comes to high-profile crime busters. We hit the jackpot with the woman. She teaches at the police academy and, not only is she female, she's also a dyke. So, we throw a bone to the gay community, too."

The AG nodded. "Perfect. Hey, didn't Elvis work as some kind of Junior Crime Fighter with the

Memphis PD?   I think he had a bunch of toy badges they gave him."

The chief of staff laughed. "Yeah, I think he did something like that. But Elvis was crazy. And dead, so we can't get him!"

"Yep, crazy as a shithouse rat," concurred Butler. He returned the list to his subordinate. "Have you contacted any of these guys?"

"I wanted to clear it with you first."

"Well, draft 'em all a letter on official letterhead. Tell 'em that the State of Arizona respectfully requests the honor of their participation on a blue-ribbon task force, blah, blah, blah, blah. Let me look at it before you send it, though."

"Will do." The chief of staff departed and Butler glanced at his watch. Time for lunch.

***

Ramses staked out Jim's small apartment complex for over a week, but the old man failed to materialize. Unless he showed up pretty soon, Ramses was going to have to confront Jim at the restaurant which, given Rosey's recent unhappy experience, he was hesitant to do. That aside, the restaurant was too public. He could, of course, simply go to Carol's apartment and retrieve the dress. There was no guarantee, however, it was even there. It would be just like the old bastard to have hidden it somewhere. But Ramses needed that fucking dress. He'd beat it out of him if he had to.

If Golden knew that a dress with Ramses' semen on it existed, he'd have a shit-fit. Fortunately, he *didn't* know. The whole fucking mess could have been prevented if Rosey hadn't been such an incompetent dumbass. Fortunately, it wasn't too late to fix things. All he had to do was wait for the old man to return home.

Ramses shifted positions slightly. Even though the bench seat in his Caprice was plush, it was still tiresome to sit hour after hour, waiting. But if the old man thought he could elude Ramses, he was dead wrong.

***

"Wow! Look at this!" Bickman handed the AG' s letter to Pam. "The AG selected me to be on his anti-corruption task force."

Pam took the letter and scanned it. "Hmm...I read in the paper that he was going to organize something like that. That's pretty cool," she smiled.

"I wonder how he got my name," Bickman mused.

Pam kissed him on the cheek. "He obviously heard of your reputation as an incorruptible police officer," she teased. "Who better to be on an anti-corruption task force? Do you know any of the other guys?"

Bickman re-read the letter. "Three of 'em I don't know. The fourth one I kinda know...he's the Chief of Detectives at Phoenix PD."

"Is he cool or an idiot?" Pam asked with apparent seriousness.

"He's okay, I guess," Bickman shrugged. "Like I said, I don't really know him, but those guys from IA were asking me about him, so I guess he's all right.

Otherwise, the AG wouldn't have chosen him to be on his task force."

"Well, I think it's quite an honor, Officer Bickman, and I'm very proud of you," Pam affirmed. "It looks like the Powers That Be have their eyes on you."

Bickman laughed. "Yeah, but maybe that isn't such a good thing!"

"There's no such thing as bad publicity," Pam responded. "So, it's definitely a good thing. Do you have to RSVP, or what?"

"It says that I'm supposed to call the AG's office and schedule a time to meet with his chief of staff." Bickman knew that being appointed to such a prestigious body as the Attorney General's task force was a great honor, and hoped that his project for Pruitt and Saturday wouldn't prevent him from participating in it.

"Good. It can't hurt to rub elbows with the big dogs, Dave. I can't wait to tell mom and dad! I've got a good feeling about this."

Bickman smiled. "I have no idea why I'm even part of the equation, but somebody must be looking out for me!"

"That 'somebody' would be me," Pam winked. This time she kissed him on the lips.

***

"Goddamn sonofabitch!" Ramses spat over the phone. "I just got a letter from the fucking AG, appointing me to some goddamn task force. "Is this a joke?"

Chief Golden patiently endured Ramses' tirade before speaking. "I know nothing about it, Oren. Nobody from the AG's office contacted me. I haven't any idea what it's about. You know as much as I do. Butler was supposed to create some kind of bullshit panel to investigate corruption, but I never heard who was supposed to be on it. I just figured it was just another political stunt intended for public consumption."

Ramses wasn't mollified. "Yeah, whatever. I think those two cocksuckers from IA had something to do with it. They must be laughin' their asses off at the irony of having me appointed to a task force that's supposed to be investigating corruption while they're investigating me...like puttin' Cuba in charge of a human-rights convention."

"I don't think IA has any pull with the AG, Oren," Golden said. "It's just luck of the draw. Besides, you *are* Chief of Detectives for the Phoenix PD so you're an obvious choice. There's nothing mysterious about it."

Ramses reflected for a moment. "Maybe," he finally acknowledged. "So, what do you think I should do? Beg off?"

"No, don't beg off. That'll look suspicious. Just graciously agree to participate and go with the flow. The fact that you were chosen to participate is actually a good thing because the AG's imprimatur will go a long way toward undermining the IA's investigation. Remember what Socrates said, 'When people speak ill of you, live so that no one will believe them.' This is the perfect opportunity."

Ramses had to confess it made sense; he'd not looked at it that way. "Yeah, okay. I'll respond to the letter and say I'm in. I'll keep you up to speed." After exchanging a few more pleasantries, he terminated the call.

Golden hung up the phone. Although he had no idea how Ramses got appointed to the AG's task force, it was obvious he had to deal with the problem of his chief of detectives sooner, rather than later.

***

Harvey lived in a rambling 1940's house in the Willo District of downtown Phoenix, not far from Jim's café, which explained why he was a regular customer. Like Jim, Harvey was a widower who resided alone so, when Jim asked if he'd mind having a house guest for a little while, Harvey responded with enthusiasm.

"Mind? Heck no! I could use the company, Jim. Stay as long as you like. You can even move in, for all I care." Harvey loved to play pinochle and checkers and secretly hoped to rope Jim into participating.

"Well, it won't be for too long," Jim assured him. "I just gotta get some things arranged at my apartment."

Harvey waived his hands dismissively. "Hey, don't worry about it. Like I said, stay as long as you want. You just gotta make some of those delicious fried egg sandwiches now and again," he grinned.

Jim thought for a moment before speaking again. "Harvey, you know my friend, Carol, don't you?"

"I don't know her, but you've talked about her. How's she gettin' on since your friend was killed?" Harvey was genuinely concerned.

"Not too good. I don't like her bein' alone now."
Jim paused. "Let me ask you something. What would
you think of two house-guests, Harvey? We'll pay rent
and it will only be for a little while."

"Pay rent? Are you nuts?" Harvey could scarcely
believe the prospect of two pinochle partners. "You
guys can stay at my place forever as far as I'm
concerned.   Like I said, your rent will be fried egg
sandwiches. I'll even supply the eggs!"

"You're a good guy, Harvey," Jim smiled. "Thank
you."

"Hey, what goes around, comes around, my
brother. I'm happy for the company."

Jim warmly shook Harvey's hand. "Lemme make
you a fried egg sandwich. On the house."

***

Bickman's efforts to locate the homeless guy
proved barren of results. Talking to bums camped in
vacant lots in the vicinity of the burned apartments
yielded nothing, nor did he have better luck with the
panhandlers occupying the freeway entrance ramps.
Bickman couldn't blame them.   What incentive did
they have to talk to the cops? Why should they rat out
a fellow unfortunate, even if they never even met the
guy? Who could blame them? Fuck the cops.

Had it been around Thanksgiving, Bickman's first
stop would have been the downtown "tent city" erected
during the holidays by the City of Phoenix. The
copious free victuals and clothing attracted the
destitute, and not infrequently the well-heeled, from all
over the state. Unfortunately, it was the brutally hot

middle of June and the homeless typically migrated to more congenial latitudes until cooler weather returned to the Valley of the Sun.   For all Bickman knew, his guy was among them.   His alternative strategy was to check the St. Vincent de Paul shelter and soup kitchen, the Salvation Army, and various other local charities and food banks, but those also yielded nothing.   Having thus exhausted all immediate options, he sat in the showroom of Imperial Chevrolet, waiting to see the general manager.

"It's a damned needle in a haystack," he complained to Pam over dinner the previous evening. "It's like creating imaginary work.   Most of the homeless people I've talked to have mental problems and just look at me with the stoicism of a cow standing in the rain," he sighed, paraphrasing Colin Wilson.

"So, what are you gonna do?" Tell 'em that you just can't locate the guy?"   Pam dished another helping of salad onto Bickman's plate.

"I've got one more idea," he said.   "I remember the guy tellin' me that he used to be the service manager at Imperial Chevy, down on Camelback Road.   He may have been bullshitting, but I'm gonna drive down there tomorrow to see whether they have any record of him. Otherwise, I don't know what else I can do to find him."

"Well, I don't know what else you can possibly do, Dave.   If he's all that important, they should be the ones looking for him, instead of just sending one person out to randomly beat the bushes."

"Hey, I called the AG's office about that task force letter. I left a message with his chief of staff, but haven't heard anything back yet."

"Mom and dad are so proud of you, Dave. Me, too," Pam grinned.

***

A surprisingly youthful man wearing dress slacks and a white shirt with an open collar strode across the polished showroom floor toward Bickman.

"I'm Stuart Rising," he said with a car salesman's smile as he approached, extending his hand. "General manager of Imperial Chevrolet. How can I help you today?"

Bickman stood and shook the GM's languid hand. Although he identified himself as a Phoenix Police Officer to the receptionist, he was in mufti, clad in Dockers, a green polo shirt, and running shoes. "Thank you for seeing me, Mr. Rising. I'm David Bickman. I'm hoping that you may be able to tell me something about one of your former employees."

Rising looked perplexed. "Perhaps...what's the employee's name?" He glanced around, then lowered his voice. "Maybe we should talk in my office. Follow me, please." He turned and retreated back the way he'd come, Bickman trailing behind.

Rising's office was surprisingly opulent; the thought momentarily flashed through Bickman's mind that he should have gone into the car business, rather than being a police officer. The general manager gestured to an overstuffed leather chair as he softly closed the door behind them.

"Now, what's this about one of my employees?" he asked as he seated himself behind a gleaming wooden desk only marginally smaller than an aircraft carrier.

"It's not one of your current employees, Mr. Rising," Bickman assured him. "My department is simply trying to locate someone we think may have been a former employee of Imperial Chevrolet. We think he may have been a witness to a crime, that's all. He's not in any sort of trouble."

"I see," said Rising. "What makes you think he may have worked at Imperial Chevrolet?"

"He told me," Bickman responded.

"Oh? You talked to him? Then why are you still looking for him?" Rising was clearly dubious, not unlike the bums Bickman encountered over the past week and a half.

"Because he's homeless. I don't even know his name. I talked to him briefly on the street a few weeks ago, but I need to talk to him again and can't find him."

"Since you don't even know his name, what makes you think Imperial Chevrolet can help you?" Bickman found annoying Rising's habit of referring to himself in the objectified third-person.

"He told me that he used to be the service manager here. If true, I was hoping that you'd have some record of him, maybe some contact information. A long shot, I realize..." Bickman smiled in an effort to assure the general manager that he was just doing his job.

"I've been the general manager of Imperial Chevrolet for the past eight years," said Rising. "And we've had the same service manager during my entire tenure here."

"Well, then, it must've been before you got here," Bickman suggested.

"Clearly," Rising responded, as if bored.

"Do you have personnel records for the time before you started working here?" Bickman asked, hopefully.

"Of course. All members of the Imperial Chevrolet family are important to our team, and we maintain scrupulous records on each member. Imperial Chevrolet has been honored with GM's 'Master Platinum Dealer' award three times," Rising added, as if it was supposed to mean something.

"Would it be too much of an imposition for you to check your personnel records to see whether you have any information on the previous service manager, or managers?"

"Don't you need a search warrant or something?"

Of course, he needed a warrant. Bickman was afraid he might encounter resistance in his effort to examine private business records. "Mr. Rising, I'm not searching for evidence of a crime; I'm simply trying to locate someone who may have *witnessed* a crime." He hoped the spurious legal distinction sounded plausible.

"I see," the general manager replied. "Well, let me check with our HR department to see whether Imperial Chevrolet may be able to provide some assistance. "He stood and walked to his office door. "Please accompany me to our customer lounge; you can wait for me there."

Bickman followed Rising down a gleaming hallway to an austere room with hard plastic chairs, vending machines, an empty coffee maker, and a blaring TV. A haggard-looking woman sat in one of the chairs, seemingly transfixed by her cell phone. She didn't acknowledge their arrival.

"I'll be just a moment," Rising said as Bickman commandeered the banged-up chair farthest from the TV. "Please help yourself to our vending machines." Bickman at first thought the general manager was joking, but quickly realized that he was as absolutely serious. The requirements for winning "Platinum Master Dealer" were apparently not too onerous.

Rising disappeared down the hall as Bickman resigned himself to a protracted wait.

***

The old man hadn't been home in days. It was obvious he was dodging him. As much as it pissed him off, Ramses couldn't exactly blame him.

He shifted positions again because his back ached. He'd spent virtually the entirety of each shift watching Jim's apartment, devoted dozens of overtime hours surveilling it, and had even ordered uniformed officers to make regular drive-bys. Nothing. It was obvious he was going to have to quit fucking around and take the bull by the horns.

Ramses glanced at his watch. The restaurant was long closed but the old man may still be hanging around. Ramses shoved the transmission into the 'D' position and pulled away from the curb.

***

Rising returned to the customer lounge 90 minutes later.   He offered Bickman a perfunctory apology, that he didn't mean, for taking so long.

"I think I may have found what you're looking for," he said. In his hand Rising held a sheet of paper.

Bickman stood. "Did you find someone?"

Rising consulted the paper. "Imperial Chevrolet has only had four service managers in its history, one of whom currently occupies that position and two of whom are apparently now dead. The service manager ten years ago was a man named 'Ed Sheets.' Mr. Sheets was terminated for reasons I can't disclose and, although we don't have his current contact information, Mr. Sheets evidently had a sister who lived locally."

"Do you have her contact information?" Bickman couldn't conceal his excitement.

"We have a phone number and address but, as I said, Mr. Sheets was terminated a decade ago. Imperial Chevrolet has no idea how accurate it is."

"May I have it?" Bickman had about all he could take of Rising's 'Imperial Chevrolet' affectation.

"Of course." The general manager handed the sheet of paper to Bickman, to which was stapled a white business card. He glanced at the paper before folding it and placing it in the pocket of his Dockers.

"Imperial Chevrolet is happy for the opportunity to have been of assistance to the Phoenix Police Department and anticipates your patronage when it comes time for your next vehicle purchase. I took the liberty of attaching the card of Imperial Chevrolet's sales manager, Casper Hughes. Mr. Hughes remains at your disposal."

"Yeah," Bickman tiredly responded.   "The Department thanks you for your help, Mr. Rising." He headed for the door, eager to follow up the information on Sheet's sister. Behind him, the haggard woman was now mesmerized by a TV commercial for an electronic fly swatter, not available in any store.

***

As he anticipated, Jim's restaurant was dark. Ramses parked on the curb and, before exiting the Caprice, surveyed the street through the windshield. Dead.

Ramses got out of the car.   Although the restaurant was obviously closed for the night, the old codger was pretty cagey and could be lurking in the back, where no light could be seen from the street. Rosey'd discovered that to his dismay. Looking up and down the street again, Ramses headed for the alley that ran along the back of the café.

Like the street out front, the alley was deserted. Because of street lights at either end, Ramses was easily able to locate the screened door to the restaurant. No light emanated from the small, barred kitchen window adjacent to it. He cautiously grasped the handle of the screened door and gently eased it open a few inches.   Beyond it a solid wood door was shut tight. Positioning himself along the exterior wall next to the door, Ramses reached over with his right hand and quietly tested the knob. It didn't budge. If the old man was inside, he'd locked himself in and was sitting in the dark. Not likely.

Ramses slipped his hand off the doorknob and headed back to the Caprice. Like it or not, he was going to have to confront Jim during business hours or, alternatively, pay another visit to the woman, Carol.

***

"Mrs. Espinoza? This is Officer David Bickman, from the Phoenix Police Department. I'm calling about your brother, Ed Sheets."

"Eddie? What happened to him now?" The voice at the other end was devoid of emotion.

Bickman couldn't believe his luck in actually talking to Ed Sheets' sister. To his astonishment, she'd not changed her telephone number in the ten years since Ed departed the Chevy dealership.

"No, no, don't be alarmed, Mrs. Espinoza. Your brother is perfectly fine." Bickman wondered whether "perfectly fine" was an entirely accurate way to describe a destitute homeless person, but could think of nothing else to say that would reassure the sister. "I spoke with him only a few weeks ago."

There was a pause at the end of the line. "So, what do you want?"

"Mrs. Espinoza, the Phoenix Police Department has reason to believe that your brother may have recently witnessed a crime. We'd like to talk to him about what he saw. Nothing more. He's not in any sort of trouble or anything."

Another pause. "I don't see Eddie very much."

"When was the last time you saw your brother?"

"I don't know. A year, maybe. I don't see him very much."

"Do you ever talk to him? Does he call you?"

"Sometimes he calls. Not very often."

"When was the last time, please?"

Another pause, longer this time. "What do you want with me?"

"As I said," Bickman patiently repeated, "we think Mr. Sheets witnessed a crime and we'd like to talk to him about what he may have seen. Your brother is our only possible witness," he added, almost desperately. Silence. "Mrs. Espinoza, would it be okay if I came over to your house so you could meet me in person? Your brother is in absolutely no trouble, I promise." He was running out of arguments.

Bickman could almost hear over the telephone the gears turning in her head. "Yeah, I guess that would be all right," she finally said.

"Are you still on Colter?" Bickman asked, with manifest relief.

"Yeah, on Colter," she confirmed. "When do ya wanna come?"

"I'll be there in half an hour, if that's okay, Mrs. Espinoza."

"Yeah, I guess that would be okay. Does my husband have to be here, too?"

"Your husband is welcome to be there, Mrs. Espinoza. It's just important that I come see you, and introduce myself, as soon as possible." Bickman feared that if she decided to wait for her husband, she might change her mind. Equally bad, she might contact her brother and warn him that the cops were looking for him.

"If it's okay with you, I'd rather that my husband wasn't here when you come," she confided. "Him and Eddie never really got along too good."

"Perfectly fine, Mrs. Espinoza," said a relieved Bickman. "I don't want to cause you any problems. I'll be there in half an hour."

"Okay, see you then," she said, somewhat vaguely.

"Thank you, I'm on my way." Bickman hung up and headed for the door.

***

The Espinozas lived in a small 1950's house on Colter Street, only a few blocks north of Imperial Chevrolet. Bickman parked his patrol car along the curb in from of the modest home and approached the front door via an oil-stained driveway. He pushed the doorbell and could hear the chime ring from somewhere inside the house. After about ten seconds, a frumpy looking woman with brown frizzy hair, wearing lime green shorts and a pale blue tee shirt with conspicuous sweat stains, opened the door.

"Mrs. Espinoza? I'm Officer Bickman." Bickman stood on the doorstep and showed the woman his Phoenix Police ID. After staring at it for what seemed an entire minute, the woman wordlessly stepped aside and motioned for Bickman to enter the dwelling, apparently satisfied with his bona fides.

"I'm Stella," she introduced herself as Bickman seated himself on the couch in the stifling living room.

"I'm sorry it's so hot in here, but we're tryin' to cut down on the utility bill. My husband bitches that it's too high, but he gets to go work in an air-conditioned building all day. He's just a dumb Mexican," she concluded, apparently satisfied that no other explanation was necessary.

Bickman wasn't sure whether to agree with her, or to protest her characterization of her husband. "I understand," he said. "It's not a problem." Stella plopped into a recliner upholstered in what appeared to be brown velvet and covered with dog hair.

"Like I told you over the phone, I don't hear from Eddie much," she began without prompting. "Ever since he pissed away his job at the Chevy dealer, he don't come around much. Besides, he and my husband never got along too good."

Bickman felt like telling her that her brother probably never came around because the interior of her house was like an oven. Instead, he asked, "When was the last time you saw Mr. Sheets?"

"'Mr. Sheets?' You mean Eddie?" Stella gazed off into space. "Six months, maybe more. See, Eddie likes his dope and my husband don't go for that. My husband likes beer because he's Mexican, but he don't go for dope. That's why him and Eddie never got along and that's why Eddie lost his job at the dealership."

"Do you know how I can get hold of Eddie? Like I told you over the phone, I just want to ask him some questions about a crime we think he may have witnessed."

"He calls here ever now and again," said Stella. "Usually during the day, when he knows my husband won't be around."

"When was the last time he called you?"

She ran a hand through her frizzy hair. "About two months ago, probably."

"Do you expect to hear from him again anytime soon?"

"It's hard to say," Stella shrugged.

"Is there any way I can contact Eddie?"

"I don't think so. He's basically a bum. Eddie don't even know where he is from one day to the next."

Bickman was becoming frustrated that this seemingly promising lead was rapidly evaporating.

"Mrs. Espinoza, if your brother calls here again, will you please tell him that I'd like to talk to him? Tell Eddie that I'm the cop that he talked to the night of the apartment fire, the cop that gave him $20."

"You gave Eddie $20?" Stella asked, incredulously. "That was dumb. All he'll do is buy dope with it."

Bickman was rapidly wearying of Stella. "Will you tell him that, please, Mrs. Espinoza?"

"Yeah, sure. No problem. Like I said, though, I have no idea when, or if, Eddie will call me."

"I understand that, Mrs. Espinoza," said Bickman, rising to his feet. He was eager to get outdoors, out of the baking house and into the comparatively cool sunlight. "Just, if he calls, please tell him to call me."

Stella clambered to her feet and took Bickman's card from his outstretched hand.

"Okay, I will." She led him to the front door. "I'm sorry it's so damned hot in here. You can thank my husband," she said, disgustedly.

"No problem. Thank you for your time." Bickman stepped onto the porch, glad to be free of Stella and her furnace-like house. "Please call me at once should you hear from Eddie."

"Will do." Stella peered around Bickman, to his patrol car parked at the curb. "Is that an unmarked car?" she asked.

"What?" Bickman wasn't sure he heard her correctly, since his car was a conventional blue-on-white police vehicle, replete with light-bar, multiple radio antennas, and the words "Phoenix Police Department" painted down each side.

"Is that an unmarked car?" Stella asked again. "I figured that, since you weren't wearing a cop's uniform, you were driving an unmarked cop car, too."

Bickman couldn't help himself. "How could it be an 'unmarked car' if it has 'Phoenix Police Department' written on it and a light-bar clamped to the roof? Does it look unmarked to you?"

"Oh," Stella mumbled, "I was just wonderin'." She closed the door and disappeared back into her house-cum-oven as Bickman returned to his vehicle, started the engine, and cranked-up the air conditioning to maximum.

***

The voice mail on Bickman's cell phone was from Stella Espinoza.

"It's me," said the message. "Eddie called and I told him you was lookin' for him. He said he already knew that because some of his bum friends already told him about you. I guess word on the street gets around pretty fast, huh?"

Bickman couldn't believe his luck, given that he was at Stella's house only three days ago. He immediately called her back.

"Did he say how I could contact him?" he asked, after hearing Stella's recitation of how Eddie had telephoned her earlier that day.

"I didn't ask him," Stella replied. "But Eddie told me that he'd come by the house in a few. I think he wants me to feed him. He won't come here when my husband's around because him and my husband don't get along too good."

Bickman glanced at his watch. "It's eleven now, Mrs. Espinoza. Okay if I come over there right now? It's really important that I talk to your brother."

"Sure. Do you want something to eat, too?"

"No thank you, Mrs. Espinoza, I already ate. But thank you for the offer."

"No big deal. I gotta feed Eddie, anyway. She lowered her voice conspiratorially. "Between me and you, I think Eddie just wants you to give him another twenty dollars."

"That's not a problem. I'm on my way." Bickman terminated the cell call and, glancing in his rear-view mirror, swung back toward Colter. He was eager to intercept Eddie before he finished his lunch at Stella's and disappeared back into Phoenix's homeless flotsam.

***

Ramses continued his stakeout of the old man's apartment, but Jim never returned home. He even drove over to Carol's apartment building a few times, though she also failed to materialize. Both of them were probably holed-up somewhere together, like fucking rodents. Failing to locate either of them at their respective homes, Ramses reluctantly focused his attention on Jim's restaurant, down the block from where his Caprice now idled, air conditioning blasting.

After studying the place for a week, Ramses ascertained that, after parking his old Plymouth in the alley behind the restaurant, Jim opened at 5:30 sharp in order to take advantage of the breakfast crowd on its way to work in the surrounding office buildings. Business slowed beginning around 9:00, but picked up again at 11:00, when the lunch crowd appeared, and was steady until around 2:00. Between 2:00 and 5:00, when the old man closed for the day, business was essentially nonexistent. Although he'd continue his surveillance for another few days, Ramses was satisfied that he'd determined the ideal time to pay a visit to the old man.

Even with the air conditioning maxed-out, Ramses' shirt was damp from sweat. He stretched his legs as best he could and arched his back. He was cramped, hungry, and pissed that he'd been reduced to this, but had no intention of pulling a Rosey by barging into the restaurant like a bull in a China shop. Tomorrow would be the day. He simply didn't have the luxury of waiting any longer. Although the broad's dress hadn't yet surfaced, Ramses was certain the old man was preparing to play his trump card. Time to put the brakes on the entire farce, here and now.

***

Bickman rang the Espinoza's doorbell, steeling himself for entry into the sweltering interior. He held the manila envelope containing the picture of the John Doe that Pruitt had given him. A wave of heat nearly bowled him over when, after a few moments, Stella opened the door, still wearing the same lime green shorts and sweat-stained blue tee shirt.

"Wow, that was fast!" she exclaimed.

"Thank you for calling me, Mrs. Espinoza. Is Mr. Sheets here?"

"He's eatin' in the kitchen," Stella responded with a jerk of her head toward the rear of the house. "I think Eddie must have a tapeworm, or something." She turned from the doorway and Bickman stepped inside, where he was immediately assaulted by a wall of heat. He reluctantly closed the front door and followed Stella toward the back of the residence.

"Hey, Eddie, does this guy look familiar?" Stella called as they rounded the corner to the kitchen.

A disheveled guy sitting at the counter looked up as they entered. "No," he said. He had half a sandwich in one hand and his beard was smeared with a paste comprised of mayonnaise and bread crumbs. "Who's he? He looks like a cop."

"That's 'cause he is a cop," Stella chortled. "I already told you that."

"What's he doin' here?" Eddie said, quizzically. He took another bite of sandwich. "Does Alfredo know you're doin' a cop?"

Stella scoffed. "I ain't doin' him, dumbass. He's here to ask you some questions. I already told you."

Eddie shrugged. "About what? I ain't done nothin'." He finished his sandwich and swiveled his head around. "Got anything to drink, Stella? It's hot as shit in here. When's your cheap-ass husband gonna let you turn the air conditioning on? He ain't in Mexico anymore, you know."

Stella opened the refrigerator door and removed a plastic jug of Sunny Delight. "Alfredo loves this crap," she said, handing it to Eddie.

Bickman stepped closer to the counter. "I'm Dave Bickman, Mr. Sheets. I talked to you a few weeks ago about an apartment fire near 7th Street and Indian School, near where you were camped. You told me that you heard somebody inside, and that you saw a guy who may have set the fire. Do you remember?" In the relatively bright kitchen, Bickman was surprised at how old the man actually was.

Eddie uncapped the Sunny Delight and took a swig. "Yeah, I remember," he acknowledged, wiping his chin on his shirt. He looked at Stella, "This stuff tastes like watered down Kool-Aid," he said.

"Nobody's begging you to drink it," Stella replied as she plopped into a kitchen chair, also covered with dog hair. "Ya wanna sit down?" she asked Bickman.

"No, I'm good," he deferred.

"I didn't set that fire," Eddie told Bickman.

"I know you didn't. But you told me at the time that you may have seen the guy who did."

"I saw a guy who almost ran over me," Eddie corrected Bickman. "All I know is that I heard some guy screamin' from inside the apartment, and some other guy tried to run me over. That's all I know." He looked at Stella. "Got any beer?"

Stella shook her head. "Alfredo drinks it faster than I can buy it."

Bickman removed the photo from the envelope and slid it across the counter toward Eddie. "Was this the guy?"

Eddie picked up the picture with a grimy hand and squinted at it, wiping the mayonnaise from his beard with the other. "He looks dead," he observed.

"Pretty much," Bickman agreed.

"The guy I saw wasn't dead. He was drivin' a car."

"Yeah, I know that." Bickman was beginning to get irritated.

Stella got up from her chair and peered over her brother's shoulder at the photo. "He looks like hell. What happened to him?"

"Didn't you hear what the guy said? He's dead," Eddie chastened her. He looked at Bickman. "What happened to him?"

"He was shot," Bickman informed them, his frustration increasing by the second. "Is that the man you saw near the apartments, Mr. Sheets? The guy who tried to run over you?"

Eddie stroked his beard thoughtfully as he examined the photo. Stella resumed her seat in the dog hair-covered chair.

"Well," he finally said, "it could be him. It's hard to say."

It was difficult for Bickman not to yell at the guy. "Mr. Sheets, I know it *could* be him. *Is* it him?"

Eddie scrutinized the photo again. "The last time I saw the guy he was pretty far away, and the first time he was sittin' in a car.   I only saw him for a second both times, but I guess he kinda looked like this guy. Hard to tell 'cause his eyes are closed. They both look Mexican."

"Maybe it was Alfredo!" Stella volunteered. "Except Alfredo don't look anything like that guy. Other than they're both Mexicans, I mean."

Bickman felt as though he'd blundered into the middle of some surreal comedy routine.

"Take another look at the picture, Mr. Sheets," he suggested with as much patience as he could muster. "See if you can tell if he's the guy you saw behind the apartments." Sweat trickled down Bickman's sides beneath his shirt because of the suffocating kitchen heat, though Stella and Eddie seemed oblivious to it.

Eddie held the photo in a grubby hand and held it close to his face.   "Yeah, this is him," he finally said.

"You sure?" Stella interjected from her chair.

"Yeah, it's him," Eddie confirmed.   He laid the picture aside before draining the Sunny Delight bottle. "Did they find the guy who burned up in the fire?" he asked Bickman.

"They found a body," Bickman told him.

Eddie nodded.   "I figured."   He tipped his head toward the photo. "He did it."

"You may be right," Bickman conceded.   "That's what we're trying to figure out."

"What's the dead guy's name?" asked Stella, indicating the counter where Rosey's photo rested.

"We don't know his name. That's why I wanted to talk to Mr. Sheets, to see whether he knew him," said Bickman.

"All I know is that he almost ran me over," Eddie shrugged. "Other than that, I never laid eyes on him before." He looked at Bickman impassively. "I'm glad he's dead."

Bickman retrieved the photo from the counter and slipped it back into the manila envelope. He just wanted to get out of Stella's broiling house. "If I need to, is there any way I can get hold of you in the future, Mr. Sheets?"

"Yeah, call his social secretary," laughed Stella. Bickman shot her an exasperated glance.

"I'm kinda hard to track down. Best bet is probably to call Stella."

"Well, where are you camping right now?"

"Here and there," Eddie evasively responded. "Nowhere in particular."

Bickman sighed, then handed Eddie his card. "Please telephone me, day or night, if you remember anything else. Okay?"

Eddie nodded, "Yeah, sure."

"Well, thanks for all your help." Bickman turned to leave.

"Hey!" Stella yelped. "Ain't ya gonna pay him anything?"

Bickman wearily slid his wallet from his pocket, removed a bill, and handed it to Eddie. Eddie glanced at it, scowled, then stuffed it into his pants pocket. Bickman headed for the front door; he couldn't get out of there fast enough.

ELEVEN

Ramses sat at a large conference room in the AG's office, along with Officer David Bickman from Phoenix PD, two uniformed sheriff's deputies from Pima County, one white and one black, and the female police academy instructor. Ramses didn't know either of the deputies or the woman, but it was obvious she was a dyke. He did recall meeting Bickman previously a couple of times but didn't consider him even a nodding acquaintance. Both deputies and the instructor were resplendent in their pressed uniforms, but he and Bickman were clad in street clothes. He wasn't sure why Bickman wasn't wearing his patrolman's uniform, but assumed it was his day off.

Like Golden said, Ramses' selection to the AG's "Corruption Task Force" made sense; after all, he was the Chief of Detectives for the largest municipal police department in the state. Who better to ramrod the whole enterprise? Bickman's presence was, however, a mystery, to say nothing of the other three bozos. With respect to the two Pima County deputies, as far as Ramses was concerned nobody lived in Pima County except ranchers and Mexicans; the sheriff's office down there spent most of its time rounding up illegals and shooting stray dogs. Why the hell did the

Attorney General waste his time carting up two guys from bum-fuck Pima County? The dyke was an obvious concession to the gay crowd.

At one end of the conference table the AG's chief of staff was lecturing them on the honor of having been chosen for such an important assignment and the gravity of the task before them. He broadly explained the AG's goals and expectations underlying the task force, and assured them that their participation would resonate in the public consciousness and significantly enhance their professional careers.

"The public rightfully demands that their public institutions remain above reproach," the chief of staff said as he distributed to each of them a thin folder embossed with the official seal of the State of Arizona. "Your job is to assuage the public's concerns and reassure them that they may repose absolute confidence in the sanctity of the body politic."

Ramses and the others flipped through their folders, which contained a handful of printed pages. The first such sheet was headed "Overview."

"So, what, exactly, are we supposed to do?" one of the Pima County deputies inquired.

"At the threshold, your jobs are to review the documents you've just been provided. They delineate potential areas of concern to the Attorney General. Take notes on what you read. After you've studied them, we'll meet with Mr. Butler to solicit your input and discuss a plan of action."

"When do you want to hear back from us?" the deputy asked.

"The Attorney General is mindful that you have regular careers and families, and that your participation on his task force represents a considerable sacrifice. Take your time to thoroughly study the materials." Bickman figured he could digest the few pages in his folder in about a half-hour, but said nothing. Just by glancing at them, though, he could see the AG's objectives were extremely vague. There must be something in the documents he was simply failing to see.

"As a token of gratitude for your participation in the Attorney General's Corruption Task Force," the chief of staff continued," the Attorney General and the people of the State of Arizona have gratefully authorized me to award each of you a plaque as a token of their profound appreciation." He gestured to a stack of laser-engraved wooden shields stacked beside him on the conference table. "Please take one on your way out today. The Attorney General and I look forward to working with each of you." With that, the chief of staff headed for the door, making it clear the meeting was over. Following his departure and a few awkward moments of fidgeting, the five law enforcement officers stood.

One of the Pima County deputies reached over the table and extended his hand to Ramses.

"I'm Mike McDonald and that's Brian Furlong," he said, nodding toward the white guy.

"I'm Linda Zerbe," said the dyke. She was built like a beer keg and sounded like a robot.

"Oren Ramses," Ramses muttered as he indifferently shook hands.

Bickman shook hands with both deputies and Zerbe. "Dave Bickman," he identified himself. "You guys are a long way from home," he said to the deputies.

"That's for damned sure," Furlong responded. "From the sound of things, we probably should've asked that guy for gas money. Does anybody have the slightest idea what we're supposed to be doing?"

Ramses had already retrieved his commemorative plaque from the head of the table. "Well, I don't know about you guys, but I'm supposed to be having lunch."

"No, seriously," continued Furlong, "did you even understand what he was talking about? I must be stupid, but it sounded like a lot of double-speak to me. Read this stuff and then what? Talk about it?"

What's this asshole's problem? thought Ramses. He can't wait to get back to Ajo to resume busting jaywalkers?

"It seems pretty clear to me," he shrugged. "We're supposed to review everything, then report back. What's so hard to understand?"

"Seems kinda pointless," said McDonald. "I think I could read this entire file in about ten minutes. He acted like it was the Oxford English Dictionary."

"I was kind of thinking the same thing," Bickman confessed. "Where's the 'task' in the 'task force'?"

Ramses was annoyed by their obtuseness. "Jesus, what's with you? Why are you makin' this so fucking complicated? Lemme draw you girls a picture. We're supposed to review this stuff, then figure out what, if anything, needs fixing. Why's that so hard to understand? "

"And for that we drove up from Tucson?" grumbled Furlong.

"You're pissed about gettin' the day off?" Ramses retorted. "Go have some lunch, look the shit over, then brainstorm it. If everything's copacetic, you still get brownie points for bein' on the AG's 'Corruption Task Force', a commendation in your personnel file and you'll be star with the folks back home. You got a problem with that?"

Ramses' pragmatism notwithstanding, Bickman concurred with the deputies' assessment and was dismayed by the attorney general's insouciant presentation. The task force appeared to be appreciably more form than substance. He would, however, withhold judgment until thoroughly reviewing the contents of his folder.

"I guess we've got to spend some time looking at the information he gave us," Bickman hopefully urged the others. "We obviously haven't had time to really study it."

"Yeah, why don't you jump on it right away?" Ramses suggested, already half-way out the door. "It's obvious the AG is in no hurry to hear back from us, but you girls can do whatever you want. I'm outta here."

After Ramses decamped, McDonald turned to Bickman. "What's with that guy? Do you know him?"

"I don't really know him," Bickman explained, somewhat apologetically. "He's chief of detectives for the Phoenix PD."

"He's kind of an asshole," said McDonald.

Although he didn't respond, Bickman agreed.

***

"I talked to the homeless guy and he said it's the same guy that he saw at the burned apartments." Bickman was in Pruitt's office. Pruitt sat behind his desk while Saturday, as usual, slouched on the sofa.

"Good work, Officer. How'd you track him down?"

Bickman recounted his meeting with the general manager of Imperial Chevrolet and his subsequent rendezvous with Eddie at Stella's house.

"Did he know the dead guy?" Saturday inquired.

"No, other than it was the same guy he saw at the apartments. He didn't know his name."

Pruitt looked at Saturday. "I think it's about time we had another chat with the ME." Saturday responded by scratching his nose.

"We heard you got picked for the AG's task force," Saturday casually changed the subject.

Bickman smiled pensively. "Yeah, such as it is. I think it's pretty much a 'task force' in name only."

"How's that?"

"All we're supposed to do is read a few reports, then report back with suggestions. Not sure what the point is," Bickman confessed.

"Who's on it with you?" asked Pruitt, idly.

"Two deputies from Pima County, Oren Ramses from Phoenix PD, and some chick from the academy."

"You know any of 'em?"

Bickman shrugged. "I kinda know Ramses, or at least know who he is. I don't know the others."

"What do you think of Ramses?"

"Like I said, I don't really know him."

Pruitt smiled, coldly. "That's not what I asked."

Bickman seemed momentarily confused. "He's all right, I guess. Seems kind of abrupt."

"That's not the word I'd use to describe him," Pruitt responded. "But we're giving you a new assignment. Keep an eye on Ramses for us." From the sofa, Saturday silently nodded.

***

Ramses parked his Caprice one-half block from the restaurant, giving him an unobstructed view of the front entrance. Nobody had entered or departed for over ninety minutes, though he couldn't tell whether there were any customers inside because the glare rendered it impossible to see through the front window. But he was tired of waiting and, moreover, feared the car would overheat because he'd been parked so long with the air conditioning on full blast.

Ramses shut the engine off, swung open the heavy door, and stepped into the street. The late afternoon heat hit him in the face like an axe. He surveyed the immediate area, then strode toward the restaurant.

The bell affixed to the door jingled when Ramses pushed it open. Interior of the restaurant was broiling. The old man was evidently too cheap to pay for air conditioning. Ramses glanced around the dining area to confirm it was unoccupied...small wonder, given the stifling heat. Jim was nowhere to be seen. Must be in back.

Ramses approached the front counter as Jim emerged from the kitchen through the swinging doors connecting it to the dining area.

"You," is all Jim said. He didn't appear surprised to see Ramses.

"Yeah, me," Ramses responded. "We're gonna have a little talk." He promptly stepped around the counter, grabbed Jim, and shoved him backwards. "You're not such a smartass when it's just you and me, huh?"

Jim thudded into the wall, fully aware of the folly of attempting to defend himself. "How come you didn't just send another hooligan?" he asked Ramses after he'd recovered. "The last one didn't do too good."

For an answer, Ramses grabbed Jim's apron and dragged him through the swinging doors into the kitchen.

"Where's the fucking dress? I'm tired of dicking with you, old man," he spat. Before Jim could respond, Ramses shoved him into the refrigerator. He was already drenched in sweat, partly from exertion, partly from nerves.

Jim drew himself upright and stood defiantly in front of Ramses, though he said nothing. Jim was far more frightened of Ramses than he'd been of Rosey, but was determined not to display it. Rosey had no skin in the game and was simply doing his job. Ramses was psychopath. Jim's shoulder, where it had crashed into the dining room wall, was already beginning to throb and swell.

"You dumb nigger motherfucker!" Ramses growled. He balled up his fist and, rearing back, directed a brutal punch to the bridge of Jim's nose. Jim careened backwards into the refrigerator, blood spurting from his crushed nose. He fell to his knees, blood from his nose cascading over his mouth, down his chin, onto the kitchen floor. "You're a pretty tough old bird," Ramses smirked, standing over him.

Jim thought the pain might cause him to pass out, but he grasped the chromed handle of the refrigerator door and used it to slowly pull himself to his feet. His apron already glistened with blood and he had difficulty breathing; he was close to vomiting because of all the blood flooding into his open mouth. Jim leaned painfully against the refrigerator, panting, and looked at Ramses. Inexplicably, he was smiling.

"What the hell's the matter with you, you stupid bastard?" demanded a nonplussed Ramses.

"My twelve-year-old granddaughter hits harder than you do," Jim managed to say.

"That so? Well, she's liable not to recognize grandpa once I get finished." Ramses grasped Jim's collar, held him at arm's length, and prepared to launch a second punch.

"Mister, you're dumber than I thought," Jim croaked.

Ramses smiled coldly. "You're the one gettin' beat up. But you can end it just by tellin' me where the dress is." He relaxed his grip slightly, to enable Jim to respond.

With painful slowness Jim raised his arm and pointed upward. Ramses' eyes followed.

"See that? Security camera. I had 'em put in after the last guy was here. Got 'em all over the place." He dropped his arm because it hurt too much to hold aloft.

Stunned, Ramses involuntarily released his grip and rapidly scanned the kitchen. Placed along the ceiling were a half-dozen tiny digital security cameras, no bigger than a button on a man's suit. He'd failed to notice them previously because of their miniscule size and, furthermore, he'd had no reason to suspect their existence. Ramses shoved Jim against the refrigerator and dashed out the swinging doors into the dining room. Identical cameras covered the entire area.

"Son of a fucking bitch!" he snarled. Ramses darted back into the kitchen, heart pounding. Jim was still slumped against the refrigerator.

"I'll kill you, you son of a bitch. Where's the tape?"

Jim looked up. The flow from his nose had slowed to a bloody trickle. "Not here; they're wireless." Despite his battered appearance, he seemed strangely serene.

Ramses grabbed the back of Jim's head and yanked it toward him.

"Make no mistake, old man, I will kill you unless you tell me where the goddamned tape is."

"You pretty much already did," Jim said, very softly. "Do what you're gonna do, 'cause ain't got the tape."

Ramses was close to panic. His picture was already on one or more of the cameras, but there was nothing he could do about it now. If the images got out, there was a chance he could be prosecuted for assault, but he could probably assert self-defense. The Chief of Detectives for the Phoenix PD would have no reason to beat up an old man and, if it came down to a swearing match, the prosecutor would certainly credit Ramses' account of the incident over that of a supposed victim with known criminal associations.

But he had to get the hell out of there before the old fucker sprang additional surprises on him.

He released the back of Jim's head. "You must think you're pretty smart," he said.

"Smarter than you, I reckon," Jim replied.

"This isn't the end of it, old man." Ramses hissed, his eyes empty, dead.

Jim smiled again, as though to himself this time. "Yeah, I know," he cryptically responded.

With a final shove, Ramses propelled Jim into the refrigerator again. He had to get out of there and think.

***

Chief Golden had been on the phone much of the morning, brainstorming with Mr. Julius and his associates on the Coast about the Ramses problem. IA's continued probing of the Dawson shooting was becoming tiresome and, because of the increasing pressure, the chief had no confidence that Ramses wouldn't do something stupid that would imperil them all. It was time to put it to bed.

"Since you managed to eradicate Rosedea," Mr. Julius had censured him, "we have no choice but to send some other people over there to take care of things."

"Mr. Julius, if Rosey hadn't been killed following the orders of Detective Ramses, we wouldn't even be having this conversation. Ramses is the problem."

"We're not unsympathetic, Chief, but the fact remains that Ramses is under your purview. You are ultimately answerable for his actions." Golden cringed at the implied threat, but preferred not to think about it. He'd hoped his supplicating phone call would constitute at least partial penance.

"We're prepared to defer entirely to you with respect to the resolution of the problem," Golden assured him, as though such a display of submission even necessary. "You have our complete cooperation."

"Yes, I know. You have no alternative."

In the end, the Coast agreed to send two soldiers over to Phoenix to sort things out. Golden expected them to arrive via a Southwest flight from San Francisco later in the afternoon. In anticipation, he called the Phoenix Police Department's on-site command post at the airport and made arrangements for them to be escorted through the VIP terminal upon their arrival. A police vehicle would then transport them directly to Golden's office at headquarters. The chief hoped the two new guys proved more reliable than Rosey had been.

***

"Oh my God, you look awful!" Carol felt like crying when she saw Jim lying in the hospital bed, bandages covering much of his face. Both of his eyes were black and his injuries rendered it difficult for him to speak.

Jim tried to smile. "I probably look better from this side."

Carol sat at Jim's bedside and caressed Jim's gnarled hand. "Did you call the police?" she asked, softly.

"Pruitt and Saturday came and talked to me here," Jim murmured. "They're the only cops I half-way trust." He paused for breath. "And maybe not even half-way."

"Did you tell them who did this to you?"

"Nope. I just told 'em that some cat came into my place, tried to rob me, and beat me up."

"Did they believe you?"

"Cops don't believe nuthin' people tells 'em, Carol." Because of his broken nose, Jim had to breathe through his mouth. "It don't matter what they believe. Pruitt just said that I was the unluckiest guy he's ever met because two guys tried to rob me in the past three weeks."

"Why don't you just tell them the truth, Jim? Tell them that it was a cop who did this to you."

"It was the cops who killed Jerry, Carol."

Neither spoke for a few moments. "Do they know you have security cameras that picked up the whole thing?" she finally asked.

"I don't think so because, when they was in my place last time, I didn't have 'em."

"So, what are you going to do now, Jim?"

Jim attempted another smile. "I got an idea, Carol."

From the hospital hallway, a stout, middle-aged nurse breezed into the room and promptly flung aside the curtain that surrounded Jim's bed. Carol had to rapidly slide her chair away from Jim's bedside to avoid being bowled over by the exuberant nurse.

"Time to take your vitals, Mr. Thompson. How are you feeling today?"

"I reckon I feel better than I look," Jim told her.

She laughed as she fiddled with the electronic monitor next to Jim's bed. "Do you need to use the bathroom first?"

"Yeah, I guess I better," he said.

Carol stood. "I'll get out of your way, then." She turned to the nurse. "How long do you think he'll be in here?"

"As long as they'll let me," Jim interjected. "It's cool, they got cable, the nurses treat me good, and the food ain't too bad, either."

The nurse scoffed. "I think he's scheduled to be discharged in a day or two. There's not much more we can do for him in here. His body's just got to heal on its own." She pushed the button on the collapsible railing that ran along the side of Jim's bed and pushed it downward, then pulled the sheet free. "Hang on while I grab a walker for you to use to get to the bathroom. Don't move." She bustled out the door.

Carol placed her hand on Jim's shoulder. "I'll be back tomorrow. Call me if you need anything."

The old man patted her hand. "I'm fine, Carol. As soon as she comes back, I'll go do my business then see what's on the dinner menu tonight. I'm actually a little tired; getting' beat-up takes a lot out of an old man," he gently smiled.

"Oh, pshhhhhh," Carol said, dismissively.

"How's Harvey?"

Carol made a face. "I'm pretty much burned out of checkers and pinochle. You better come home soon so I can have a break."

Jim chuckled as the nurse returned with a walker. "Here we go," she declared. "I'll change your bed while you're in the bathroom, then we'll check your vitals."

Carol stepped aside as the nurse positioned the walker beside Jim's bed and began to assist him swing his legs to the floor. "See ya tomorrow, Jim," she promised.

"You better," he warned with a wink. Jim winced as, with the help of the nurse, he slid forward to the edge of the bed and grasped the walker. A trickle of blood began to ooze from beneath the bandage covering his nose.

"Take good care of him," Carol told the nurse.

"I promise," she smiled. She helped Jim to his feet and grasped one frail arm as he steadied himself. "You okay, Mr. Thompson?"

"Never better," he said. "You go home now, Carol. I'll tell you my plan when I see you tomorrow." Jim feebly began pushing the walker toward the bathroom, shuffling his feet as he went. Carol reluctantly departed.

***

Bickman, McDonald, Furlong, and Zerbe sat in the AG's conference room. It had been just over two weeks since their initial meeting with Butler's chief of staff and, having completed their assigned homework assignment, they were prepared to provide their assessment. Despite the fact they'd been sitting for 45 minutes, however, neither Butler, nor his chief of staffed, had deigned to make an appearance.

"Maybe it's me," observed McDonald, "but the AG doesn't seem too interested in his own task force."

Furlong nodded. "I hate to say it, but it seems like kind of a joke. The stuff he gave us to look at was basically a bag of air. Not sure what recommendations we're supposed to make."

Although he was initially flattered to be chosen to be a member of the task force and wanted to give the AG the benefit of the doubt, Bickman had to agree. The slim folder given them by the chief of staff contained a mish-mash of documents on various state agencies, replete with multi-colored pie charts, Venn diagrams, and graphs. Although he understood the gist of most of it, Bickman remained unclear on the purpose of such plebian information. What, exactly, were they supposed to do with it? And what did it have to do with corruption? Bickman was obviously failing to recognize the underlying significance of the material and presumed the AG would, when he arrived, clarify matters.

"So, where's the other guy?" Zerbe asked Bickman. "Don't you guys work together?"

"Well, we both work for Phoenix PD," Bickman told her. "He's the chief of detectives but I'm only a patrolman. I wouldn't say that we 'work together.'"

"Whatever," Zerbe dismissively responded. "How come he isn't here? Can't be bothered?"

"Can't say that I blame him," McDonald conceded. "Not sure why *I'm* here. I'm thinking he may be right to bag it. None of this crap means diddley-squat to me." He gestured toward the folder on the polished table before him. "Hell, I didn't even vote for the guy."

The door to the conference room opened and Attorney General Butler strode in trailed by his chief of staff, who was carrying a stack of folders.

"Good morning, lady and gentlemen," Butler greeted them. None of the four officers knew whether protocol required them to stand when the AG entered the room so, not knowing what else to do, they remained seated at the conference table.

"Good morning," McDonald responded. Bickman and Furlong glanced at each other but said nothing.

Butler glanced quizzically at his chief of staff. "I thought there were five members on the task force."

"There are," his aid confirmed. He looked at the seated men. "Any idea where the fifth member is?"

McDonald and Furlong both made 'don't-ask-me' faces.

"We were just discussing that," Bickman volunteered. "He may just be running late."

"Understood," Butler nodded, seemingly satisfied. He slid the chair out at the head of the conference table and sat. His chief of staff occupied the chair immediately adjacent. "I'm glad you all were able to come here today," the attorney general began. "As you know from your initial meeting with my chief of staff, we asked you to join my task force because of your outstanding law enforcement expertise. We specifically enlisted your help in order to review the fiscal policies of certain agencies that have lately come under public scrutiny. To that end, we provided you with folders containing pertinent budgetary information to assist your analysis. I hope you've had opportunity to study those materials and are prepared to share your conclusions." Butler smiled benignly and leaned back in his chair. His chief of staff appeared bored.

The four law enforcement officers at the table looked at each other in perplexity. They thought they'd been chosen to sit on task force investigating institutional corruption, a subject about which they admittedly knew very little; now they were being asked to assess mundane accounting practices, a subject about which they knew even less.

"Mr. Butler, I'm not sure I understand. I thought we were here to discuss corruption," Bickman said. "Isn't this a *corruption* task force?"

"Yes, of course you're right," the attorney general tut-tutted. "But corruption typically betrays itself through financial irregularities. The Romans, of course, said it best, 'per aspera ad astra.' Given your broad law enforcement backgrounds, we were confident that any fiscal improprieties would reveal themselves to your collective scrutiny."

Bickman thought the attorney general sounded like he was making a speech.

"If you suspect that monies have been misappropriated, why don't you just undertake a forensic accounting?" he suggested. "Given what you just said in English, it seems like more of an accounting issue than a law enforcement issue at this point."

The attorney general looked at Bickman indulgently. "Officer..." he paused and looked expectantly at his chief of staff.

"Bickman," grunted the chief of staff.

"Bickman," continued Butler, "the electorate is clamoring for action. They demand transparency and accountability in their elected officials. A 'forensic accounting,' as you call it, will appear as nothing more than a diversion, bureaucratic time-wasting. The people want results, not nitpicking; genuine accomplishments, not wild goose chases." He lowered his voice conspiratorially. "Besides, between you and me, who is better suited to identify and ferret-out corruption? An army of pasty accountants who probably couldn't spot a criminal if their lives depended on it, or someone with specific law enforcement experience? Whom would you trust? Let me put it another way, if someone was breaking into your home, intent on harming your family, who would you call? An accountant or the police?" He paused, clearly pleased with his spontaneous example. "That is the exactly situation we have here," Butler continued, "though on a broader scale, allegations that criminals are looting the public treasury." The attorney general looked at them triumphantly.

"So, what are we supposed to do?" Furlong asked.

"You've had the opportunity to review the materials provided by the attorney general's office," the chief of staff interjected, "what are your impressions? Does anything jump off the page at you?"

"Impressions? I had no idea what I was looking at, or why I was looking at it," confessed McDonald.

"Well, is it safe to say that your analysis thus far has revealed no evidence of misappropriation of funds or other suspicious activities?" prodded the chief of staff.

Furlong, McDonald, and Bickman looked at one another.

"I guess," McDonald finally said, with obvious hesitation.

"We are gratified to hear that." The attorney general soberly nodded his head.

His chief of staff abruptly stood and gathered the folders on the table before him.

"We've prepared additional materials for your review," he said as he walked around the table and handed a folder to each member of the task force. "Who will give our fifth member his copy?"

McDonald and Furlong looked at Bickman. "I guess I will," he sighed.

"Splendid," Butler smiled.   He stood. "You are doing a great service to the community for which you should be very proud." He walked around the table and shook hands with each of them. "If you have any questions, don't hesitate to contact my chief of staff. I hope to see all five of my task force members here after you've read and digested the new materials." He and his chief of staff then departed.

Furlong looked at the others. "Does anyone have any idea what the hell that was about? What are we doing here?" None of them had a response.

***

Pruitt and Saturday sat in the medical examiner's Oriental-motifed office.

"It smells like a dorm room in here," Saturday observed, referring to the scent of incense that permeated the room. "I thought incense went out in the '70's. What's with this guy?"

Pruitt chuckled. "Yeah, all he needs is a Jimi Hendrix black-light poster."

The door opened and McKeever walked in, wearing his customary cowboy boots. His face fell.

"What do you want?" He brusquely greeted them.

"Good afternoon, Dr. McKeever," Pruitt evenly responded.

"What do you want?" the medical examiner repeated. He walked past them and sat behind his desk.

"We just came by to give you an update on your John Doe," Saturday informed him. McKeever tried to appear apathetic. "We know who he is."

McKeever's face betrayed no hint of surprise. "And?"

"He's Georgio Rosedea."

McKeever forced a smile and shook his head. "Impossible. I told you last time you were here, I autopsied Rosedea months ago. You'll have to do better than that."

"Bullshit," Saturday countered. "We've got a witness who positively ID'ed him. We showed him the autopsy photos." Saturday was mindful that Eddie Sheets did not, in fact, identify the body as being Rosey. But McKeever didn't know that.

"I don't give a damn what your supposed witness said. I outta know who I autopsied," McKeever replied.

"That's exactly what we were thinking, too," Saturday agreed, amiably. "By the way, our witness also saw Rosedea kill some guy a few weeks before the old man at the restaurant plugged him. He set a fire over off Indian School Road that ended up frying a material witness. How do you suppose a guy you supposedly autopsied 'months ago' managed to do that?"

McKeever didn't respond. Pruitt imagined that he could almost hear the gears churning in the medical examiner's head.

"You know, "Pruitt suggested, "it isn't too late to dig yourself out of whatever you've gotten yourself into. I'm guessing that bodies occasionally get mixed up; it's an honest mistake. Shit happens, right? Now's your chance to make things right, Dr. McKeever. Nobody expects you to take the fall."

"I don't know what you're talking about," McKeever snorted.

"Hmmmmmm...that's too bad, because when the roof caves in on your little charade, it's gonna crush every one of you lying bastards."

"You can't talk to me that way!" McKeever snapped.

"Sure, he can. He just did," Saturday corrected him.

McKeever rose from behind his desk. "Get out."

Pruitt sighed, then he and Saturday stood. "Think about what I said, doc. The shit's gonna hit the fan and, when it does, you're gonna be standing right in front of it."

At their car, Saturday started the engine and flicked the air conditioner to "high." Just walking the short distance from the medical examiner's office to the parking lot left them soaked with perspiration and the interior of the vehicle already felt like an oven. They let the cold air blow over them in silence.

"Do you think he'll fold?" Pruitt finally asked, more-or-less rhetorically.

"Yeah, I think he will," Saturday responded. "It all depends of who he's more afraid of, us or Ramses."

Pruitt slipped the transmission lever into "D" and began backing out of their parking spot.

***

The two soldiers from the Coast referred to themselves as "Red" and "Doc." Notwithstanding his moniker, Red was bald with a neatly trimmed white beard; Doc appeared to be Asian. Both of them looked utterly banal as they sat in Golden's office in Phoenix Police Department headquarters on Washington Street but, since they were evidently hand-picked by Mr. Julius, he wasn't about to question their bona fides.

"We were real surprised to hear about Rosey," Doc remarked.

"Yeah, he was a good guy," Red added.

Golden considered it something of an overstatement to characterize Rosey as a "good guy," but simply nodded without saying anything. No sense starting off on the wrong foot.

"Is it always this hot here?" Red groused.

"It cools off in the winter," the chief assured him.

"That's not sayin' much. I don't see how it could get any hotter," Red opined.

Doc transitioned to the business that brought them to the sweltering desert.

"We were told that you'd fill us in on the particulars about Rosey," he said to the chief.

The soldiers' arrival in Phoenix was prompted by a DVD that Golden received earlier that week. Addressed to him personally at the Phoenix Police Department, the disc was accompanied by no correspondence and didn't bear a return address, though its postmark revealed that it had been mailed from Phoenix. The chief received a substantial volume of personal correspondence at his office, virtually all of it from crackpots. Mail delivered to department headquarters on Washington Street was routinely x-rayed before being distributed to its various addressees throughout the building, though Golden seldom actually saw any of it. Letters addressed directly to him were opened by his staff and either ignored, sent a perfunctory response or, if warranted, flagged for further action. Someone in the chain of command evidently considered the disc laying atop his desk suitable for further action. Golden disinterestedly slipped it into the DVD player in his office and sat down to watch it.

"Rosey's dead because we've got a bull in a China shop," Golden informed them. "Mr. Julius thought you two could have a sit-down with him."

"Yeah, we could do that," Doc assured him. "How long do you want the sit-down to last?"

"Forever."

"Not a problem," replied Doc.

***

Other than junk mail and bills, she rarely received an ordinary old-fashioned letter anymore, so Teddi Ramses was surprised to see the small, unprepossessing package in her curbside mail box when she braved unrelenting heat in order to retrieve the mail. Occasionally, her sister in Earlham, Iowa, sent her a clipping from their hometown newspaper but, otherwise, they communicated exclusively by email. Maybe she intended the package as a surprise, or simply forgot to tell Teddi that she'd mailed her something during one of their regular email exchanges. No matter.

Teddi gathered up the mail, carefully closed the mailbox, and rapidly retraced her steps up the walkway to her house. The early afternoon sun was blinding and she wanted to get indoors without a moment's delay. The mysterious package promised to relieve some of the tedium of her day.

The interior of her home was like an oasis and Teddi laid the package on a counter while she rapidly sorted through the rest of the mail, depositing most of it, unopened, into the kitchen garbage can. She then turned her attention to the package.

Neatly wrapped in what appeared to be a fragment of a brown paper grocery bag, the package appeared to be either a CD or a DVD: thin, square, and about the right size. Although the package bore no return address, its postmark established that it had been mailed from Phoenix two days previously. Because she didn't recognize the hand writing, however, Teddi double checked to confirm the package hadn't been misdelivered by the mailman. It hadn't. Intrigued, she tore it open.

As she anticipated, the package contained a clear plastic jewel case containing a shiny electronic DVD. Laying atop the disc was a small sheet of paper with a hand-written name, "Gail," and, beneath it, a local telephone number. The paper was signed "A Friend." Teddi opened the jewel box and removed both the sheet of paper and the disc.

The conventional Memorex disc had obviously been created by a private individual and bore no label. As she carried the disc and note to the living room,

Teddi wondered whether Gail, whoever she was, had made and sent it to her. If so, why? She didn't even know anyone named "Gail." Teddi slipped the DVD into the player, sat on the couch, and used the remote control to turn it on.

The black-and-white image that immediately appeared on the screen was perfectly clear but had no sound. It revealed the interior of a room throughout which were positioned several tables and booths. A restaurant, evidently. Based on the angle, the camera was positioned close to the ceiling, pointing downward into the room, which was devoid of activity. Teddi watched the image with increasing curiosity.

After several seconds, a figure appeared at the top of the picture. It was her husband. Notwithstanding the angle, there could be no doubt of his identity. Ramses briefly glanced about the room, seemingly oblivious that he was being filmed. Apparently satisfied, he walked toward a counter at the opposite end of the room when a second figure, an elderly black man, appeared at the bottom of the screen. Seeing him, Ramses stepped around a counter, roughly grabbed the old man, and shoved him backwards into the wall. Teddi literally gasped. Although there was no sound, the old man's reaction to the abrupt assault left no doubt of its violence.

Ramses leaned down, grasped the old man's apron, and yanked him to his feet. Still holding the apron, he dragged him through a set of swinging doors and disappeared from the camera's view.

It wasn't over. Another camera instantly switched to different scene, a kitchen. The same elderly man stood with his back toward a refrigerator and Ramses towered over him. Ramses appeared to be saying something to the man when he abruptly shoved him backwards. The man crashed into the refrigerator, but quickly straightened and turned to face Ramses again. Ramses continued talking to the man, then abruptly balled up his fist and propelled it into the man's face.

The old man thudded into the refrigerator again. The clarity of the DVD was such that Teddi could easily discern blood spurting from his crushed nose. She was horrified and sickened by the spectacle of her husband beating a defenseless old man.

The man sagged to the floor then, after a moment, struggled to his feet by grasping the refrigerator handle and pulling himself upright. Although it was difficult to see because of the blood flooding his mouth, it appeared to Teddi that he was smiling. Ramses stepped forward, grabbed the old man by the collar, and prepared to punch him a second time. Teddi could see the man begin talking to Ramses while shakily pointing upward with his left hand, evidently toward the camera that was currently filming them. Ramses looked up, directly into the camera, then released his grip on the man. He abruptly turned and stepped from the camera's field of view, only to return a minute later. The black man remained slumped against the refrigerator. Ramses grabbed the back of his head and, although she couldn't hear the words, it was obvious he was screaming at the helpless man. After a harangue lasting a few seconds, Ramses gave him a final shove and once again disappeared from view. This time he didn't return. After a few moments, the elderly man stood upright and turned his battered and bloody face upward, toward the camera, which then went dark.

Teddi sat on the couch, stunned. Although the entire DVD scarcely lasted a total of two or three minutes, she was shocked by her husband's undisguised brutality. At no point did it appear that the unidentified black man provoked Ramses, nor did he attempt to defend himself against the barbarous assault he suffered. The images on the screen made it manifestly clear that Ramses simply attacked him. Who was he? Why did Ramses attack him? Who was 'Gail' and what relationship to Ramses or the victim did she have?

Teddi was shaking and felt like vomiting. She briefly considered watching the DVD a second time, but the thought of it sickened her.   Although Ramses wasn't exactly a paragon of husbandly devotion, he'd never physically struck her. His marital abuse manifested itself through a combination of scorn and indifference. Teddi realized that, at least occasionally, his job with the police force involved at least a measure of violence. She'd seen enough cop shows on television to know that. But she had no inkling that her husband attacked inoffensive old men.

She placed the remote control on the couch beside her and studied the note with Gail's telephone number. Whether it was Gail, or someone else, who actually sent Teddi the disc, it was apparent that Gail played some role in it. Why else would they have enclosed a note with her telephone number?

Holding the slip of paper in one hand, Teddi retrieved her cell phone and dialed Gail's number. It rang four times before anyone answered.

"Hello?" said a flat, female voice.

"Is this Gail?" Teddi was trembling and she couldn't prevent her voice from cracking.

"Who's this?" Gail guardedly responded.

"This is Teddi Ramses. Oren Ramses is my husband."

***

"You what?" Carol wasn't sure she'd heard Jim correctly.

"I sent the disc to the chief of police and his wife. I also sent his wife his girlfriend's phone number". Jim's face was still bruised and he wore a bandage over the bridge of his nose.

They were sitting at Harvey's kitchen table, having just completed a second game pinochle. Harvey poured another round of diet soda.

"How do you know where the guy lives?" he idly asked.

"I just asked around," Jim replied. "There ain't too many secrets on the streets, especially when it comes to somebody as unpopular as Detective Ramses."

"I don't understand. Why didn't you just give it to the two cops you told me about? The ones that come to the restaurant?" Carol gently scolded him. "I guess I can understand sending it to the chief of police, but what was the point in mailing it to his wife?"

Jim placed his gnarled hand over Carol's. "Do you trust the police, Carol?"

"You know I don't. But if you don't trust the cops, why did you send it to the police chief? And why his wife?"

"I sent it to the chief of police because I figured he ought to know what kind of men he's got workin' for him. I sent it to his wife because, who do you think will be more apt to do something about the disc? The police or a pissed-off wife?"

"I can answer that," Harvey chuckled as he resumed his seat. "There's nuthin' worse than a pissed-off wife! Good thing she'll be able to talk it over with the guy's girlfriend. I wouldn't wanna be there when that happens!"

"Yeah, right." Carol shook her head. "You two are worse than a couple of little kids."

"I don't know about that," Jim responded. "But what I *do* know is that, chances are his wife will be curious enough to call that number and, like Harvey said, she'll end up talkin' to Ramses' girlfriend. And when she does, she's gonna learn all kinds of stuff about her husband that she maybe don't wanna know."

"So how does that help us?" Carol asked. "Won't that just be hurtful to Ramses' wife? And if you want the police department to know what an asshole Ramses is, why didn't you just give the disc to those two cops you know?"

"I don't know if it helps us or not, Carol," Jim sighed. "I just know that I'm tired of us bein' hurt. If nuthin' else, don't you think his wife ought to know what kind of man she's married to?"

Carol was unmoved by Jim's asserted altruism. "You didn't send Ramses' wife the disc, or his girlfriend's phone number, because you care that she's married to a jerk.   You did it to hurt her. I don't know why you just didn't give it to those other cops."

Harvey looked at Jim expectantly, curious to hear his response to Carol's challenge. He hoped they'd wrap up their conversation because he was eager to start another game of pinochle.

"You're right, Carol," Jim finally conceded, very softly. "I want to hurt her because I figure that, if I hurt her, she'll hurt him.   I don't give a damn about her. Hurtin' Ramses is all I care about. I didn't give it to the two cops that come into the restaurant because they're low down on the totem pole and, for all I know, they're Ramses' friends."

"Hell, hath no fury like a woman scorned," Harvey added, knowingly.

"How do you know the chief of police isn't in bed with Ramses, too?" Carol dismissively responded.

Jim sighed. "I don't, Carol. I just figured that somebody in the police department outta know what kind of man Ramses is and, if you want somethin' done, go to the man in charge. That's why I sent it to the chief of police instead of givin' it to those other two cops. Maybe that makes me a bad man. Maybe I'll go to hell," Jim continued. "But I already killed a man and, at this point in my life I don't really care much."

"If ya go to hell, I'll have your bed turned down for you," Harvey assured Jim as he took a drink of diet soda. Carol was silent. Harvey looked at the kitchen clock. If they didn't start a new game soon it would be bedtime. "I'm glad we worked everything out," he said, hopefully.

Carol shot Harvey a dubious glance. "I don't think we worked anything out, but I don't know what the answer is," she confessed.

Jim smiled wearily. "There ain't no 'answers,' Carol. If I knew the answers, I'd be sittin' on a beach somewhere, drinkin' cold beer, instead of playin' pinochle in Harvey's kitchen." He turned his attention to their host. "Not that I mind," he gently smiled. Harvey beamed.

"Speakin' of that," Harvey reminded them, "if we're gonna get another game in, we'd best get started."

"Carol, I can't unring a bell," Jim concluded. "I'm not a bit sorry I sent everything to Ramses' wife, and would do it again in a heartbeat. All I can do is live with it." He turned to Harvey. "I want to play pinochle now."

***

"How long since you've seen Ramses?" Pruitt asked.

"A while," replied Bickman. "I don't even know whether he's still part of the AG's waste-of-time task force. For that matter, I'm not sure why *I* am."

"How's that?" Saturday idly inquired as he bit down on a tortilla chip.

Bickman shook his head. "It's just a lot of make-work. Nothing gets accomplished. I'm not sure what the point of the whole thing is."

"Welcome to reality," Saturday shrugged.

They were eating lunch at mom-and-pop Mexican restaurant on south Central Avenue.

"The point," Pruitt said in response, "is to show the voters that Butler is watchin' out for 'em. Aside from that, nothing is supposed to get accomplished." He took a sip of Coke.

"I guess," said Bickman.

"There's no 'guess' about it," Saturday added, indifferently. "There's nothin' to guess about. Butler doesn't care one way or the other whether you find any corruption; in fact, he hopes you don't. That way he can tell the voters that everything's hunky-dory and everybody can go back to watching 'Dancing with the Stars.'"

"I'm thinking about talking to someone and blowing the whistle on the whole farce," Bickman asserted.

"Oh, yeah?" Saturday skeptically responded. "Who would you talk to? You got contacts in the media, Mr. Ambassador? Even if you did, you think they'll get all excited about what you have to say? Who they gonna believe, some disgruntled Phoenix PD piss-ant patrolman or the attorney general? Besides, you trash the AG and you might as well shitcan your whole career. But be my guest." He ate another tortilla chip. "Ya know," he said to Pruitt as he brandished a chip, "these are pretty good. Usually, they're either cold or too greasy. These guys know how to make chips!"

Pruitt turned to Bickman. "Here's what I want you to do: meet Ramses somewhere. Think of some pretext. Find out what he's been up to. Maybe he'll talk to you, since he won't talk to us."

"How am I supposed to do that?" Bickman asked. "It isn't like we're best buds. I barely know Ramses.

Besides that, he's Chief of Detectives and I'm just a lowly patrolman. Why would he talk to me?"

"I'm sure you'll think of something," Pruitt opined. "Besides, you don't have a choice," he continued, matter-of-factly. "If you ever want to be promoted to detective, you'd better start acting like one." He looked at Saturday as he popped a tortilla chip into his mouth. "You're right, these are pretty good!"

TWELVE

Ramses' house was dark when he wheeled up. Notwithstanding that it was nearly 2:30 a.m. Theodora's Nissan wasn't parked in the driveway, although she should have retired hours ago. Despite the fact that he didn't feel like talking to her in the first place, he couldn't imagine why Theodora's car wasn't there. An ominous feeling came over him. He'd hoped to watch a little TV, drink a beer or two, then go to bed, but that didn't look like it was going to be in the cards. Ramses needed something to take his mind off his problems.

A gravel path led from the driveway and Ramses padded toward the rear of the home, which was cloaked in darkness. As he turned the corner, he immediately saw the back door was slightly ajar. Ramses instinctively reached to the small of his back and grasped the Walther PPK holstered there.

Ramses crept to the door, blood rushing in his ears. Why was all this shit happening to him now? And where the hell was Theodora?

Police protocol dictated that he retreat and call a squad car. Although he'd cleared houses without assistance in the past, he'd not done so since he actually worked the streets many years previously and didn't feel like undertaking it by himself. Before calling for backup, though, he flattened himself against the back wall and placed his head near the open door, straining to hear any sound from inside the unlit house. Silence.

Ramses returned to the front of the house and hastily dialed the Phoenix Police Department's confidential back line on his cell phone. 911 was for chumps. An operator answered after two rings and Ramses rapidly identified himself, explained the situation, and requested backups. She assured him that help was en route and instructed him to await their arrival at the curb one-half block east of the residence. She also cautioned him not to enter the home. Glancing once more toward the darkened house, Ramses headed for the rendezvous point.

Two police squad cars, their lights off and without sirens, slithered to the curb just as Ramses arrived. Two uniforms emerged from one car, while a single officer stepped from the other. Ramses immediately recognized Bickman as he approached.

"I heard the call and was in the neighborhood," Bickman explained. The other two cops, whom Ramses didn't know, huddled around them.

"My wife's car isn't in the driveway and the back door was open," Ramses tersely explained. "I couldn't tell if anyone's still inside."

"How do you want to play it?" one of the nameless officers asked.

"I'm not wearing armor, so I'll follow you guys. We'll go in the back; it opens into the kitchen and I'll flip the lights on as soon as we're in."

Although it was left to their individual discretion by the department, most officers wore body armor beneath their uniforms while on duty. It was hot and uncomfortable, but a generally effective barrier against common handgun calibers.

"Do you think we should call in S.W.A.T.?" the other cop asked, somewhat anxiously.

"No." Ramses immediately dismissed the suggestion. "I don't want this thing turning into a circus. As far as I know my wife isn't even home, so we're not dealing with a hostage situation and I don't want every knothead from the department traipsing through my house."

"Okay," said Bickman, "if that's how ya want to do it. Where's your house?"

"Down there." Ramses gestured with his head toward the end of the street. "Follow me." He unholstered his PPK and led the way, the three cops trailing dutifully in his wake.

***

Theodora's car was still absent from the driveway and the darkened house unchanged. Ramses instructed the two uniforms to creep around one side of the structure and rendezvous at the back door as he and Bickman made their way around the opposite side. It was now 3:05 a.m. and the air was still hot and muggy, though that didn't fully explain the sweat that streamed copiously down Ramses' sides and soaked his shirt. On the sidewalk in front of the house they split into the two pre-arranged teams and melted into the darkness.

Bickman stepped ahead of Ramses, his service pistol grasped in his right hand. Both of them flattened themselves against the outside wall as they crept around the exterior of the home, heading for the back door. As he rounded the corner of the structure, he spotted his two counterparts already pressed against the back wall, weapons drawn. The closest of them pointed wordlessly toward the partially open kitchen door. Beyond it yawned a black void.

Bickman motioned for Ramses to close the distance between them. "The door is already open," he whispered.

"Go on," Ramses ordered.

With Bickman leading, he and Ramses silently approached the near side of the kitchen door; the other two cops stole closer to the door from its opposite side. Because they were less than ten feet away, Bickman could see them clearly, even in the gloom. He paused to allow his excited breathing to slow to a normal cadence, though his heart was pounding.

Catching the attention of the first cop, Bickman pointed to his chest and held up one finger. He then pointed to his counterpart and held up two fingers. The other cop nodded. Making certain the cop was still watching, Bickman held his hand aloft and, in exaggerated fashion, slowly began counting one, two, three, on his fingers. At the instant he reached "three," Bickman lowered his shoulder and barreled into the door, flinging it fully open with a bang. As he spilled into the unlit house, Bickman hoped to hell that the other three guys were right behind him.

As Bickman crashed into Ramses' kitchen, the other cop promptly thudded into him, nearly knocking him off his feet. If there was someone else inside the house, any element of stealth or surprise they may previously have possessed instantly vaporized.

"Get the lights," Bickman shouted. He darted out of the middle of the floor, to a less exposed position, just as the kitchen lights blazed on.

Standing immediately behind him, looking wildly about, was the second cop. The third cop was behind him, while Ramses was framed in the doorway, one hand on the light switch adjacent to the door, the other on his PPK.

The kitchen was an exemplar of ordinariness: stainless steel appliances, granite countertops, white cupboards. A plate and glass rested in a wire rack adjacent to the sink, drying, and a pink tea towel was threaded through the handle of the refrigerator. A ceiling fan, evidently wired to the light switch, spun merrily. Other than the four cops, the kitchen was unoccupied.

"Theodora?" Ramses called from the doorway. No response. He nodded toward the arch that connected the kitchen with the dining room. "There."

Bickman tentatively approached the arched entryway, pressed himself against the wall, and peered into the dining area. The two uniforms took up positions on the opposite side of the aperture, though Ramses remained where he was. The illumination from the kitchen rendered it easy for Bickman to scan the confines of the unlit dining room.

Like the tidy kitchen, the prosaic dining room was orderly, if uninspired. A dark, heavy table occupied the center of the carpeted floor and a matching china cupboard was placed along the opposite wall. A faux-crystal chandelier was suspended over the table which, judging from the cobwebs that dangled from it, saw little use. Bickman glanced back at Ramses.

"Nuthin'," he informed him.

Ramses abandoned his post at the kitchen light switch and approached Bickman. He poked his head through the archway.

"Theodora?" he called again. Hearing no acknowledgement, Ramses reached around the corner, into the dining room and blindly groped along the interior wall until his hand encountered a light switch. Ramses flicked it on. "Try the living room," he ordered Bickman.

It was becoming increasingly apparent that no one other than them was in the residence. Bickman and the other two cops ducked into the dining area then, somewhat incautiously, proceeded to the living room. It, too, was unoccupied and, like the first two rooms, remarkably unremarkable. Ramses trailed after them from the living room down the hall, toward the bedrooms at the rear of the house, flicking lights on as they went.

"Theodora?" he periodically muttered as they penetrated deeper into the house. Although Ramses still clutched the Walther, Bickman and the other two officers restored their weapons to their holsters, as it was obvious the house was empty.

Except for customary furniture, the first two bedrooms were vacant. Like the dining room, it appeared to Bickman that neither had ever been utilized for their intended purpose. They tramped out the door of the second bedroom, en route to the master bedroom at the end of the hallway.

"Can you think of any place your wife may have gone," Bickman asked from the head of the column. "A girlfriend, maybe?"

"Where would she possibly go at three in the morning?" Ramses scoffed. "Besides, she doesn't have any girlfriends that I'm aware of."

"A boyfriend, then?" Ramses shot Bickman a baleful look but didn't respond.

The master bedroom, though neat, at least gave the appearance of actually having been used. The counterpane on the king-sized bed was slightly bunched, as if something had been placed on it or someone had been sitting there. On the far side of the room, a closet door was slightly ajar and Ramses bounded to it. He flung it open as one of the cops ducked into the adjacent bathroom in order to satisfy himself that no one was lurking there.

"Her clothes are gone," Ramses announced to nobody in particular, staring into the empty closet. Bickman wandered over and poked his head into the closet. He said nothing, though it was apparent that Ramses' wife had decamped.

Ramses abandoned the closet and turned his attention to an ornate dresser situated against the wall opposite the foot of the bed. One after the other he slid the drawers open, then slammed them shut. Like the closet, all were empty.

"Son of a fucking bitch," he spat.

Bickman and the other two cops clustered near the bedroom door, looking at each other in awkward silence.

"Is there anything you want us to do?" Bickman finally asked.

"Yeah, leave," Ramses said. He sat on the edge of the bed and looked at them expectantly.

Surprised by their abrupt dismissal, the three officers had no choice but to nod their goodbyes and make their way back to the kitchen.

"Looks like the old lady flew the coop," one of them remarked.

"Looks that way," the other agreed. Although Bickman said nothing, he couldn't help but feel sorry for Ramses. If nothing else, it had to be embarrassing to come home and find out that your wife had run out on you. On the other hand, what the hell was Ramses doing out at three o'clock in the morning? One of the perks of being chief of detectives was that Ramses kept regular hours. Wherever he was at 3:00 a.m., he wasn't working. Bickman couldn't help but speculate that, maybe if Ramses been home more often, his wife would still be there.

As soon as he returned to his squad car, Bickman radioed the dispatcher with a brief update, saying only that the house was secure. Everybody has problems, even cops, he concluded as he twisted the key and pulled from the curb.

As soon as the three cops departed, Ramses rose from the bed, walked to a PC on a small table in the corner of the bedroom, and flicked it on. When the screen flickered to life, he went online and typed in the web address for the bank where he and Theodora maintained their joint accounts. When he clicked on "my accounts," his suspicions were confirmed. The bitch had liquidated all their accounts, a combined withdrawal exceeding $10,000. Sonofafuckingbitch.

Ramses turned the computer off and returned to the bed, where he sat on the edge. He was effectively broke and his wife had disappeared. God knows where she was, who she was talking to, or what kind of bullshit they were feeding her, or she them. Ramses didn't know exactly how, but that old nigger was behind all of this. He just should have finished the job when he was at the restaurant instead of allowing himself to get spooked by the supposed security cameras. They were probably fake anyway. The old man sure as hell didn't have brains enough to install security cameras. Ramses felt like a fool for letting Jim buffalo him. Who the hell did he think he was? Those two assholes from IA might also be involved, but he doubted it. That wasn't the way IA generally worked. Ramses glanced at the beside clock: 4:15 a.m. No sense going to bed now; he couldn't sleep even if he tried. Besides, it would begin to get light in less than an hour.

Ramses sighed. As if he didn't already have enough on his plate, now he had to deal with this crap. He'd head over to Gail's house and ponder his options over there. She'd probably have some suggestions about what to do. He stood and headed for the door.

***

"So wifey took a powder, huh?" Bickman, Pruitt, and Saturday were eating lunch at a gyros place not far from Bickman's apartment. "Maybe she's not as dumb as we thought," Pruitt said.

"She couldn't be," Saturday observed. "But she was dumb enough to stick around with Ramses for as long as she did." He took another bite of gyros, then turned to Bickman. "They make a good sandwich here. You eat here often?"

"First time," Bickman replied.

"You should eat here more often. Bring your old lady," Saturday advised, taking another bite. "They make a good sandwich," he repeated. "Must be real Greeks runnin' the place," he observed, looking around. "See, a real gyros is made with lamb. Lotta gyros places are too cheap to buy lamb, so they substitute beef, instead. It's not the same," he authoritatively opined.

"I'll remember that," Bickman assured him.

Pruitt steered the conversation back to Ramses. "So, did Ramses say anything when he found out that his wife had split?"

"Not to me," Bickman responded. "And I don't think he said anything to the other two guys, either. It was obvious that he wasn't happy about it, though."

"Yeah, I'll bet," Saturday snorted.

"Ok, here's what you're gonna do," Pruitt said. "Starting now, you're gonna be Ramses' BFF. You're gonna commiserate with him about what a treacherous, perfidious bitch his wife is, you're gonna locate her, and you're gonna find out what caused her to bail. Women just don't hit the bricks for no reason. She learned something about Ramses and I want to know what that was. Maybe she discovered a girlfriend, but maybe it was something else. Whatever it was, you're gonna find out."

"What if he won't talk to me?" Bickman asked.

"Why wouldn't he? Like I said, you guys are BFF's. Don't BFF's tell each other everything?" Pruitt took a bite of gyros. "This would be a lot better if they used beef," he told Saturday.

"Hey, I almost forgot, how's the crime-busters task force going?" Saturday asked Bickman, changing the subject.

Bickman scoffed. "It's a joke. We just look over reports and make up stuff to say about 'em. We never see the AG, but his assistant, or whatever he is, seems satisfied with whatever we're supposed to be doing."

"Isn't it a volunteer position? Sounds like they're gettin' their money's worth," Saturday remarked.

"Has Ramses been attending?" Pruitt inquired.

Bickman shook his head. "He was there for the first session, but the only time I've seen him since is when we showed up at his house the other night. The night his wife left."

"Doesn't Butler say something about the fact that Ramses is never there?"

"Nobody's said anything to me about it," Bickman shrugged. "Even if Ramses was there it wouldn't make any difference since we don't accomplish anything, anyway. I don't even know why *I'm* there."

"I already told you why you're there," Pruitt said. "You're former Phoenix Police Officer of the Year, David Bickman, poster-child for the AG's Crime Task Force, or whatever it's called. You're there to give the impression that the AG's all over the corruption business like a cheap suit. Who could possibly question the integrity or dedication of an Officer of the Year?"

"Bullseye," Saturday added. "Except about the gyros, I mean."

"But that isn't what's happening," Bickman protested. "Like I said, we do nothing but read stuff and making up stuff to say about it. The whole 'task force' is a farce."

"You're missing the point," Pruitt said. "You sell the sizzle, not the steak. Nobody really cares if anything actually gets accomplished. Butler sure as hell doesn't. He just wants it to *look* like something's happening 'cause he knows that's all the voters care about. If you actually found corruption, he'd have to get off his butt and actually do something about it instead of fixing parking tickets for his friends and making PSA's on TV about keeping your kids safe around water."

Bickman didn't really appreciate Pruitt's cynicism, but it was difficult to refute. He ate the rest of his lunch in silence.

***

Welch's good faith attempt to set things to rights had been a bust. True, it had inspired Butler to create his corruption task force, but that enterprise appeared to be stalled at the gate. Welch hadn't heard anything substantive about it, anyway. He feared Butler was just playing to the electorate, that the whole thing would eventually sputter out once the AG or, more importantly, the voters grew bored with it. But it was worse than that. If anybody from Sunstone got wind that Welch had attempted to blow the whistle on the Dawson shooting, Welsh would promptly end up in a neighboring plot. In hindsight, it would have been better if he'd kept his mouth shut from the get-go. But he couldn't unring a bell. Welch looked up as the hostess escorted coroner McKeever to his table.

"Hey," Welsh listlessly greeted him.

"Hey,   Earl."   McKeever   responded   with corresponding lassitude as he sat down.

The hostess handed him a menu that was about an inch thick. "Jarrod will be your server," she informed him, as though the identity of their waiter was a meaningful revelation. McKeever took the menu wordlessly.

"Haven't seen you for a while," Welch said after the hostess departed.

McKeever found the city manager's observation to be simultaneously true and peculiar, given that they rarely needed to see one another.

"Yeah, been busy," is all he said.

A young, heavyset guy sporting colorful tattoos along both arms and his neck, multiple nostril rings, ear   lobe   plugs,   and   a   zebra-striped   Mohawk materialized at their table: Jarrod.

"I'll be serving you today," he said with forced enthusiasm. "Have you eaten with us before?" Like Jarrod cared.

"Bring   me   a   whisky,   neat,"   Welch   ordered, ignoring Jarrod's ice-breaking question.

"Two," McKeever added, holding up two fingers.

"My pleasure, gentlemen," Jarrod assured them. He was lucky the hostess seated these two booze-hounds in his station, as it appeared likely that a good tip would be forthcoming. "Can I start you with an appetizer, as well?"

Welch glanced at McKeever, who shook his head. "No, just the drinks for now."

With a semi-bow, Jarrod retreated from their table.

"Christ, where do they find these freaks?" McKeever marveled to Welch.

"Beats the hell out of me," Welch said. "That kid belongs under the big-top, not serving food in public. Kinda makes me lose my appetite."

"Must be the owner's kid," McKeever speculated. "Otherwise, I can't imagine why they'd hire him. Just one more example of the narcissistic 'Notice-Me' syndrome."

"Yeah, well, he's gotta earn enough money to pay for all those tattoos and piercings," Welch observed.

Jarrod returned with their drinks. "Gentlemen..." he said, carefully placing an absorbent coaster on the table in front of each man, then setting their respective glasses atop the coasters. He stepped away from the table. "Have you had a chance to look over the menu?"

"I think I'm just going to have drinks for now," Welch responded. "Keep 'em coming."

"I'll have a French dip," McKeever said, handing his menu to Jarrod.

"I'll bring you some water, too," Jarrod said, gathering up both menus.

When Jarrod bustled away, McKeever took a sip of his drink. "Why'd you want to see me, Earl?"

Neither McKeever, nor anybody else, knew about Welch's anonymous, abortive call to the AG's office, and Welch intended to keep it that way.

"I just wondered whether you've talked to anyone," Welch vaguely replied. He downed his drink in one gulp.

The medical examiner looked puzzled. "Talked to anyone about what?"

"You know, Dawson...whatever," Welch responded. "I guess I just wanted to talk to somebody..." his voice trailed off.

McKeever wasn't sure whether he was being set-up and tried to appear nonchalant.

"A couple of cops from Phoenix PD talked to me about a John Doe who was killed in a robbery a few weeks ago. He's on ice down at my office because they won't let me release the body to the mortuary. Is that what you're talking about?"

Welch leaned forward and lowered his voice. "Is it Rosey? I heard somebody shot him."

"Rosey?" McKeever looked genuinely surprised. "Rosey was killed last year! It's just a John Doe." He swallowed the rest of his drink and looked around for Jarrod.

Welch leaned back into his seat. "You can tell me, you know."

"Tell you what, Earl? What do you want me to tell you?"

The city manager searched the coroner's face for any expression of reassurance.

"Nothing, I guess," he finally muttered. Then he brightened. "Have you talked to Golden?"

"Yeah, he and I talked a while back. About the John Doe."

"What'd he say?" Welch asked, a little too eagerly.

A beaming Jarrod arrived at their table bearing McKeever's sandwich.

"Here we go," he said, sliding it before him.

"Our water?" McKeever reminded him.

"Oh, yeah.   Forgot."   He looked at Welch. "Another drink?" The city manager nodded. "Be right back with the waters and your drink. You okay drink-wise?" he asked McKeever.

"Bring me another one when you bring his," McKeever instructed Jarrod. He dunked the sandwich into the accompanying cup of *au jus* and took a bite as Jarrod scuttled away. "The meat on this is like rubber bands," he said, disgustedly, and returned the sandwich to the plate. "Our waiter must've made it."

"What did you and Golden talk about?" Welch probed.

McKeever looked noncommittal. "Nuthin' much. We just talked about why the cops seem to be taking a particular interest in the John Doe."

Welch watched him intently. "What if they find out it's Rosey?"

A pained expression crossed McKeever's face. "Earl, shut the hell up. Rosey's dead and cremated. Is that what you want to talk about? Really?"

Jarrod returned to their table. "Here we go, gentlemen, two whiskys, neat." He plucked the empty glasses from their coasters and replaced them with fresh drinks.

"Our water?" McKeever asked again.

"On its way," Jarrod assured him before billowing away.

McKeever's abruptness distressed Welch. "Aren't you afraid somebody will figure something out?" he hazarded.

"How would they do that unless somebody said something?" McKeever pointedly asked. "Like they say, a lot more people have talked themselves into jail than have talked themselves out of it." He paused and sipped his drink, studying Welch over the rim of his glass. "Who have you been talking to, Earl?"

The unexpected question caught the city manager by surprise. He hurriedly took a drink.

"Me? Why would I talk to anyone?" he responded, flustered.

McKeever looked at him coldly. "You're the one who's got his panties in a wad over the John Doe."

"For Christ's sake, Larry, I was just asking a question," Welch sullenly responded. He drained his whisky.

"Look, Earl, Golden and I just talked about whether there was any cause for concern. We both concluded that there's not." McKeever wished he actually believed it.

"What do you think's the worst-case scenario?" Welch tried to sound as though he was engaging in mere philosophical speculation.

"The worst-case scenario is that the earth will explode tomorrow, in which case none of this will matter. Other than that, we're just gonna have to ride it out. Nobody from the PD has talked to me in a while, so maybe it's already blown over."

"Nobody's talked to me," Welch said. He sounded mildly disappointed.

"That's a good thing, Earl. Do you really want people sticking their noses up your ass?"

Jarrod breezed back to their table, sans water. "How are we doing, gentlemen? How's the sandwich? Can I get you another drink?"

McKeever looked at Welch. "I'm about finished," he said.

"Would you like a box?" Jarrod asked, pointing to the French dip.

"No, it's not worth eating," McKeever informed him.

Jarrod's face assumed a pained expression. "Oh, I'm sorry to hear that. Would you like something else from the menu?"

"We'll just take the check," Welch interjected.

"Very good. Be right back." Jarrod was actually glad they'd decided to leave, as they were becoming somewhat cranky. He sped away to retrieve their check.

"So, what are you gonna do?" Welch asked.

"I'm gonna go back to my office and do some paperwork. Exactly what you should do."

"Lemme ask you something."

"What's that?"

Welch lowered his voice. "Do you trust Golden and Ramses?"

"I trust them as much as I trust you," McKeever replied.

Welch was about to respond when Jarrod returned with the tab. "Who gets the honor?" he asked.

"I'll take it." Welch reached for the bill.

"Thanks for coming in today. I hope to see you guys again soon." With that, Jarrod was gone.

"Thanks for the drink. I'll let you know if I hear anything else," McKeever promised as he stood.

"Yeah, me, too." Welch glanced at the check, removed three tens from his wallet, then tossed them onto the table. "I'm gonna finish my drink. I'll talk to you later." McKeever departed without saying anything further. He wanted to get back to his office and call Golden.

THIRTEEN

Ramses must make a pretty good salary as chief of detectives; Bickman couldn't understand why he'd want to waste his time working as a part-time bouncer at a crappy neighborhood bar.

He was in uniform and it was early evening when he walked into the Gallows. Although the place was devoid of customers, Ramses sat at one end of the vacant bar chatting with the bartender. They looked up when Bickman pushed open the tavern door, momentarily flooding the dim interior with sunlight. Ramses and the bartender suspended their conversation and watched in silence as Bickman approached them across the empty floor.

Bickman hadn't seen Ramses since the evening he and the other two cops had reported to Ramses' home, notwithstanding there'd been another task-force meeting at the AG's office earlier that week. Ramses had been conspicuous by his absence.

"Hey," Bickman said, hoping he didn't sound too chipper.

"Yeah, how ya doin'," responded Frank, the bartender. "Help you with something?"

"I'm here to see Detective Ramses," Bickman said. Frank look quizzically at Ramses, then slowly stepped toward the opposite end of the bar, wiping it with a wet cloth as he went. Ramses looked at Bickman impassively without moving from his bar stool as the latter drew up an adjacent stool. Bickman plopped a pile of folders onto the bar between them.

"From the AG," he explained.

Ramses glanced at the folders disinterestedly. "What am I supposed to do with 'em?"

"We're supposed to read 'em."

"Yeah, that'll happen. Want something to drink?"

"Sure."

"Hey, Frank," Ramses yelled at the bartender, "bring us a couple of Diet Cokes."

Although Bickman's ostensible reason for stopping by the Gallows was to provide Ramses copies of the latest materials pertinent to Butler's corruption task-force, he was actually there under orders from Pruitt.

Frank filled two glasses with soft drinks and carried them down the bar. He wordlessly placed them next to Ramses and trudged back to the far end.

"That thing still goin' on?" Ramses asked Bickman, taking a drink of Diet Coke.

Bickman laughed. "The task-force? Yeah, such as it is. Pretty much a waste of time, I think."

"I figured that much out in the first five minutes."

"Yeah, well I guess you're smarter than me."

"I've just been around longer," Ramses shrugged.

Bickman took a sip of his soft drink. "That why you quit coming?"

"Yep."

Bickman inwardly debated before asking his next question. He knew, however, that Pruitt would expect to know.

"Did your wife ever show up?"

The unexpectedness of the question caught Ramses off guard.

"What did you just say?"

Bickman rapidly backtracked.

"Sorry, I didn't mean to be presumptuous. I just meant that I know you were worried about her, and just wondered if she got home okay." He feared he may have overplayed his hand. After all, he barely knew Ramses and, moreover, was his nominal subordinate.

"The fuckin' cunt served me with divorce papers," Ramses said, indifferently.

"So, she's okay?"

"I guess. She may be okay but I sure as hell ain't." Ramses drained his Coke. "Hey, Frank!" he yelled at the bartender as he held aloft his empty glass and rattled the ice cubes in it. He looked again at Bickman. "The fat bitch wants the house, my pension, alimony, every fuckin' thing that isn't nailed down."

Frank made his way back down the bar, retrieved Ramses' glass, and refilled it.

"You good?" he asked Bickman, who nodded in reply. He retreated down the bar.

"I'm sorry to hear that," Bickman told Ramses because it seemed the appropriate thing to say when somebody tells you that their wife is divorcing them. "So, what are you going to do, if you don't mind my asking?"

"I don't know yet. Hire a lawyer, I guess. I'll be damned if I let that cow get any of my fuckin' pension, and I'm not gonna pay her alimony. Screw her."

"Well, sorry about the hassle," Bickman commiserated.

"Thanks. It isn't like I don't have a ton of other shit on my plate right now. Dealing with this crap is the last thing I needed."

Bickman was about inquire about the other things going on in Ramses' life when the front door opened and two men strolled in from the street. Though their precise features were difficult to discern because they were silhouetted in the brilliant sunlight that streamed through the door, one was clearly bald with a neatly trimmed white beard, while the other appeared to be Asian. Both were wearing suits, sunglasses, and looked like bankers. The pair scanned the interior of the tavern as the door swung shut behind them.

"Help you gents?" Frank called from behind the bar.

The Asian immediately zeroed in on the two men sitting on barstools at one end of the bar. They made their way across the room and stood directly in front of Ramses. The one with the beard turned to Bickman.

"We need to talk to Detective Ramses," he said. "Why don't you go write some traffic tickets." Puzzled, Bickman looked at Ramses.

"Who are you?" Ramses asked, his voice betraying no emotion.

"Friends," smiled the Asian. "We need to talk to you about a dog."

Ramses shook his head. "I don't think so. I don't even like dogs, but I heard that Chinks like to eat 'em."

The Asian smiled again. "Yeah, I heard that, too."

Although neither of the men had done anything overtly hostile or threatening, their presence seethed with menace.   The one with the beard looked at Bickman again, who hadn't moved from his stool next to Ramses.

"Something wrong with your hearing?"

Bickman wasn't sure how he should react, so he turned toward Ramses. "You got this?"

Ramses' eyes never left Doc. "Yeah, I got it."

"That dog I told you about?   It belonged to the chief. He said we needed to talk to you about it," the Asian resumed. "You don't want to upset the chief, do you?"

Without averting his eyes from the Asian, Ramses muttered to Bickman, "You better get goin'. We'll talk later."

Bickman hesitated, then slid off his stool and turned to look at Frank, who stood at the far end of the bar, watching the developments with interest.

"Don't forget your homework," Bickman told Ramses, nodding toward the pile of folders on the bar.

The bearded guy moved slightly aside to allow Bickman to pass. With a final glance at Ramses, he stepped around him and walked slowly to the front door of the Gallows. Ramses' gaze never wavered from the Asian's face, who stood directly in front of him.

Once he'd returned to his squad car and cranked up the air conditioner, Bickman wasn't sure what he should do. Neither of the men had actually threatened them, so he couldn't justify radioing in an "officer in distress" call. Yet his instincts told him that their ominous appearance didn't bode well. Bickman removed his cell phone from his uniform pocket and punched in Pruitt's number. Characteristically, it immediately went to voice mail.

"Hey, it's me," he said. "It's 6:30 and I was just with Detective Ramses at the Gallows and two guys came in, a white guy and an Asian. I didn't recognize them and they didn't introduce themselves, but they wanted to talk to Ramses in private. Not sure what they wanted, but figured you ought to know." He terminated the call and pulled away from the curb, heading home.

Inside the bar, the bearded guy informed Ramses, "Our car is in back. Let's blow this dump."

"I kinda like it here," deferred Ramses. "Besides, I'm working."

"Hmmm.... That's too bad, because the chief really wants to see you," said the Asian. "Now."

"If Golden wants to see me, why didn't he come?"

"Because he sent us," replied the Asian, as though it was the most obvious thing in the world. "Let's go, he's waiting."

Although Ramses had no idea who the two guys actually were, their explanation that they were emissaries from Golden was entirely plausible. They were clearly not neophytes and, since Ramses didn't recognize them, it was possible they were from the Coast. They may, in fact, have been sent over specifically to replace the recently departed Rosey.

Ramses slid off his stool.

"I'll be back in a little while. Keep an eye on my stuff," he told Frank, meaning the folders Bickman previously deposited.

"That's cool. It shouldn't be too busy tonight," the bartender, who remained standing at the far end of the bar, assured him.

The Asian pointed to the door and, with the bearded guy in the van, the three men exited the bar. They walked around the building to the gravel parking lot in the rear, where a black BMW sedan was parked. The bearded guy unlocked the car and got behind the wheel, while the Asian opened a rear door and gestured for Ramses to climb in. Ramses complied, somewhat warily, and the Asian slid in beside him.

"You guys got names?" Ramses asked as the bearded guy cranked the engine over and flicked the air conditioner on.

"I'm Red and that's Doc," the bearded guy responded from the front seat, watching Ramses in the rearview mirror.

"I don't think I've seen you around."

"We're from the Coast," Red explained, confirming Ramses' suspicion. He put the BMW in gear and pulled from the parking lot. "I can't say I care much for the weather around here."

"Yeah, well, get in line," Ramses remarked. He glanced out the tinted window. Although the burnished sun was beginning to drop behind the office buildings on the west side of the bar, the air temperature still exceeded 100 degrees. "Where we headed?"

"The chief wants to talk to you," said Doc. "It shouldn't take too long."

They drove in silence. Although Ramses was far from sanguine about being basically shanghaied by Doc and Red, he knew that resistance would have been folly. Sunstone didn't hire amateurs.

Red drove south on 7th Street, toward the Salt River. The Salt had been dammed upriver more than a century earlier, leaving a desiccated channel that cut like a gaping scar through the center of Phoenix. The dry riverbed was utilized as a landfill, a camping spot for vagrants, the location of a few wrecking yards, and the site of several commercial sand-and-gravel operations. A handful of construction companies also maintained storage yards along the waterless course of the Salt. Beyond that, the city wouldn't permit the construction of permanent structures because of the fear they'd be swept away in one of the flash floods that periodically roared down the otherwise dry riverbed. Ziggurat Contracting stored most of its heavy equipment, including scrapers, graders, dump-bellies, flatbeds, backhoes, and cement trucks at a fenced enclosure in the bed of the Salt River.

When he reached the north edge of the broad Salt, Red slowed before turning west onto a one-lane asphalt road that ran along the edge of the lifeless riverbed. He lowered the BMW's visor because they were now heading directly into the sun, suspended, immobile, above the distant Estrella Mountains. It burned a hole in the torpid air. After driving about five minutes, Red slowed again and turned south, into the dry riverbed itself. He flipped the sun visor up. Through the BMW's windshield, Ramses could see Ziggurat's construction yard directly in front of them, encompassed by a ten-foot chain link fence surmounted by razor wire. The hulks of heavy equipment bearing Ziggurat's logo, a stepped pyramid, loomed before them behind the fence.

"Golden thought it would be safer to meet here," Doc explained as the BMW drew to a halt before a double gate with large "No Trespassing" and "Prohibido el Paso" signs affixed to it. Red threw the BMW's transmission lever into "P," then exited the vehicle to unlock the gate. He swung one-half of the gate open, returned to the car, and drove into the yard. Once inside the fence, Red paused only long enough to shut and lock the gate before returning to the car and driving slowly toward the small office building at one end of the enclosure.

From the back seat, Ramses peered around. "Where's Golden's car?" he asked. He was becoming uneasy about the way things were developing.

"He's on his way," Red answered as he pulled before the structure, put the transmission in "P," and shut the engine off. He removed his sun glasses and placed them carefully atop the dashboard.

Ramses was beginning to regret his decision to leave the bar with these two guys. His PPK still nestled in the small of his back in a holster clipped to his belt; Ramses found its presence reassuring. If they intended to do him harm, they would certainly have searched him, or at least asked if he was packing, neither of which they did. Hopefully, things were exactly as Doc represented and the chief had simply sent them to retrieve Ramses for a strategy session. Nothing sinister about that.

Red exited the driver's seat and held the rear door open to allow Doc and Ramses to climb out. The sun had finally dropped completely behind the Estrella's and it was beginning to grow dark. Ramses was struck at how much cooler it was in the low-lying riverbed than it was in the center of town, scarcely five miles away.   Although he could see the lights of the city twinkling in the distance, they seemed a million miles away.   Ramses' shirt was damp and a slight shiver thrilled down his spine, whether from the comparative coolness of the evening air, or for some other reason, he was unable to say.

The three men walked to the building, gravel crunching beneath their shoes, where Red unlocked the door. He reached inside and flicked the lights on; a harsh neon glare filled the interior.   Red stepped across the threshold, followed by Ramses and Doc.

It was really more of a workshop than an office. Arranged along the interior walls was an assortment of large power tools: metal lathes, pipe benders, table and band saws, drill presses.   Clear sheeting was draped over most of the equipment and large areas of the cement floor were covered with heavy, blue plastic, tarps. A pyramid of gallon cans was stacked in one corner and the place smelled like paint.

"They're paintin' the interior," Red explained. He dragged a folding office chair from a corner and placed it near the center of the room, on top of a blue tarp. "Might as well make yourself comfortable while we wait."

Doc carted two more office chairs over and plopped them down near the first chair, more-or-less in a circle.

"Why don't you make us some coffee?" he amiably suggested to Red. As his partner made his way to the

Bunn coffee maker sitting on a rickety table in one corner of the room, Doc sat down next to Ramses.

"What time'd he say he'd be here?" Ramses asked.

Doc glanced at his watch. "I'm surprised he's not already here," he said.

"Do you know what he wants to meet about?"

"He didn't say. He just told us where you'd be and asked us to bring you."

Ramses looked pensive. "I guess it's kinda good that you guys are here because I wanted to talk to the chief about a job, anyway."

"What kinda job?"

"A guy's been giving me problems. I need somebody to take care of him. I talked to Golden about it before."

"Bring it up when he gets here," Doc suggested.

Ramses paused. "Did you know Rosey?" he finally ventured.

"How do you want it?" Red called from across the room, his back to them.

"Black for me," Doc told him.

"Black," Ramses seconded.

"Yeah, I knew him," Doc replied. "Too bad how he ended up." Ramses didn't reply.

Red filled two Styrofoam cups with coffee when Doc turned his head slightly, listening.

"Did you hear that? I think that may be Golden." Ramses didn't hear anything. "Lemme look."

Doc got to his feet as Red turned from the coffee maker holding two Styrofoam cups and began walking toward them. He proceeded slowly to avoid slopping the hot beverage onto his hands from the uncovered containers. Doc went to the door and peered out into the darkness.

"I guess it was nuthin'," he announced and shut the door.

Doc returned to the center of the room at the same time Red arrived with Ramses' coffee. Doc stood behind Ramses' chair as Red reached forward and handed the cup to Ramses.

"Here ya go."

As Ramses reached out to grasp the cup, Doc pulled a snub-nosed .357 revolver from his waistband, placed the muzzle vertically on the crown of Ramses' head, and pulled the trigger. The bullet plowed straight down Ramses' spine, killing him instantly with virtually no effluence of blood. Ramses' body flopped forward and slid onto to plastic tarp. Hot coffee spilled over his lifeless hands.

"Goddamn, that just about deafened me!" Red exclaimed.

"Yeah, me, too," Doc complained. Red handed him the other cup of coffee. Doc took a sip. "There's no quiet way to shoot somebody in a closed room."

Holding his cup of coffee in one hand, Doc squatted, flipped open Ramses' jacket, and removed the PPK from its holster. He tugged Ramses' watch off his wrist.

Red nodded in silent agreement. "Occupational hazard," he concluded.

Doc stood and crammed Ramses' PPK and watch into his trouser pocket then walked over and propped open the workshop's door. He returned to Ramses' prostrate body. The two men grabbed the tarp and half-lifted, half-dragged, the tarp and its lugubrious cargo toward the door.

"Mother fucker, this guy's heavy," Doc panted as they proceeded, crab-like, along the building's concrete floor. "Wait a minute, I gotta rest." Both men were already drenched in sweat.

They set the tarp down. Red walked over to a rack of implements and, after, surveying them a moment, removed an axe. He propped it against the door frame before returning to the tarp containing Ramses' body.

"C'mon," he urged Doc, grabbing his two corners again.

With an audible sigh, Doc complied and together they carried the tarp outside, where they deposited it onto the gravel parking lot, near the rear of the BMW.

"Grab a flashlight and that axe," Red instructed him. "And bring another tarp."

Doc disappeared into the office and returned a moment later with all three items. He flicked the flashlight on as Red rolled Ramses' body off the tarp onto the dirt, face up. He arranged Ramses' limbs in spread eagle fashion. While Doc held the flashlight, Red took the axe and, after removing his suit jacket, rapidly proceeded to dismember the body. As he worked, Red tossed Ramses' arms, legs, thighs, calves, feet, and head onto one tarp. When he'd finished his grisly task, he and Doc scooped the trunk of Ramses' body onto the second tarp and wrapped it up, tamale-like. Doc popped the Beemer's trunk and they lifted the parcel into the vehicle, after which Red slammed shut the trunk lid.

"No fuss, no muss," he said.   Notwithstanding Red's vigorous use of the axe, there was a surprising paucity of blood on the ground because they'd left the torso largely intact.

They returned to the remaining tarp and folded it around Ramses' limbs and head. Doc stuffed the flash light into his rear pocket and together they lugged the tarp back into the office, Red kicking the door closed with his foot as they crossed the threshold.

"Carry it over to that band saw," Doc directed, motioning with his chin as they carried what was left of Ramses across the room. "I'll get his teeth and cut him up while you go out and cover the blood in the parking lot with some dirt." He handed Red the flash light.

They dropped their burden with a thud next to a large band saw and Red went to locate a shovel. Doc dragged one of the folding chairs over and hung his suit coat over the back. Next, he went to a nearby work bench that was littered with hand tools. Locating a pair of pliers amongst the clutter on the workbench, Doc returned to the band saw and removed the clear plastic sheeting draped over it. He plopped down onto the folding chair, flipped the tarp back to reveal Ramses' body parts, smoothed the plastic sheeting over his lap and part-way up his chest, and leaned down to retrieve Ramses' head.

Placing the head in his lap, Doc opened the mouth and, with the pliers, systematically began to extract Ramses' teeth, placing them in a neat pile on the floor next to his chair. Twisting the teeth out of each jaw was laborious and Doc was quickly drenched

in sweat. He momentarily looked up from his task.
Red must've found a shovel because he'd disappeared.

About fifteen minutes into the process of
removing Ramses' teeth, Red returned from the
parking lot.

"Zoop, zoop," he announced. "The construction
crew will obliterate whatever's left of it when they drive
into the yard tomorrow morning." He wandered over to
watch Doc work. "Got another one of those plastic
drop cloths?" he asked after a few minutes.

"I took this one off the band saw. Get one off one
of the other pieces of equipment." Doc gritted his teeth
as he strained to yank out a molar.

Red walked over to a table saw and whipped the
sheeting from it. He folded it roughly into quarters,
then snipped a diagonal from the upper right-hand
corner with a pair of heavy shears. When he unfolded
it, the square drop cloth had a diamond-shaped hole
cut neatly in the center. Red slipped it over his head;
it hung just past his knees. A cheap plastic poncho.

"Not bad, eh?" he said to Doc.

Doc chuckled. "You look like the Man with No
Name."

Red returned to the tarp holding Ramses' limbs.
He punched the rocker switch on the band saw and it
roared to life with a loud screech. Red picked up an
arm and unceremoniously guided it into the saw's
whirring blade.

The humming blade initially spattered bits of
flesh onto Red's poncho, but Ramses' clothing
absorbed most of the offal. The saw quickly
encountered bone, which it severed with loud
screeching noises. The stench of burning bone quickly

filled the room. Red turned the arm first this way, then that way, cutting it into sections about four inches long. He tossed each section back onto the blue tarp. He then did the same with the second arm. Ramses' feet he simply cut in half.

"Wanna spell me?" he asked Doc, who was still industriously engaged in removing teeth. The mound of teeth at his side had grown appreciably.

"Perfect timing." Using both hands, Doc tossed Ramses' head back onto the tarp at his feet, where it landed with a thump. He stood and tucked the drop cloth into his shirt collar, then grabbed one of Ramses' calves as Red stepped away from the churning saw.

As Red had done with Ramses' arms, Doc quickly reduced the remaining limbs to four-inch chunks. He then turned to the head.

"Quarter it?" Red suggested.

"Yeah, that sounds about right," concurred Doc.

"I'll find something to put his teeth in."

As Doc fed Ramses' head into the saw, Red scoured the office for an appropriate container. He finally found an old baby food jar filled with screws. He dumped the screws out and replaced them with Ramses' teeth.

Doc switched the band saw off, which powered down with a shudder.

"Done and done," he said. They'd previously discussed with the Coast the best way to dispose of Ramses' body. It was agreed that his limbs would be sawed into manageable pieces, while the trunk would be left intact; it was simply impractical, to say nothing of messy, to cut up Ramses' trunk. As to the former, they would be dumped into the large rotating drum on one of Ziggurat's cement trucks. Once in the drum, Ramses' limbs and skull would be indiscriminately mixed with the cement slurry that Ziggurat intended to pour as part of the foundation for the new Phoenix City Hall; Ziggurat had been awarded the right to build city hall under the terms of a no-bid contract. Red and Doc would chauffeur Ramses' torso north on Interstate 17 that night, to the border of neighboring Yavapai County, tossing Ramses' individual teeth out the window of the moving car. There were precipitous drop-offs along remote stretches of freeway in that area, and they'd simply fling the torso over one of them. The headless, legless trunk would tumble down the incline several hundred feet and lodge in the rocks and bushes below, concealed from the roadway. Ramses' torso would probably never be found and, even if it was, the insects, coyotes, birds, and other scavengers that inhabited the area will have rendered it unidentifiable. All usable traces of DNA will have become completely degraded due to prolonged exposure to the elements and, because of their proximity to an interstate highway, the remains could have originated anywhere in the country. The authorities would have no option but to write them off as "unidentified male" and call it a day.

"Another job well done with our usual speed and accuracy," declared Red. He slipped his poncho off and wadded it up.

"You hungry?" Doc asked. "Let's stop by a burger place on the way out of town, clean up, and get something to eat."

"Yeah, I could eat something," Red agreed.

"Who's gonna deal with that?" Doc pointed to the blue tarp where the fragments of Ramses' limbs were heaped.

"Somebody from the construction company is supposed to be here in about half an hour to toss everything into a cement mixer."

"What about the saw?   It's pretty fucked up."

"Same guy's gonna haul it off. Ain't our problem." Red slipped the baby food jar containing Ramses' teeth into his pocket. "Let's blow," he said and they strolled out the door.

***

Carol, Jim, and Harvey were having lunch at the restaurant. Following his discharge from the hospital, Jim paid to have the air conditioning repaired, so they were able to eat in comfort. They were the sole diners.

"You know, you guys can stay at my place for as long as you want," Harvey assured them again as he took a bite of tuna fish sandwich.

"That's sweet, but we can't stay there forever," Carol smiled.

"Why not? With Jim doin' the cookin' and you providing' the scenery, everything's great!"

Although his face was largely healed, Jim still had difficulty chewing. He listened to the conversation between Harvey and Carol as he sipped a Pepsi through a straw.

"No, Carol's right," he finally said. "You been a good friend, Harvey, but I'm thinkin' everything's all right now."

Carol put her sandwich down. "What makes you think that?"

"I ain't heard nuthin' from Ramses since I mailed the disc to his wife. That's a good sign, ain't it?"

Jim's simplistic mindset puzzled Carol.

"That probably only means that he's just biding his time, plotting what to do next. What if he comes back here, or to your apartment? He just about killed you last time; what do you think he'll do next time?"

"Good thinking," Harvey said. "You better keep staying' at my place, Jim."

"Even if I stay at your house, I still gotta restaurant to run, Harvey. Ramses, or anybody else, can find me here anytime they want. Besides," Jim smiled ruefully, "I don't want you getting' beat up, too."

Carol placed her hand over Jim's. "So, close the restaurant, Jim. Live off your Social Security. You don't need this place but I need you."

Jim held her hand. "I can't do that, Carol. I got too many people depending on me. For a bunch of my customers, I may be the only other person they see all day! They need me, too." He paused, his dark eyes searching her face. "Besides, I'm tired of being threatened and bullied. Everybody thinks they can do whatever they want to an old man and a young woman and, up 'til now, they have. But I ain't gonna run no more, Carol. I did wrong, tellin' Jerry to run; I see that now. I can't run no more."

FOURTEEN

Bickman and Saturday sat in Pruitt's second-floor office. Saturday handed Bickman a cup of coffee, then resumed his seat on the couch.

"So, neither of them identified themselves?" Pruitt asked.

Bickman sipped his coffee. "Nope."

"Tell me again what they looked like," Saturday directed from the couch.

"Slight builds, dark suits, one guy was Asian, the other guy was white and had a little beard. They looked like car salesmen."

"And you didn't recognize either of them?" Bickman shook his head.

"Did Ramses know 'em?"

"He didn't act like he did," Bickman replied.

"Which one of 'em was in charge?"

Bickman reflected a moment before responding. "The Asian did most of the talking."

"Did he have an accent?"

"Neither of 'em had accents."

"Tell me again exactly what they said to Ramses."

"The Asian just said they wanted to talk to him. He said they were from the 'chief.'"

"The 'chief'? Police chief? Fire chief?"

"Maybe Sitting Bull sent 'em," Saturday volunteered. Pruitt ignored him.

"I don't know," Bickman replied. "He just said 'chief.'"

"Did they say they had a car, or what?" Pruitt probed.

"They never mentioned a car, though I assume they had one. There wasn't a vehicle parked out front when I went to my squad car, but they may have parked in back."

"So how did it finally end up?"

"Ramses told me to split, so I did. The whole thing lasted less than five minutes. I went back to my car and called you. I have no idea what happened to Ramses, or the two guys, after I left the bar." Bickman sipped his coffee. "Did you talk to Ramses?"

Saturday leaned back on the couch and laced his fingers behind his head.

"Well, that's the thing. Ramses has vaporized. He didn't return to the bar that night and hasn't been to work since. We're thinking' those guys from the bar may have taken him on a little vacation."

Bickman frowned unconsciously.

"Even though they didn't look like garden variety bad asses, I don't think I'd want to screw with either of those guys. They gave off a bad vibe." He turned to Pruitt. "Ramses was bitching about his wife divorcing him. Do you think she has anything to do with anything?"

"Not likely," Pruitt said. "The guys you're describing were obviously pros, *way* out of the old lady's league. If a pissed-off wife wants to put the hurt on hubby, she hires a dumbass truck driver, not a professional.   Whoever hired those guys had some serious coin."

"Who, then?" Bickman asked.

"Sitting Bull," Pruitt smiled, mysteriously.

***

People were eating at two booths, and another customer was seated at the counter, when Pruitt and Saturday walked in. They seated themselves at a table as Jim emerged from the kitchen, carrying a plate containing a hamburger and a heap of potato chips.

"Man! What happened to you?" Saturday exclaimed. The vestiges of Ramses' beating were still visible on Jim's face.

Jim deposited the plate in front of the customer at the counter and hobbled to their table. "I cut myself shaving," he said.

"You must've shaving with a chainsaw."

"Something like that. What's your pleasure?"

Pruitt looked closely at Jim.

"We came by here a coupla times during the week but the place was buttoned up tighter than a tick. You okay?"

"Never better," Jim replied. "You two gonna eat, or did you just come by just discuss my health?"

"Bring us each a burger and a Pepsi," Saturday directed. He paused. "Hey it's actually cool in here. What's with that?"

Jim smiled. "I had the a/c fixed. Glad somebody noticed."

"That must explain the other customers," Saturday said, looking around.

"I'm blessed," Jim acknowledged. "Business been pickin' up lately." He headed back to the kitchen to prepare their lunch.

"Looks like somebody wanted to get his attention," Saturday observed after Jim left.

"Think they succeeded?"

Saturday looked puzzled. "I don't know. He seems pretty chipper for just gettin' thumped."

"Think he'd tell us who did it?"

"Sure, when hell freezes over."

Pruitt shrugged. "Let's ask him. What's he gonna do? Not invite us to his birthday party?"

Jim returned with two glasses filled with ice and two Pepsis, which he placed on their table. As he turned away, Pruitt touched Jim's hand.

"What really happened to you, Jim?"

"Nuthin'. I told you."

Wanting to gauge Jim's reaction, Pruitt took a chance. "Detective Ramses has disappeared."

Jim paused. "Say again?"

"Ramses. He vaporized," Saturday said. "We thought you might be interested."

Jim looked puzzled. "What happened to him?"

"That's what we're tryin' to figure out. You wouldn't know anything about it would you?" Pruitt asked.

"I run a restaurant. Folks disappearin' is your business, ain't it?"

"Yeah, it's our business. Just like the people who help 'em disappear is our business," Saturday retorted.

Jim turned to face him.

"Mister, if you're sayin' that I had something to do with somebody's disappearance, you best put me in jail right now. I could stand to have somebody cook for *me* for a change. Otherwise, I'm gonna go finish your lunches." He looked at Saturday defiantly.

Pruitt appreciated the old man's mettle.

"Naw, we don't think you had anything to do with it but, then again, who would have believed that you waxed Georgio Rosedea? You're full of surprises, Jim."

"Who?" Jim asked.

"The guy you blew away with the shotgun," Saturday informed him.

"He said his name was 'Adolph'," Jim corrected him.

"Yeah, right," Saturday scoffed. "If he was 'Adolph,' then I'm your Uncle Fud."

"Well, Uncle Fud, unless you want a burger that tastes like charcoal, I better get back to the kitchen," Jim told him.

"You free to talk for a minute after you bring our food out?" Pruitt asked.

"I'm here all day," Jim replied. "But if it's all the same to you two, I'd like to feed my other customers before you run 'em off."

Pruitt laughed. "We'll be here."

Jim nodded and limped away. En route to the kitchen he stopped at the two occupied booths and briefly chatted with the diners, then paused to exchange pleasantries with the guy sitting at the counter. The detectives' burgers were frying in a skillet with the gas flame turned low, so when Jim finally returned to the kitchen, he had only to flip the patties and begin preparation of each bun.

As he worked, Jim reflected on Pruitt's revelation about Ramses' disappearance. He wasn't convinced they were even telling the truth; like his mother used to say, some people would rather climb a tree and lie than stand on the ground and tell the truth. He'd just have to talk to Pruitt and Saturday and try to figure out the truth. He assembled the burgers, placed them on plates, and dumped some potato chips onto each plate from an industrial-sized bag he'd purchased at Sam's Club. Balancing a plate in each hand, he headed back to the dining room.

Although one booth was still occupied the other customers had departed. Jim set the detectives' plates before them then immediately turned to clear the dishes from the other tables. The diners had simply paid their respective tabs by leaving money behind.

"You doin' okay?" he called to the other booth while he hauled dishes back to the kitchen.

"Doin' fine," the elderly man assured him. "I was afraid you went out of business, Jim."

The old man smiled. "You don't have to worry 'bout that. I just took a few days off."

"Oh no, Jim. You're not allowed to take days off." I'll starve to death!" the man grinned.

Jim returned to the table where Pruitt and Saturday were eating their burgers, pulled a chair out, and sat down.

"How do you know Ramses disappeared?"

Pruitt wiped mustard from the corner of his mouth with a napkin. "He hasn't been to work in a few days and nobody seems to know where he is."

"What happened to him?"

Saturday looked at Jim patronizingly. He'd already consumed nearly his entire burger.

"We don't know; that's why we said he's 'disappeared.' If we knew what happened to him, we wouldn't be having this conversation."

"Ramses left a bar a few nights ago with two guys," Pruitt resumed. "He hasn't been seen since."

"Maybe they were friends of his," Jim suggested.

"Doesn't look that way. We think somebody sent 'em to get rid of Ramses."

"Which they did," Saturday added, picking potato chip crumbs from his plate and licking his fingertips.

"I don't go to bars," Jim said.

"I know. We just thought maybe you knew something."

"I run a restaurant," Jim replied. "Why would I know something? Besides, it ain't my turn to watch Ramses." He looked at Pruitt skeptically. "Don't you two get paid to protect people? How come the folks you're supposed to be protectin' seem to end up either missin' or dead? How do you figure that? I'm startin' to think you're overpaid."

"When was the last time Ramses was here, Jim?" Pruitt asked.

"What makes you think he was here?"

"Because we think he did that to your face," Saturday said, matter-of-factly. "Either that, or he sent somebody to do it."

"I told you what happened to my face."

"Yeah, I know what you told us," Saturday acknowledged. "It's bullshit."

Jim turned to Pruitt. "Have you asked Ramses' wife where he is?"

"How do you know he has a wife?"

Jim shrugged. "Just guessin'."

Pruitt was dubious. "Yeah, well, we talked to her. Problem is, she's divorcing his ass and couldn't care less where he is."

Jim reacted with surprise. "Divorcing him? Too bad."

"Yeah, ain't it," Saturday grunted.

"Why's she divorcing him?" Jim asked.

"Probably because she hates his guts," Saturday speculated. "What's it to you?"

"Just makin' conversation," Jim told him.

"Ever heard of anybody named 'Doc' or 'Red,'" Pruitt asked.

"Sure," Jim replied. "I call my doctor 'doc.' Don't know anybody named 'Red,' though. Why?"

"They're the guys Ramses left the bar with the other night."

"Don't know 'em," Jim repeated.

"You never answered Pruitt's question," Saturday reminded the old man.

"Which question?"

"When was the last time Detective Ramses was in here?"

"I'm old and don't remember things like I used to. Why don't you ask him when you find him?" Jim responded.

"Okay, lemme ask it another way, when did you cut yourself shaving?"

"Couple of weeks ago, maybe a little better."

"So, either Ramses, or somebody he sent, was in your restaurant a couple of weeks ago. And when he was here, he beat you up," Saturday conjectured. "Do I have that right?"

"You're the one doin' the talkin'," Jim said.

Pruitt quietly listened as Saturday resumed.

"We know that's what happened because you blew away the first guy that Ramses sent," he pointed toward the kitchen, "and it's not likely that he was real happy about it. We're thinking that Ramses personally returned to finish the job. The funny part is that Ramses didn't finish the job but, right after he's here, his wife initiates divorce, then he completely disappears." He looked dubiously at Jim. "Why do you suppose that is?"

"Like I said, you can ask him when you see him," Jim said. "I already told you what happened. Maybe Ramses just didn't like my cookin'."

"So, he *was* here."

Jim shrugged. "That's what you keep sayin'."

Pruitt looked at Jim earnestly. "We've been square with you. Why don't you return the favor? Why is Ramses so interested in you? Whatever it is may have gotten him killed. You don't want any part of that, do you?"

"I been part of it since you shot Jerry," Jim sighed, "but I don't know anything about Ramses' disappearing." He paused. "I won't say I'm sorry, though."

"Why did he send Rosedea to hurt you? Why would he do that?"

"You mean 'Adolph?'" Jim corrected him again.

Pruitt gave him a wry look. "Whatever."

"Even if you don't know anything about Ramses' disappearance, blackmail is a crime, too," Saturday warned.

"I wouldn't know anything about that," Jim said. "But if you want to arrest me, have at it."

Pruitt furrowed his brow in thought before speaking again. "Can you think of anyone who might know something about Ramses' disappearance, Jim?"

Jim smiled enigmatically. "Like I said, if it was me, I'd talk to his wife again. Maybe even the chief of police."

"There's that 'chief,' again," Saturday remarked.

FIFTEEN

"I have recently been informed, gentlemen, that professional commitments have conspired to render it necessary for one of our members, Phoenix Chief of Detectives, Oren Ramses, to resign his appointment to the attorney general's organized crime task force."

They were seated around the conference table in a room in the attorney general's office during one of their irregular status meetings. Although the task force had deteriorated into comedy among the remaining members, Bickman pulled the chief of staff aside at the beginning of the session to inform him that Ramses would not return. Bickman figured that, if "professional commitments" included being dead, the chief of staff's explanation was probably reasonably accurate.

"The attorney general is grateful for Detective Ramses' contributions to the task force. Now, do any of the remaining members have comments or contributions since our last meeting?" the chief of staff concluded, looking around the table.

Because Ramses had attended only the single, initial session of the task force, Bickman knew he was unlikely to be missed. In fact, he suspected that

Ramses had passed from their minds long ago. His absence would therefore prove a matter of indifference.

"Nothing from me," Furlong said. "If you want to know the truth, I don't even know what I'm looking at half the time." He pointed to the stack of folders in front of him on the table.

The chief of staff smiled patiently. "I'm sure you do yourself a disservice, Officer Furlong. The attorney general has every confidence that their background and experience renders every member of the task force uniquely qualified to analyzed and comprehend the materials that have been entrusted to them."

Whatever, Bickman thought.

"You will be pleased to learn that the attorney general has scheduled a press conference next week to disseminate the findings of the task force to a grateful public," the chief of staff continued, completely ignoring Furlong's reservations.

***

They were sitting in his office when McKeever walked in. Shit.

"Your secretary said it was okay if we waited. You got some nice stuff in here," Saturday said, gesturing with his hand.

"What do you want?" McKeever stepped over Saturday's outstretched legs and sat behind his polished desk. "I'm busy, so be quick."

Saturday looked hurt. "You don't act like you're very happy to see us. You should be, because we've got good news. You can stop worrying."

McKeever refused to take the bait. "Great. You can show yourselves out." He raised his eyebrows expectantly, though he knew they wouldn't be easily compelled to leave.

"What Saturday's trying to tell you," Pruitt interjected, "is that Oren Ramses has disappeared. We think he's probably dead, though we can't prove it yet."

The coroner couldn't mask the surprise that crossed his face. Golden had said absolutely nothing to him about Ramses since their last meeting though, admittedly, they'd not spoken in a few weeks. On the other hand, Pruitt may simply be lying. Assuming what they said was true, McKeever was uncertain whether Ramses' purported disappearance was a good thing or a bad thing. He needed to talk to Golden.

"What's that to me? Aren't missing persons the bailiwick of the police department?" he casually responded.

"Yeah, of course. We just figured you'd be interested because you two worked together on the Rosedea thing." Pruitt looked at McKeever intensely. "With Ramses out of the picture there's less chance of that whole thing coming around to bite you in the ass. You know, 'too many cooks spoil the broth.'"

"On the other hand," Saturday mused, "Ramses may have been only the first to get it. Whoever eliminated him might have been hired to do the same with everybody else involved in the charade. Eliminate all the loose ends. It's tough to say."

"Yeah, I guess that's true," Pruitt reflectively concurred. "I'd not thought of that."

McKeever looked dubious. "What 'charade?'"

Pruitt ignored him and looked at Saturday. "It just occurred to me that one of the guys that Ramses was last with was named 'Doc.' Did you think of that?" Without waiting for an answer, he turned back toward the medical examiner. "You're a doctor..."

"After a fashion," Saturday observed.

"...you weren't with Ramses and another guy at a bar week or so ago, were you?"

"Don't be absurd," McKeever snorted. "I wasn't at a bar with Ramses or anyone else. I resent your attempt to implicate me in his disappearance if, in fact, that's really what happened."

"No need to get testy. Besides, it's easy enough to confirm," Pruitt said. "Don't take our word for it. Call the chief and ask him."

"Chief Golden?"

"No, Chief Sitting Bull," Saturday amiably suggested. "How many chiefs do you know, for Christ's sake?"

McKeever cast a sour look at him. "Whatever happened to Detective Ramses, if anything, isn't my problem. "

Pruitt stood. "You know, Doctor McKeever, I admire your grit. If somebody told me the guy I was in cahoots with may have been murdered, I'd probably piss my pants 'cause I'd be worried that I might be next in line. But you're one cool customer, I gotta give you that." He and Saturday made their way to the door. "Call us after you talk to whoever else is involved in this thing. Even if you can't see it, it's unravelling."

The medical examiner watched them depart wordlessly. As soon as the door shut behind them, he grabbed the phone on his desk and rapidly dialed Golden's direct line at police headquarters. To his relief, the chief picked up.

"Golden," the chief muttered, as if distracted.

"Hey, it's me," McKeever breathlessly greeted him.

"What's up?"

"What the hell happened to Ramses?" McKeever abruptly blurted.

A long pause ensued. McKeever wasn't sure they'd not been disconnected.

"Bob?"

"Yeah, I'm here," Golden finally responded.

"What the hell happened to Ramses? Those two cops just left my office and said that he was missing, maybe murdered. What are they're talking about?"

Another pause. Finally, "The only thing I heard is that Ramses hasn't been to work for a couple of days. It's no big deal, Larry. His wife's divorcing him, so he probably just needed some time away. He's probably been out lawyer-shopping."

McKeever clucked his tongue. "That's not what those two cops made it sound like. They're pretty much convinced that somebody killed him."

"Good God, Larry, why would anyone want to kill Ramses? Quit lettin' those guys get into your head! You're overreacting to their bullshit, just like they want you to."

"First Rosey gets killed, then Ramses disappears. Who's next, Bob?"

"Nobody's next, Larry. Rosey got killed because he was an idiot. And Ramses' probably out drunk or whoring somewhere. He'll drag his ass back in a day or two. Why are you letting those two IA assholes fuck with you?   You're making it sound like an Agatha Christie novel."

The chief's explanation, while reasonable, relieved McKeever only slightly.   "They said Ramses disappeared after meeting two guys at a bar."

"You mean Ramses and two of his drinking buddies left a bar together a coupla days ago?   Is that what you're telling me, Larry?   Yeah, you're right. That's about the most suspicious thing I've heard in a long time.   We'd better bring Interpol in on this one!"

McKeever resented the chief's condescending manner, but remained silent.

"Look, Larry, here's what happened," Golden continued. "Ramses and a couple of guys he knows went out on a bender and are still sleeping it off.   Who could blame him?   Ramses' wife bagged him and is suing his ass for divorce. His life is basically in the shitter.   Those two IA guys don't have brains enough to put two-and-two together, or pour piss out of a boot so, since they can't find Ramses, they decided to screw with you again.   Why do you let them get to you?"

Maybe he was making too much out of it, McKeever thought.   Why did he allow them to rattle him so much?

"So, you think Ramses is alive?"

"Why wouldn't he be?" Golden rhetorically answered. "Let me ask you, what would happen even if he wasn't?" Without waiting for McKeever to respond, the chief continued. "If Ramses completely disappeared, which isn't going to happen, that might not be such a bad thing because we could theoretically dump everything on him and he wouldn't be around to refute it!   Even better, he'd be unable to implicate anyone else and drag everybody else down with him. After hanging everything on Ramses, IA could just pack up its bat and ball and go home: 'Rogue Cop Commits Crimes and Vanishes'. Another job well done by the Internal Investigations Division of the Phoenix Police Department. People could then turn their attention to more important things, like the Bachelorette." Golden was surprised by how easy it was proving to plant the seed.

McKeever had to admit that he'd not considered the chief's hypothetical scenario. "And when Ramses shows up?" he asked.

"Then we're no worse off than we were before. Status quo ante. I keep telling you that absolutely nothing has changed, Larry. Why do you keep letting those IA guys buffalo you?"

Everything the chief said made perfect sense. "I don't know. I guess I got rattled when they told me that somebody killed Ramses," McKeever sheepishly admitted.

"That's what they're counting on. They're hoping you'll freak out and do something stupid." Golden hesitated. "Don't do something stupid, Larry."

"I won't. I just wanted to talk to somebody, Bob." McKeever invariably felt reassured after the chief explained matters. Where did those IA jerks get off trying to intimidate him? Who the hell did they think they were?

"Just don't freak out," Golden cautioned. "And don't call me every time somebody tells you something you know can't be true. If I hear anything important, I'll contact you."

"I had lunch with Earl Welch the other day," McKeever confessed.

Golden groaned inwardly. This thing was getting out of hand. "What'd he want?"

"He asked about the John Doe."

"What about him?"

"He asked whether it was Rosey."

"What'd you tell him?"

"I said how could it be Rosey when Rosey was killed months ago? I told him that, as far as anyone knew, it was just some guy who was shot during a botched robbery."

"Did Welch say whether he'd been contacted by anybody from the PD?"

"He didn't say, but I got the impression they haven't. I think he would've said something. Have you talked to him?"

Golden reflected a moment before responding. "No, I haven't heard from Welch, but let me know if you hear from him again. He makes me nervous."

"Yeah, I will," McKeever promised. "Thanks for talkin', Bob."

"No problem. Like I said, I'll contact you if I hear anything."

Golden replaced the receiver onto its base. McKeever's recurring hysteria was bad enough, but now he had to rein Welch in, too. The chief was tired of having to be the designated babysitter. As long as everybody remained cool, they'd easily ride the storm out, but the idiots, McKeever and Welch, were running around in a panic like little girls. Although he'd managed to talk McKeever off the ledge today, Golden had no idea how long that would last, especially if

McKeever remained in contact with Welch, who was like a cancer. He sighed. It was also only a matter of time before it became apparent that Ramses was gone for good and IA would show up on his doorstep again.

***

"We fear your husband may have been the victim of foul play, Mrs. Ramses."

Pruitt and Saturday were sitting in Teddi's living room. She was wearing a new skirt and blouse, heels, her hair was recently coiffed, and she was wearing too much makeup. Teddi also smelled as if she'd bathed in perfume. Pruitt thought her preternaturally composed, given the circumstances.

"Were you aware of any threats recently directed against your husband?"

"No, but we seldom actually talked," she replied. "Oren wasn't home much. I guess, being a police officer and everything, I shouldn't be surprised that somebody might want to hurt him."

"Pardon me for asking, but is that what prompted the divorce? That Detective Ramses wasn't home very much?"

Teddi looked at Pruitt in surprise. "No, I was accustomed to that."

"When did you last see your husband?" Saturday asked.

She crossed her ankles demurely and stared into space. "I don't know, two weeks, maybe. It was right after I left him."

"After you moved out?"

"Yeah. We met for lunch. He wanted me to come back."

"But you didn't?"

Teddi looked at Saturday disgustedly.

"No, I didn't. Oren never cared about me. He was angry that I left and cleaned out the bank accounts. That's all he cares about. I came home only after somebody from the police department called and told me that Oren had disappeared. They wanted to know if I knew anything which," she quickly added, "I don't. I didn't even know he was missing."

Pruitt interceded. "Did Detective Ramses ever mention the names 'Doc' or 'Red' to you?"

"No. Who are they?"

"A couple of guys your husband was seen with."

"Never heard of 'em but, like I said, Oren and I seldom talked. What did they say about Oren?"

"We haven't been able to talk to them," Pruitt admitted.

"Well, if they were hangin' around with Oren, they must've been jerks," Teddi opined.

Pruitt somehow expected Teddi's derisive response. "Well, I don't know about that. They're just somebody we'd like to talk to."

"You want to know what kind of man Oren was?" Teddi abruptly asked. "Let me show you who've you've got working for you."

Teddi stood and walked across the living room to an entertainment center. She pulled a clear plastic jewel case from a shelf, removed a shin

"Somebody sent me this," she explained as she flipped on the adjacent TV and static filled the screen.

"It came in the mail. I don't know who sent it or how they even found me." The TV screen flicked to life.

The black-and-white image that immediately appeared on the screen was perfectly clear but had no sound. It revealed the interior of a room throughout which were positioned several tables and booths, a restaurant, evidently. Based on the angle, the camera was positioned close to the ceiling, pointing downward into the room, which was devoid of activity.

"What's this?" Saturday grunted.

"Just watch," Teddi told him. They focused on the scene unfolding before them, their curiosity piqued.

"That looks like Jim's place," Pruitt remarked.

"Just watch," Teddi repeated as, after several seconds, Ramses appeared at the top of the picture.

***

"You owe me a hundred bucks," Saturday announced.

"For what?" Pruitt dubiously responded. They were en route to a Mexican food restaurant on Seventh Avenue.

"I told you it was Ramses who beat the old guy up."

"Yeah, well, I never took the bet," Pruitt dismissively responded.

Saturday scoffed. "It doesn't matter. You lost by default."

"Oh yeah? Well, in that case, I'll let you buy me lunch and we'll be even," Pruitt suggested.

"How do you figure that?" Saturday laughed as he wheeled into the restaurant's parking lot and pulled into a space. "Chinese algebra?"

"Yeah, something like that," Pruitt said. "Me thinkee we outta have a chat with Jim and Sitting Bull."

Saturday swung his car door open. "How come you figure the old man just didn't give us the disc? What's with sending it to Ramses' old lady?"

"He didn't give it to us because he doesn't trust us," Pruitt replied as they walked across the restaurant's parking lot. The heat from the asphalt boiled up and the blistering sun ricocheted off the other parked cars. Pruitt tried to wipe the perspiration from his face with his shirt sleeve. "The cops killed his best friend. Who could blame him?"

"So, what'd he think the old lady could do?" Saturday opened the door and they ducked into the building's cool, dark interior.

"I gotta think about that," Pruitt confessed. "Maybe he was just pissed off, but I suspect he has plan. Or thinks he does, anyway. What I *do* know is that he doesn't trust the cops." He held up two fingers when he caught the attention of the hostess. They suspended their conversation while the hostess led them to a booth in the back of the restaurant, threading her way through tables occupied by other lunchtime diners.

"So, did the old man have a hand in killing Ramses?" Saturday mused after sliding into the booth.

"Doubt it. Jim doesn't have a pot to pee in, let alone money to hire pros."

"Hmm...who, then?" The hostess returned with two glasses of water. After she left, assuring them that their server would be right with them, Pruitt resumed.

"Assuming that Ramses didn't just disappear of his own initiative, for the hell of it, or that somebody offed him out of the blue, who'd want him dead? And why?"

"His wife, I guess. She's divorcing him, anyway."

"Why should she care whether Ramses' dead? Like you said, she's divorcing him, so she has no incentive to kill him. Besides, wifey is more interested in scoring some young cock than in killing her husband. She was dressed like a floozy, or didn't you notice? On top of that, she doesn't have the dough, or the brain power, to arrange a professional hit."

"So, who does?"

"Whoever Doc and Red work for."

"Gee, really? Who's that?"

Pruitt frowned. "I'm thinkin' it was a business deal that went south. But what kind of business? And why was is necessary to eliminate Ramses?"

"Lemme ask you something," Saturday proposed as he opened a menu. "How do we know that Ramses is even dead?"

"If he isn't dead, where is he? More to the point, why, assuming what Bickman told us is right, did Red and Doc tell Ramses that 'the chief' sent 'em?"

Saturday looked up from his menu. "You think Chief Golden killed Ramses? What the hell for?"

"Look, Ramses was a piece of shit. I don't know who killed him, but even the guys who did it said that 'the chief' sent 'em. Bad cops are like cockroaches, if

you see one, there's a shitload more that you *don't* see.
If it looks like a duck and flies like a duck and quacks
like a duck, it's probably a duck."

"Or a cockroach," Saturday noted.

"I'll put money that Jim mailed a copy of that disc
to Chief Golden, too, because he doesn't trust the
cops, including us. He must've had a pretty good idea
that, once Golden saw it, Ramses would mysteriously
disappear." Pruitt couldn't help but smile.

"So, like I said, why'd he mail a copy to his wife?
What was the point?"

"To fuck with him. Even if Golden shredded his
copy the disc or just ignored it, Jim figured that wifey
would shit a brick when she saw it, which she did.
She was his fallback strategy. I'm guessing the disc
wasn't the only thing Jim laid on the old lady.
Whatever it was, it was enough for her to promptly
dump Ramses' ass." Saturday glanced at his menu as
their server approached their booth. "Give us a
minute," he instructed her.

"What makes you think the old man sent a copy
of the disc to Golden?" Saturday asked.

"We already know that Ramses' old lady was
mailed a copy of the disc. The only person who would
have had any reason to send it to her was Jim. But
other than throw his ass out or divorce him, there's
not much else his wife could do to hurt Ramses. So,
Jim decided to hedge his bets by sending a copy to the
disc to someone else, someone who could really put
the hurt on Ramses, the chief of police. Who better to
send it to than him? A meter maid? Jim figured that
one of two things would happen, if the chief and
department were honest, Ramses would eventually

lose his job. If the chief and department are crooked, though, Ramses would probably disappear completely. Either way, it would be a win-win for Jim."

"Why didn't the old man just give us the disc and let us run with it?"

"Like I said, he doesn't trust us. By sending it directly to the chief, Jim knew that something, one way or the other, would happen. If he gave it to us, he had no guarantee that we just wouldn't bury it, or that the chief would even *see* it. By targeting the top of the food chain, he figured the department would have no choice but deal with it. It's not that Jim trusts Phoenix PD; he just figured the chief would have to do something once he saw Ramses beating up a defenseless old man. At a minimum, Ramses would probably lose his job. But the disc did a hell of a lot more than that. For whatever reason, it touched a nerve and Ramses ended up dead, or so it seems. It worked out better than even the old man anticipated." Pruitt looked triumphantly at Saturday. "That old man is manipulating everybody, including us."

Saturday looked skeptical. "Lotta 'ifs.' Assuming the old man sent a copy of the disc to Golden, how did he know that Golden wouldn't just ignore it? And how do we know that the disc had anything to do with Ramses' disappearance?" He spotted their waitress cutting her way back toward their table. "I'll have the lunch special," he told her when she arrived.

"Two," Pruitt added, folding his menu and handing to her. "And two iced teas with lemon." After she departed, he resumed. "Jim basically told us he did. Remember last time we were at his place? I asked him if he knew anyone who might know anything about Ramses' disappearance and he said Ramses' old lady and the chief of police! Remember? Why would he specifically suggest them unless he knew they had some dirt on Ramses? And the reason they had dirt on Ramses is because he mailed it to them!"

"Why would anybody kill Ramses just because he punched-out an old man?   Big deal. Lose his job, maybe, but I don't even know about that.   It doesn't make sense.   Sounds like overkill, if you ask me." Saturday smiled wickedly at his unintentional pun.

"You're right, the disc may have nothing to do with Ramses' disappearance," Pruitt admitted. "Maybe it was all just coincidental. But the fact remains that the two guys who met Ramses at the bar told him that 'the chief' sent them, and the chief evidently received his copy of the old man's disc right before they showed up. If something happens, it must be possible." Pruitt took a sip of water as he watched Saturday's reaction.

Their waitress returned with their specials. "Careful, hot plates," she cautioned as she slid them onto the table. "I'll bring your teas in a sec."

"Thanks," Pruitt smiled as she bustled off.

Saturday adjusted his plate, picked up a fork, and began idly jabbing his food. "So, like I said, you think Golden arranged to have Ramses killed?" What the hell for? Because his chief of detectives roughed up a guy who runs a greasy spoon?"

"Here's an idea," Pruitt suggested as the waitress returned with their teas. "Let's ask him."

***

Golden knew it was just a matter of time before IA showed up again. After all, they had to do *something* to justify drawing a paycheck. When Saturday called, the chief told him that he'd set aside a half-hour and meet them in his office later that day. Other than a handful of people in the department, nobody was yet aware of Ramses' absence and Golden hoped to keep it that way. The last thing he needed was the media to get wind of the story. They'd have a field day over the "Mysterious Disappearance of the Celebrated Chief of Detectives of the Phoenix Police Department." He already had enough to deal with without also having to play the tiresome media game.

His secretary buzzed him from her office. "The two gentlemen from Internal Affairs are here," she informed Golden.

"Tell them I'll be with them shortly," the chief instructed her. "Let 'em twist in the wind a while."

"Will do."

Golden rapidly flipped through a report on his desk, indifferently jotting a few notes as he read. He then picked through his accumulated phone messages and tossed most of them into the waste basket at the side of his desk. Finally, realizing there was nothing else he could do to forestall them, Golden buzzed his secretary. "Escort them in."

Moments later, his secretary gently rapped on his office door before gently opening it.

"Inspectors Saturday and Pruitt," she announced. She stood aside and allowed them to enter Golden's office.

Golden looked up from his desk but did not stand to greet them.

"Please sit down." While not exactly hostile, the chief's invitation was less than cordial.

"Thank you, Chief Golden," Pruitt responded, seemingly oblivious to the cool reception. He sat in a leather office chair directly in front of Golden's desk while Saturday plopped onto an upholstered loveseat along one wall. "We're here about Detective Ramses," Pruitt announced.

"Oh, how so?"

"We have reason to believe that he may have met with foul play," Saturday remarked from his loveseat.

"Detective Ramses has taken a leave of absence," Golden informed them. "Nothing more."

"A 'leave of absence' is something of an understatement," Pruitt said. "We suspect that Detective Ramses may actually have been murdered."

"Murdered? Please!" the chief scoffed. "That's absurd. Although Detective Ramses certainly had enemies, everyone in police work has enemies. It comes with the job. I don't know whether you're are aware of it, but Detective Ramses and his wife are going through some rough times right now. They're confident they'll be able to work things out but, for the time being, Detective Ramses needed a little alone time."

"Yeah, we heard they were having a hard time," Saturday acknowledged. "In fact, we talked to Ramses' wife."

"His wife? Why?" Golden chastened him. "Don't you think it best that they be allowed to work out their marital problems quietly, in their own time?"

"She doesn't even know where Detective Ramses is," Pruitt corrected him. "It's kinda hard to work out problems with your husband when you don't even know where your husband is."

"But let me ask you something else," Saturday abruptly changed the subject. "Who are 'Red' and 'Doc?'"

"Who?" Golden's expression betrayed no hint of surprise.

"You know, Red and Doc. They said they were friends of yours."

"I've never heard of them," stated the chief. "They're no friends of mine. Should I know them?"

"Well, they know *you*. They said that you sent them when they met with Detective Ramses, the last time he was seen," Pruitt informed the chief. "You sure you don't know them?"

"I just told you I don't know anyone named 'Red' or 'Doc'," Golden snapped.

"Hmmmmm... here's something else you probably don't know," Saturday continued. "Before he disappeared, Detective Ramses had two meetings with the US Attorney. Any idea what they were discussing?"

This time, Golden was unable to mask the alarmed expression that animated his face.

"The US Attorney? What are you talking about?" Beads of sweat abruptly broke out on the chief's forehead and he could feel his heart begin to race.

"Yeah, the US Attorney. We called their office but couldn't pry anything out of 'em. Do you have any idea why Detective Ramses would want to meet with the US Attorney just before he disappeared?"

Although Pruitt and Saturday were unaware of any meetings between Ramses and the US Attorney, they dangled the bait just to gauge Golden's reaction. They weren't disappointed.

"Detective Ramses would have no reason to meet with the US Attorney," Golden stammered. "Your information is obviously wrong."

Saturday shook his head. "I don't think so. You could call the US Attorney yourself and ask, but I doubt if they'll talk to you; they wouldn't talk to us, anyway. You know how the feds are."

"If you know where Detective Ramses is, we can just call him and ask," Pruitt suggested. "We need to talk to him about some other matters, anyway."

"I think he's on a fishing boat somewhere," the chief lamely responded.

"Can you call his cell?"

"He may not have coverage where he is, but we can try," Golden reluctantly acknowledged. He poked a button on his desk phone. "Charlene, call Detective Oren Ramses' cell, please."

An awkward silence ensured. After an eternity, Charlene finally buzzed the chief. "Detective Ramses isn't picking up. I left a voice mail," she said.

Golden looked smugly at Pruitt. "Like I said, he's fishing."

"When's he scheduled to be back?"

"My guess is that Detective Ramses has accrued quite a bit of unused vacation time," the chief replied. "He may be gone a while."

Saturday spoke. "Chief, did you and Detective Ramses ever talk about the fact that IA was looking into the Jerry Dawson shooting?"

"Who?" Golden started perspiring again.

"Jerry Dawson. Detective Ramses was the investigator on that case."

"Oh yes, I remember now.   No, he and I never discussed it.   As you know, my job is administrative, not field work. I'm also the primary liaison between the Department and the city council."

"So, Detective Ramses never told you that IA was looking into the Dawson investigation?"

"Not that I recall," stated the chief.   "I seldom have occasion to talk with Detective Ramses on *any* subject.   He has his job, I have mine," he vaguely concluded.

"Has anybody talked to you about Detective Ramses within the last, say, three months?"

"Other than you, not that I remember," Golden said. "Why would they?"

"No one?"

Golden paused. "I think I've adequately answered all your questions for today," he finally demurred. "Please schedule an appointment with Charlene if you feel the need to resume your little inquisition."

"Just one more question, Chief, did you recently receive an anonymous DVD in the mail?"

"Have a good day, gentlemen." Golden terminated eye contact and began flipping through papers on his desk.

Pruitt glanced at Saturday. They simultaneously rose to their feet and wordlessly exited Golden's office.

"You get it?" Saturday asked Pruitt in the hallway outside.

Pruitt grinned. "Got it." He patted the electronic recorder tucked in his jacket pocket.

"I'll get a copy of Golden's visitors' list," Saturday said. "Let's see who the chief's been seeing."

***

Golden wasn't sure what to do about Saturday's assertion that Ramses had been talking to the US Attorney. It was probably bullshit but, where Ramses was concerned, anything was possible. One thing he needed to do immediately was call McKeever and caution him not to reveal that the two of them had been in communication about Ramses or, for that matter, anything else.

To his credit, Ramses had been right about how potentially dangerous the old man was. The only possible way IA could have known about the DVD is if Jim told them. This whole damned thing was starting to unravel at the seams. Golden needed to contact the Coast for guidance. He removed the telephone handset from its receiver and began dialing.

***

"Besides his wife and the chief of police, who else might know something about Ramses' disappearance?"

"How would I know?" Jim responded. They were sitting at the restaurant's lunch counter, Pruitt and Saturday having just finished eating. "Ain't that the kind of thing you guys are supposed to know?"

"Jim, you know a lot more than you let on," Pruitt said. "Besides, we're cops. You know a lot more about what's actually happening on the streets than we do."

"I run a restaurant," Jim reminded him.

"I guess," said Saturday as he plucked potato chip fragments from his plate.

Jim looked at him defiantly. "Mister, nobody's beggin' you to eat here."

"Let's see, Alto Murphy ate here and he's dead. Georgio Rosedea ate here and he's dead. Detective Ramses ate here and he's dead. I'm starting to think that eating here is the equivalent of playin' Russian roulette. I might as well start smoking again." Saturday looked at Jim, inviting a response.

"Like I said, nobody's holdin' a gun on you. Go eat somewhere's else if you're afraid of keelin' over."

Pruitt felt like his was stuck between two eight-year-olds. "Jim, how's your friend? The one who identified Ramses' picture."

Jim smiled broadly. "She's good. She went back to work drivin' a limousine."

"That's great! I'm glad she's back on her feet."

"I don't know about that," Jim said, "but you gotta work if you wanna eat. Besides, workin' gets folks' minds off their problems."

"That's true," Saturday concurred. "Speakin' of which, we confirmed something that we already knew was true. It was Ramses who beat you up."

Jim looked at him benignly. "It took you this long to figure that out? No wonder they stuck you two in Internal Affairs." Saturday ignored the slight.

"Ramses' wife showed us the disc you sent her," Pruitt said. "What was the point, Jim?"

"After killin' his gorilla, I was pretty sure Ramses would come here himself. That's why I had those cameras put in. I figured it was the only way to protect myself."

"Why'd you send the disc to his wife and the chief of police? Why didn't you just give it to us?"

Jim looked directly at Pruitt. "Would you guys have given it to the chief? No, you would have taken back to the police department and given to someone else, who would have given it to someone else, who would have given it to someone else, who would have given it to Ramses. Then what do you think would have happened to me? That's why. By sending it directly to the chief, I figured he'd have to do something because he couldn't have a liability like Ramses walkin' around."

"So, you don't trust us?" Saturday asked, rhetorically.

"Nope. I trust the Lord, Carol, Harvey, and me. They're the only ones I trust," Jim affirmed.

"Well, we think the chief did more than just 'something,' Pruitt said. "We think he had Ramses killed."

"If that's true, it wasn't because Ramses beat me up. Cops beat people up all the time and nothin' happens to 'em." Jim looked pointedly at Saturday. "If your chief, or anybody else, had a hand in killin' Ramses, it was because he was into something a lot bigger than beatin' up an old man. That may have pushed it over the edge, but there was more to it than just that."

Pruitt looked thoughtful. "So that brings me back to my first question, who might know more about it?"

Jim looked circumspect. "I know somebody who might know something," he finally revealed. "But she sure as heck won't talk to you two."

Saturday perked up. "She? Who is 'she'?"

"It don't matter who she is," Jim informed him, "'cause she ain't gonna talk to no cops."

"But she'll talk to you?" Pruitt quietly asked.

"She'd be more apt to talk to me, but that don't mean she will," Jim said. "People around here don't trust cops, and if they think I'm workin' for the cops they won't trust me."

"Jim, even if you don't trust me, I trust you. If you vouch for this person, and her information turns out to be accurate, we could probably see that she receives some monetary compensation. Maybe some for you, too. I'm not promising anything, but there's a program like that available."

"I don't want none of your money," Jim snorted. "I ain't doin' this for money. I'm doin' it for Jerry and Carol."

Pruitt was afraid he'd offended the old man. "I know that, Jim. Nobody's trying to buy you. I just figured you could use some help paying for getting your air conditioning fixed."

"I don't need no help," Jim repeated. "Keep your money."

"Ok, fair enough. But do you think your friend might need a little extra money?"

"Everbody needs money," Jim acknowledged.

"Well, would you ask her whether she knows anything about what happened to Detective Ramses? You don't have to tell her that you're asking for us."

"I won't *have* to tell her," Jim laughed. "Who besides the cops would give a hoot about Ramses?"

"Well, do what you think best, Jim. Like I said, if she'll talk to you and her info is legit, we'll try to get her some money. Nobody has to know where it came from."

"I'd only do it if it'd help Jerry," Jim said, "but I'll think about it."

SIXTEEN

Butler was pissed. From his chair on the stage, he could see the ballroom at the Airport Hilton wasn't even close to being full. The press release distributed to the media by his chief of staff clearly stated that he intended to discuss the progress of his crime task force, so where was everybody? But for the free coffee and pastries on tables at the rear of the room, he feared the turnout would be even thinner. Four unattended video cameras on tripods were aimed at the lectern positioned near the front of the stage.

"Where the hell is everyone?" he complained to the chief of staff sitting next to him. Arrayed along the stage in folding chairs on either side of them, looking awkward and uncomfortable, were Furlong, Bickman, McDonald, and Zerbe.

The chief of staff surveyed the room. "They'll be here, don't worry about it," he responded with a noticeable absence of conviction. "Remember, this entire hare-brained task force was your idea. I've been doing my best to gin up interest in the damned thing."

"Yeah, well," the voters aren't gonna remember your 'best,'" Butler grumbled.

"Based on the polling I've seen," the chief of staff replied, "most people basically have an "if-it-ain't-broke-don't-fix-it" attitude toward the task force. If I were cynically disposed, I might even suggest that many of them basically see it as publicity stunt."

Butler swiveled to face his chief of staff. "Maybe, but you should know better than anyone, there's no such thing as bad publicity. As long as they remember the task force, that's the important thing."

The chief of staff scanned the ballroom. A herd of reporters hovered around the coffee and pastry station in the back, while smaller groups clustered about the room in threes and fours, chatting. In one hand they carefully balanced plates weighed down with donuts and, in the other, cups of coffee.

"We'll give 'em a few more minutes, then get started," the chief of staff said. "You gonna have any members of the task force address the media?"

Butler shook his head. "I just want the media to see that there really *is* a task force."

"Understood," concurred the chief of staff. "I think that's probably the safest way to handle it." He cast a brief look down the row of folding chairs to his left, where Bickman and Furlong quietly chatted. Both were in uniform, bolstering the decorum of the occasion.

The chief of staff finally stood and stepped to the lectern. Grasping its sides, he leaned into the microphone.

"Ladies and gentlemen," he intoned after the feedback subsided, "please take your seats so we can get started." Groups of reporters momentarily interrupted their murmured conversations to glance toward the stage, then resumed chatting with their peers. The chief of staff waited a few moments before repeating his request.   This time, the knots of reporters scattered throughout the ballroom reluctantly concluded their colloquies and began drifting toward their chairs, still grasping pastries and coffee.

"Thank you, ladies and gentlemen," smiled the chief of staff.   He stood at the podium, patiently waiting as, after much rustling, whispered salutations, and handshaking, the bulk of the reporters finally sat down and directed their collective attention to the assemblage on the stage.   The video operators assumed their positions and fiddled with their cams while a few die-hards remained defiantly gathered around the coffee and pastry station at the rear of the room.

"Thank you for coming today, ladies and gentlemen," the chief of staff began. "As you know, in response to citizen concern, a task force was recently assembled by your attorney general.   In addition to Attorney General Butler, seated behind me," the chief of staff extended his arm like a circus ringmaster introducing the next act, "are members of the task force. We previously informed you of their bona fides and you all know who they are. Their qualifications are beyond dispute, their reputations above reproach." The chief of staff paused as a smattering of anemic applause rippled through the audience.

"Since its inception, the task force has been engaged in a relentless crusade to uncover instances of alleged malfeasance in the public sector.   The attorney general and his task force have been unsparing in the execution of this task, the exposure and extirpation of criminality at every level of the body politic.   To this end, the task force has devoted countless hours poring over records and memoranda, accounts and ledgers.   Nothing was sacrosanct, nothing inviolable because, as a wise man sagely observed, 'sunlight is the best disinfectant.'"   Listening to the chief of staff's oratory, Bickman momentarily wondered if he was describing a different task force.

"Today, the task force is pleased to take the opportunity to apprise the public and media of its progress."   Here, the chief of staff stepped away from the podium and, with a flourish, urged Butler to his feet.   Beaming, the attorney general stood and stepped forward to the lectern.

"Good morning, ladies and gentlemen," he greeted the assembled reporters.   The chief of staff discreetly returned to his seat before Butler launched into a grandiloquent disquisition about the success of his crime task force.

Bickman glanced up and down the row of chairs at his fellow task force members. All of them appeared utterly bored.   He was uncomfortable and his butt was beginning to hurt because of the folding metal chair. He shifted positions, steeling himself against an interminable morning of speechifying.

***

Chief Golden didn't watch the attenuated coverage of the AG's presser on the local evening news. He seldom watched the local news, anyway, because its content was invariably comprised of lame happy-talk about brave cancer survivors, unethical garages, and the proper way to cook zucchini. Besides, he received a personal briefing every morning at his office, covering all the pertinent news. He did, however, read a brief article about the press conference in section "B" of the morning paper, sandwiched between a review of a new micro-brewery and the obituaries. Per the article, attorney general Booth's task force had discovered no evidence of corruption or malfeasance. Big surprise.

"Chief, we're not exactly sure why you're calling," said Mr. Julius, unctuously. "It was our understanding that you only required assistance with respect to one of your police officers, which we were happy to provide. We confess, however, that we're more than a little surprised to hear from you again so quickly."

Golden literally winced. Although he dreaded calling the coast, he knew that Sunstone had operatives in the Phoenix office of the US attorney who might be able to provide additional information about Ramses' clandestine meetings there.

"We're very grateful for all the help you've provided," the chief quickly assured him.

"Are you losing control of the situation over there, chief?"

"Not at all, Mr. Julius. I guess you could say that I'm calling simply to give you a sort of status report."

"Yes, I could say that," Mr. Julius agreed. "I could say a great many things. But what *are* you saying, chief?"

Golden thought quickly before responding. "At the threshold, I called to let you know that the attorney general's probe found nothing untoward, Mr. Julius. I knew you'd be glad to hear that."

"Yes, we are gratified to learn that," he responded, non-committedly. "However, our people over there previously informed us that Mr. Butler's task force yielded nothing. Your attorney general is clearly positioning himself to run for governor, perhaps more."

Golden was chagrined by Mr. Julius' rebuff. "Yes, that seems to be the consensus of opinion," he stammered. "But there's another matter that I felt should be brought to your attention."

"Oh?"

"I recently received information that Detective Ramses may have met with the US attorney here in Phoenix. The source of my intel is questionable, but I felt it important to pass along, none-the-less."

Silence. "We've heard nothing about any such meeting from our people over there," Mr. Julius finally stated.

"Well, like I said, I'm not sure how reliable my intel actually is," conceded the chief.

"Who is your informant?"

"The two IA officers investigating Detective Ramses."

"Did they tell you how they supposedly acquired their information?"

"They didn't say."

More silence ensued. Golden could feel rivulets of perspiration flow down his sides, beneath his dark blue uniform, notwithstanding that his office was almost uncomfortably cold. He looked out his fifth-floor window, to the traffic on Washington Street below. Despite the reflective glass, the blistering sunlight outside was nearly overwhelming. Golden felt like needles were being thrust into his eyes and he was starting to get a migraine.

"That's most interesting, chief," Mr. Julius eventually said. "We'll look into it and talk again. Anything else for now?"

"Nothing else, Mr. Julius. Thank you very much."

"Of course, chief. We are always at your disposal." The call abruptly disconnected.

Golden replaced the telephone on its cradle, unsure of what to do now. The good news, if there was any, is that Mr. Julius didn't volunteer to send Red and Doc back over to Phoenix.

***

Chris was behind the bar.

"Katrina in?" Jim asked.   He mopped his perspiring face with a plaid handkerchief. Chris nodded wordlessly toward the unlit recesses at the rear, then turned his attention back to his magazine. Jim ambled farther into the interior.

"Greetings, Jim."   Katrina's mellifluous voice wafted from the void. "You're getting' to be a regular, regular."   Her doughy bulk loomed in the dimness, holding court in her customary booth. Katrina wore a faded negligee that struggled to contain her massive breasts.

"I don't know about that," Jim said as he eased himself down opposite her. "You been okay?"

Katrina shrugged in the gloom. "For a fat old broad. But I guess I'm a hell of a lot better than the people eatin' down at your place."

"How's that?"

"I heard you plugged some dumb bastard," she indifferently replied.

Jim couldn't restrain a tiny smile. "Yeah, I guess I did. He was tryin' to rob me."

It was Katrina's turn to smile, though skeptically. "Yeah, right. That ain't what I heard."

"What did you hear?"

"I heard that somebody put a hit out on you."

Jim paused before responding. "Yeah, that's really what I finally figured, too."

"Well, congratulations on gettin' him before he got you. Who'd you piss off?"

"I got a pretty good idea," Jim said. "I know something else, too, Detective Ramses is dead. Even though you and me talked about him when I was in here before, that didn't have nothing to do with it," he quickly added. "He didn't know anything about what you and me talked about. You got nothin' to worry about."

Katrina stared at him impassively. "Yeah, I already heard that Ramses bought the farm. But do you really think I give a hoot whether Ramses may have gotten himself killed because of our little chit-chat? I was only worried that if word got out that I'd talked to you about him, Ramses would come in here and break my neck, not that somebody might kill him. At any rate, that isn't a problem now. I'm startin' to think, though, that your friends have a high mortality rate."

"Ramses wasn't no friend of mine," Jim corrected her.

"Whatever. But you're in good company, 'cause I don't know anybody that's exactly broken up over the fact that he's dead."

Jim looked intently across the cigarette-burned table at Katrina. "Do you know what happened to him?"

"I heard some stuff," she vaguely acknowledged. "But most of what I hear is pretty much bullshit."

"Like what?"

Katrina's expression betrayed her distrust. "What's it to you? I thought Ramses wasn't your bud. Why do you give a crap what happened to him?"

Jim sighed. "'Cause I think he's the one who hired the guy to kill me."

Katrina scratched her black roots while she pondered Jim's revelation.   She squinted at her yellowed fingernails in the half-light before responding. "Could be. I heard Ramses, and half of city hall, was ass-deep in that shit with Jerry."

"So, how'd he die?" Jim persisted.

Katrina resumed scratching her head. "Well, the way I heard it, he's relaxing in a landfill after a coupla out-of-towners thumped him."

Jim was dubious. "Out-of-towners? Why would anybody from out of town wanna kill Ramses?"

"Couldn't tell ya. That's just what I was told. It's nothing to me, one way or the other. Like I said, most of what I hear is bullshit, anyway." Katrina peered at Jim through the slits in her face that served as eyes. "So, tell me about the dude you wasted in your place. It ain't often that we get a dyed-in the-wool vigilante in here. Just like Charles Bronson!"

"There ain't much to tell. Ramses thought I had some bad stuff on him, so he sent his gorilla over to get it."

"He got it, all right!" Katrina snorted. "What kinda bad stuff?"

"Just some stuff," Jim evasively replied.

"If you say so, but I heard there was something screwy about that whole thing, too."

"How's that?" Katrina had piqued Jim's interest.

Katrina leaned forward slightly and plopped her thick arms, which resembled ham hocks, onto the table. "The guy you killed, what was his name?"

"Adolph."

"Well, that may have been what he told you, but that wasn't his real name."

"I figure criminals use fake names all the time. "

"Yeah, they do," Katrina agreed. "But the guy you killed is supposedly the same guy Jerry wasted. But tell me something: how can somebody get killed twice by two different people? How does that work? The guy musta been an effin' Houdini!"

"They can't," he said.

Katrina smiled wickedly. "Right. What'd they do with the stiff?"

"The guy in my restaurant?"

"Yeah, after you plugged him, what happened to his body?"

Jim thought a moment. "I don't know. The cops took it away. I guess they buried him."

Katrina shook her head, causing her multiple chins to sway. "Naw, they don' bury 'em right away if they died while committing a crime but they can't identify 'em. I'll bet 'Adolph' is frozen in a meat locker down at the coroner's office. They turned the stiff into a stiff!" she chortled.

Jim recalled Saturday's previous revelation that 'Adolph' wasn't the dead guy's real name. "So, do you know what his name was?"

"George Rosicrucian, or something like that."

"How come he called himself 'Adolph?'"

"Like you said, criminals use fake names. What else is new? But whatever his name was, the stuff you had on Ramses must've been some heavy shit. Heavy enough to warrant sending somebody over to step on you." Katrina watched Jim with a mixture of curiosity and admiration.

"I reckon so," is all he said.

Katrina yawned, covering her cavernous maw with a pudgy hand. "So what else you wanna talk about, other than the guy you blasted in your restaurant?"

"I just figured you might have wanted to know about Ramses," Jim explained.

"I told you, I already knew," said Katrina, yawning again. "But I don't know why you give a crap. I'd think you'd just be happy he's dead."

Jim sadly shook his head. "I'm never happy when somebody passes, Katrina, even bad ones. I just wish they wasn't so many bad ones."

"Who?"

"People, bad people."

"It is what it is, Jim," she philosophically replied.

He was silent a minute. "Would you fix it if you could? Or at least try?"

"Huh?"

"Would you fix things if you could?"

Katrina feared the old man was losing it. "What are you talkin' about?"

"I'm talking about tryin' to make things better, Katrina."

"Better how?" she skeptically asked.

"Better by takin' some trash out."

"Seems to me you already got a jump on takin' out the trash when you blasted that stooge in your restaurant. How much more you intend to take out?"

Jim smiled. "As much as I can carry."

"I don't get it," Katrina said. "What's in it for you? Or, more important, for me?"

"Nuthin'."

"So, what's the point? If I wanted to save the world, I'd be dishin' out breakfast to the winos down at the Lighthouse Mission."

"I never said nuthin' about saving the world. I just said that I want to take some trash out. You can help, or not. I just figured you might be interested." Jim looked around the seedy interior of the bar. "It ain't like you got a whole lot goin' on around here."

Katrina laughed. "You noticed, huh?" She looked intently at him. "What trash you talkin' about?"

"Whoever had a hand in killin' Jerry."

"Yeah, well, I think you may need help with that. I'm thinkin' there may be a lot more trash than you think."

Jim smiled again, his teeth almost luminescent in the gloom. "That's why I asked if you wanted to help."

Katrina reflected a moment before responding. "Ya know, Jim, I'm generally not too big on helpin'. Helpin' is for chumps," she finally said. She paused. "But I guess I might not mind putting a few lumps on the heads of those fat-cat bastards at city hall, just for the hell of it. After all, I don't imagine I'll live forever and what do I have to lose except this paradise?" Katrina spread her arms expansively, indicating the squalid interior of the bar. "Besides, with Ramses dead, I don't have to worry about him."

"I know a couple of cops who say there might be some reward-type money available," Jim volunteered.

"Screw the cops and their money," she derisively replied. "If the cops think they can buy me, they're dumber than I thought. If I do anything, it'll be because I want to, not because those pricks think they own me. So exactly what kinda help are you talking about?"

Jim chuckled. "Call the chief of police and tell him that you're Ramses' girlfriend and that he told you everything."

"That's a laugher. I'm probably the only broad in town that *wasn't* Ramses' girlfriend!" Katrina looked puzzled. "'Everything' what?"

"It don't matter. Whatever he knows about Jerry he'll tell you. And if he don't know anything, it won't matter."

"I guess," Katrina shrugged. "That all?"

"You said that Adolph's body is probably still down at the coroner's office?"

Katrina nodded. "Yeah, that's what I figure. They can't bury him until they know who he is. They'll eventually figure it out. That's one reason the cops have been talkin' to you."

"How do you know they been talkin' to me?" Jim asked, defensively.

Katrina laughed. "Why else would you be here, Jim? Besides, they told you about the reward money."

"Well, I told 'em that I wasn't interested in no reward," Jim said.

"I already knew that, too. So, what about the coroner? "

"Call 'em and tell 'em that you know who 'Adolph' really is."

Katrina shrugged. "Okay, but I don't know what you think all of this is gonna accomplish."

"When I was a boy in Texas," Jim explained, "me and my friends would go down to this fishin' hole behind my house. When it was hot and the fish was too lazy to bite, we'd either have to 'jug' for 'em or throw sticks of dynamite into the water to stir 'em up. That's exactly what we're gonna do, stir 'em up and see if they'll bite."

"Well, I'm not gonna call anyone from here," Katrina warned. "You're gonna have to bring me a cell phone that I can pitch-out afterward."

"Like this one?" Jim reached into his pants pocket, withdrew a cheap phone, and placed it on the table between them. "I bought it at Safeway," he said. "It only cost five bucks."

Katrina reached out and dragged the cell phone toward her, the fat on her arms jiggling. "They can put a man on the moon," she marveled at its diminutive size. "So, what are the numbers I'm supposed to call?"

I gotta get 'em. Didn't want to take too much for granted," Jim smiled.

"Right," Katrina said, with palpable skepticism. She picked up the phone, briefly squinted at it in the dimness, then tucked into her ample cleavage. "Get me the numbers and I'll call 'em. Who knows? It might even be fun, like one of those 'sting' operations the cops run. Give 'em a taste of their own medicine! Me and you are like fuckin' spies, Jim!"

He stood. "Thanks for helpin' me, Katrina. I'll pray that the Lord blesses you."

"The Lord gave up on me a long time ago. I'm not doin' it for Him," she said. "I'm doin' it because I got nuthin' else to do."

"I know," Jim softly replied. He turned for the door.

***

Pruitt and Saturday sat in the latter's office on the second floor of police headquarters, scrutinizing the chief's visitors' log.

"Dr. Lawrence McKeever, the coroner, went to see Golden twice over the past six weeks, but no other times for the entire year before that. What do you suppose they talked about," mused Saturday.

"Stiffs?"

"Yeah, but *what* stiffs? Why would the coroner suddenly want to talk shop with Golden? And why would the chief of police be interested in what the coroner's doin'?"

"When did Jim Thompson kill Rosedea?"

Saturday frowned as he thought. "Three weeks ago," he said.

"And when was the first time the coroner went to Golden's office?"

Saturday consulted the log. "Three weeks ago," he announced. "But get this, two guys visited Golden in his office a week before Ramses disappeared. Take a guess what their names were."

"Frick and Frack?"

"Try 'Jack Ruby' and 'Dr. Doolittle'. I'm not kiddin', the guy wrote his name down as 'Dr. Doolittle."

"Red and Doc?"

"In the flesh."

"Methinks we should have another talk with McKeever," Pruitt suggested. Let's ask him if he talked to Golden, about anything, over the past coupla months, and see what he says. If he denies it, we'll tell him he's damned liar."

Saturday smiled wickedly. "Let's go. I know a good taco place on the way."

***

McKeever flipped through the accumulated phone messages his secretary handed him the moment he walked into his office. The coroner as returning from a four-day weekend in Mexico, where he'd hoped the time away would clear his head. It didn't.

He apathetically tossed two-thirds of the messages into the trash can adjacent to his desk. Napoleon instructed his secretary not to respond to any of his correspondence for at least three weeks, explaining that, at the end of three weeks, most of it wouldn't require a response. McKeever found Napoleon's observation to be largely accurate and adopted the practice in his own office.

"Those two police officers also came by," his secretary informed him.

McKeever's heart sank. "Did they say what they wanted?

"Only that they wanted to talk to you."

"Did you tell them where I was?"

"Only that you were out of the office and would be back today."

Shit. That means they could waltz into his office at any time. McKeever nervously glanced at his watch. "If they come back, tell them that I'm still out."

"Okay. Should I tell 'em when you're expected back?"

He shook his head. "No. Just tell them you don't know when I'll be back. But let me know when they arrive and when they leave."

"Will do. But I don't think that's gonna dissuade them," she warned. "I don't know what they're after, but they're persistent as hell."

McKeever sighed. "I know. I don't know what they're after, either, but whatever it is, I wish they'd leave me alone."

"What *do* they want, Doctor McKeever?"

He spread his fingers in a helpless gesture. "I'm not sure. I think they're investigating the John Doe that was killed in that restaurant hold up, but I have no idea why they keep harassing me. It's not like I know anything about it."

His secretary clucked her tongue sympathetically and was about to respond when the intercom buzzed in the waiting room.

"Be right back," she promised as she scurried out, closing the door behind her.

McKeever sat at his desk and stared blankly out the window. This can't go on. His intercom beeped, startling him.

"It's them," she whispered. "What should I tell them?"

McKeever was close to panic. "Tell them that I'm not here and you don't know when I'll be back."

"Will do." The intercom clicked off. McKeever's heart was pounding. He quietly stood and crept across the Oriental carpet to the door, against which he pressed his ear. Although it was a fire door, impervious to sound, McKeever imagined that he could hear Pruitt and Saturday in the next room.

"Dr. McKeever isn't in and I don't know when he'll be back," his secretary informed the two detectives.

"That's weird," said Pruitt. "His county-issued car is in his parking space. If he's not here, who's driving his car?" He looked at Saturday. "Don't you think that's weird?"

"Big-time weird," agreed Saturday. "Besides, I thought McKeever was supposed to be back today."

Pruitt turned back to the coroner's secretary. "No matter. We'll wait a little while. You never know when he might show up."

"I think it would be better if you came back another time," she ventured, hopefully.

"Naw, it's too hot to go out again," Saturday deferred. "We're already sweatin' like butchers. We'll just cool off in here."

"As you wish, but I'll be going to lunch in a little while," she persisted.

"You know," Pruitt patiently said, "this would be a whole lot easier if Dr. McKeever just quit hiding in his office."

"Who said he's hiding in his office? Who said that?" the secretary demanded, as though affronted.

"He did," said Saturday, indicating Pruitt as they sat down to wait.

On the other side of the door, McKeever wasn't sure what was going on. He couldn't risk cracking the door to peek out, nor could he sneak out of his office because it disembogued directly into the waiting area. His secretary hadn't beeped him to say that Pruitt and Saturday had departed, so he was forced to conclude they were still on site. Doing what? McKeever had been reduced to the status of a prisoner in his own damned office. He felt like screaming with frustration.

He stole back across the room to his desk and quietly dialed Golden's private number. Maybe the chief could call the dogs off.

***

"I'm not sure everyone was convinced about the accomplishments of the task force," the chief of staff said. "In fact, I'm not entirely convinced that anyone was even listening."

Butler laughed. "No, they were listening all right, if only in hopes of hearing me fuck up! In fact, I thought it went pretty damned well. Like the old expression says, 'I don't care what they say about me as long as they spell my name right'. You worry too much."

"I'm not worried, Booth. I'm just telling you what I saw."

The attorney general waved his hand dismissively. "It doesn't matter what you saw. We accomplished exactly what we wanted to, a spot on the evening news and a write-up in the papers. The task force is functioning exactly as I'd hoped."

He stood and walked to the mini-refrigerator in the corner of his office. Removing two bottles of beer, he returned to the pair of heavy leather chairs in the center of the room and handed a beer to his chief of staff.

"As long as we're able to keep my name in the collective mind of the electorate, that's the main thing."

The chief of staff twisted the cap off his beer and tossed it into a waste can. "Well, I guess you're doing that. I just hope it doesn't come back to bite us both in the ass."

"Res quanto est maior tanto est insidiosior," toasted Butler, clinking the neck of his beer against that of his chief of staff. "Syrus, Maxims."

"Whatever," he responded, taking a swig.

***

Bickman and Pam walked back to the parking lot after catching an afternoon matinee.

"They showed that clip again on the news this morning. You looked soooooooo handsome!" Pam gave him a peck on the cheek.

"I guess," he said. "I felt like a doofus sitting up there. The attorney general is a pompous windbag and his chief of staff is really slimy."

"I don't care about them, you looked great! Mom and dad were really impressed! Dad thinks the task force will do wonders for your career."

They arrived at their car where Bickman unlocked the doors. He looked at Pam over the roof of the vehicle. "I'm thinking about quitting the task force."

"What? Why?"

He slid into the driver's seat and Pam plopped onto the passenger's. The interior was broiling, the steering wheel too hot to touch. Bickman jammed the key into the ignition, started the car, and flicked the air conditioner on full blast. Neither of them spoke as the cold air washed over them.

"The task force is a waste of time," he finally said. "The people on it are okay, but we almost never see the AG and, like I said, his chief of staff is a slime ball. Being on it takes time away from being with you and we never seem to accomplish anything, anyway. All we do is read reports but, other than that, nothing really happens. Hell, I don't even understand half of what I'm reading." Pam knew nothing of his association with Pruitt and Saturday; he didn't bother to tell her that, because Ramses was no longer around, the essential raison d'etre for remaining on the task force no longer existed.

Bickman gingerly touched the steering wheel to confirm that it had cooled sufficiently to grasp. Satisfied, he glanced in the rearview mirror, put the car in "R," and backed out of their parking spot.

"But what about your career?" she frowned.

"It won't hurt my career. They can replace me in about two seconds. I already talked to some people." Bickman had come to realize that members of the task force were fungible.   Butler's chief of staff didn't actually care who served on the task force, provided they were associated with law enforcement in some capacity and looked good in a uniform.

"Well, I *would* like to see more of you," Pam admitted. "I guess mom and dad are just gonna have to reconcile themselves to the fact that their son-in-law doesn't want to be a media star."

Bickman laughed. "You can tell Ernie that it's still not too late to get my autograph."

"Maybe I'll sell 'em on eBay," Pam winked. "Seriously, though, I just want you to know how proud I am of you. I just want you to be happy."

Bickman turned the car onto the street fronting the theatre and headed back toward their apartment.

"Believe me, getting off the task force will make me happy. But what would really make me happy right now is something from Dairy Queen. I'll even buy."

"I might be induced to accompany you," Pam grinned, "but only because you're buying."

"The story of my life," Bickman sighed. "My riveting personality isn't enough. I'm reduced to bribing 'em with Dairy Queen."

"Oh? Who else have you bribed with Dairy Queen?"

He turned into the restaurant's parking lot and whipped into a parking spot. Reluctant to turn the air conditioning off and step into the scorching heat, Bickman let the car idle and turned to Pam.

"Well, I'll tell you if you promise not to tell anyone else. When I was in high school, I think the only reason my date agreed to go to prom with me is because I promised I'd take her to Dairy Queen afterward."

"Oh, you poor baby," Pam commiserated. She leaned over and kissed him on the cheek.

"Well, the fact that she weighed about 275 pounds may have had something to do with it," Bickman conceded. "But you should've seen the rack on her!"

"You jerk," Pam laughed and playfully slapped his arm. "I hope she ordered four of everything on the menu!"

"Speakin' of which, are you ready to eat? I'm starving!" Bickman switched the engine off and they bailed out of the car, racing for the door.

***

"She called again." Clearly annoyed, Charlene handed Golden the latest telephone message. He took it from her without looking up.

"What's she want?" The chief sat at his desk, reviewing a new anti-prostitution ordinance for the consideration of the Phoenix city council.

"She said her name is 'Susan Hayward' and that she's a friend of Detective Ramses," Charlene tiredly replied. "This is about the umpteenth time. She's probably just some nut case who wants to tell you about the mysterious floating lights she's seen hovering over her trailer park."

Golden looked up, startled. "She knows Ramses?"

"That's what she said."

"Where's she live?"

"I tried to get her address but she refused to give it."

"How old did she sound?"

Charlene looked perplexed. "I don't know. Not that old, I guess. Hard to say."

Golden scrutinized the telephone message, which had a local area code. "Did she say exactly what she wanted?"

"Only that she wanted to talk to you, and *only* you. She wouldn't leave a message other than her call-back number." Charlene pointed to the slip of paper clasped between Golden's fingers.

The chief had been out of his office most of the last few days. Aside from having to attend multiple city council meetings, he'd been busy discretely trying to get more information about Ramses' purported trysts with the US Attorney. His efforts proved unavailing. Awaiting him when he finally returned to his office were multiple messages from 'Susan Hayward', as well as calls from Larry McKeever. Golden really didn't feel like talking to the medical examiner right now, so he put McKeever's messages aside without looking at them. His immediate priority was to figure out who 'Susan Hayward' was. And, more to the point, what she wanted.

SEVENTEEN

The coroner's secretary opened the sliding glass window that separated her office from the waiting area.

"I'm going to lunch and have to lock the office up," she announced. Pruitt and Saturday had been there more than two hours. During that period, she could tell from the lights that blinked on her office phone that the medical examiner had placed several calls, though she had no idea to whom. She felt terrible that he remained trapped in his office while these two lazy-ass turds sat on their butts, reading magazines and relaxing. What if Dr. McKeever had to use the bathroom?

Saturday looked up from a copy of 'National Geographic.' "If you lock the office up, what do they do with the bodies that come in while you're eating lunch? Leave 'em on the curb?"

She looked at him patronizingly. "I don't lock up the entire building. Just Dr. McKeever's office. The building itself is open 24 hours. By law, someone always has to be here to receive bodies."

Pruitt tossed his magazine onto a table. "Well, I guess if McKeever isn't man enough to come out and talk to us, we'll be going."

"I told you, Dr. McKeever isn't here," she reiterated.

"Yeah," said Pruitt, "I know what you told me. When he emerges from his office, you may want to tell him that next time we come, it'll be with an arrest warrant. If he wants to make things easier on himself, have him call me. He's got my number."

Saying nothing further, the two detectives rose and departed. As soon as they exited the office, she rose from her chair, raced across the waiting area, and locked the door behind them. She then returned to her office and quietly knocked on the adjoining office door. Opening it slightly, she poked her head in. McKeever was sitting at his desk.

"They're gone."

The coroner looked as though he was approaching utter collapse.

"Did Chief Golden call?" he managed to croak.

"Nobody called," she said. She fully opened the door and stepped across the threshold into McKeever's office. "Everybody except those two jerks thinks you're out of the office."

He nervously massaged his forehead with his fingertips. "I thought they'd never leave."

"*You?* I've been sitting out there for the past two hours with 'em. I thought that one guy was gonna barge his way back here!"

McKeever smiled ruefully. "Thanks for running interference for me."

She sat on the edge of the leather couch.

"Look, Dr. McKeever, I don't know what any of this is about, and I know it's none of my business. But whatever it is, it has nothing to do with you. I think you should maybe talk to those guys. They said they're coming back to arrest you next time."

"I don't know what it's about either," he lied. "Maybe I should hire a lawyer." He looked at her imploringly.

"Only guilty people hire lawyers," she declared. "Why do you need a lawyer? You just need to talk to those guys and find out what the heck they want. Look at you! You're a nervous wreck!"

"So Chief Golden didn't call?" he asked again, hoping for a different answer the second time around. McKeever had placed three calls to the chief while imprisoned in his office.

She shook her head. "No. I wish somebody had; it would have broken the monotony of having to stare at those two idiots."

McKeever was dismayed and angry in equal measure. He'd left detailed, if hushed, messages about his predicament, but Golden apparently couldn't be bothered to return his calls. This is bullshit!

"So, what are you gonna do, Dr. McKeever. I don't think those guys are going away."

"I don't know, I don't know," he muttered, more to himself that to her. "Go ahead and go to lunch; let me know if you still see them hanging around outside or in the parking lot. And make sure to lock your door when you leave."

She nodded and backed out of his office, softly shutting the door behind her. McKeever sat at his desk, closed his eyes, and rested his head in his hands. He was trembling uncontrollably.

***

Chief Golden learned there were more than three dozen 'Susan Haywards' in Phoenix, ranging from infants to old ladies. He figured Ramses wouldn't have been screwing the former or the latter, but wasn't entirely convinced of that, either. Besides, that scarcely narrowed the field. Although dubious, he decided the only way to get to the bottom of it was simply to return her call. He reluctantly removed the receiver of his desk telephone from its cradle and slowly dialed the number.

"This is Susan," said a dulcet recorded voice. "Don't be shy; leave a message and I'll call you back."

"This is Chief Robert Golden of the Phoenix Police Department returning your call," the chief officiously stated in his gruffest voice. He provided only his private cell number before terminating the call. Done.

He was torn whether he wanted Susan Hayward, whoever she was, to return his call.

***

"Do you know someone named 'Susan Hayward'?" Having returned from lunch, McKeever's secretary retrieved the single telephone message that had been left during her absence.

"Susan Hayward was an old actress," McKeever wearily informed her. He was sick of talking to people, sick of being harassed.

"Well, whoever she is or was, she called while I was at lunch and said that she wants to talk to you about the John Doe killed in the restaurant robbery."

"What about him?"

"She didn't say. Her message just said that she wanted to talk to you."

Shit. Golden wouldn't return his calls and now he had some stranger calling him out of the fucking blue about Rosey. What was he supposed to do now? "She didn't say anything else?"

"Only that she wanted to talk to you."

McKeever felt like vomiting.

"What's her number?" he sighed. She handed him the written telephone message; he glanced at it but didn't recognize the number. "Are those two cops still hanging around?"

"If they are, I didn't see 'em," she assured him.

The coroner looked at the telephone message again. "Do you suppose 'Susan Hayward' is working with them?" he speculated.

"I have no idea, Dr. McKeever, "but there's one way to find out. Maybe she has information about the John Doe that'll get those guys off your butt. In fact, she may even know why they're harassing you."

McKeever nodded. "Yeah, I guess I should call her back," he said without conviction.

"Look, John Doe can't stay in the back, frozen, indefinitely. If she really has information about who he is, you need to pursue it, especially if it'll convince those two cops to back off."

"Yeah, you're right." Since he already knew the identity of the body in his freezer, McKeever wasn't sanguine about whatever additional intelligence Susan Hayward purportedly possessed. He handed the message back to his secretary. "Call her back and beep me when you get her on the line," he directed.

"Okie dokie," she smiled. "I feel good about this, Dr. McKeever. I watch those forensic shows on TV. It's unexpected breaks like this that lead to solving crimes."

McKeever watched her as she exited his office. He hoped she was wrong.

At her desk, the secretary punched in the number from the telephone message pad. After four rings a live female voice answered.

"This is Susan. Who's this?"

"Hello, this is the office of Medical Examiner Dr. Lawrence McKeever," she said, smoothly, "returning your call from earlier today."

"Oh, yeah," said the voice. It was impossible to ascertain her age, though she sounded relatively young. "I have information about a body you have down there. I know who it is."

"May I have your address, please?"

"No, you may not. Are you the coroner? If not, let me talk to the coroner," the female voice imperiously demanded.

McKeever's secretary was not unaccustomed to dealing with cranks over the phone. "Hold on, please, and I'll see whether Dr. McKeever is available.

"If you don't know if he's available, why are you even calling me?"

"Hold please." She pushed the 'hold' button and beeped McKeever. "Susan Hayward's on line one."

"Okay, got it," he said with a dearth of enthusiasm. McKeever cleared his throat, hesitated, then punched the appropriate button. "This is Dr. McKeever."

"Are you the coroner?" asked a skeptical female voice.

"I'm the medical examiner, yes. How can I help you?"

"Well, Mr. Medical Examiner, it's not so much a question of your helpin' me, as much me helpin' you."

"How do you mean?"

"I mean I know who the guy is you've got laying on the slab down there, the guy that tried to knock over that old man's restaurant. I know who he is. I also know that he wasn't there to rob the old man."

"I'm just the medical examiner. Why don't you go to the police with whatever information you have?"

"Yeah, I could do that, I suppose. Is that what you really want me to do, Mr. Medical Examiner?"

"Well, that's what the police are for, aren't they?" McKeever stumbled and bumbled. "Like I said, I'm just the medical examiner."

"Suit yourself. I just figured you and me might could do some business, just between us two girls. But if you'd feel better about bringin' the cops in..." Her voice trailed off.

"No, wait!" McKeever blurted, thinking of Pruitt and Saturday. He paused. "Do I know you?"

"Yeah, maybe you saw that movie I was in, 'I Wanna Live.' That's me, I wanna live."

"Are we talking about money?"

"I don't know what you're talkin' about, but I'm talkin' about a dead guy you've got on ice. Nobody said anything about money."

McKeever was growing anxious and impatient. "So, what do you want?"

"I want to talk."

"We're talking now, aren't we?"

"No, I want to talk face-to-face. I like to see who I'm talking to. But if you don't want to talk, I'll take your advice and just call the cops. I know *they* like to talk."

"Now hang on," McKeever cautioned. He didn't like the way conversation was headed. "Do you work for the police?"

"If I worked for the police, don't you think I'd already have talked to them? For an educated guy, you're not too smart."

"Well, this is all new to me," McKeever conceded.

"What's new to you, Mr. Medical Examiner? Pretending that you don't know who the dead people laying on your slab really are?" The voice paused. "Don't worry, we'll meet in a public place. Unlike your friends on the police department, I don't intend to kill you. Your bein' dead wouldn't help me one bit."

"When?"

"I'll call you back. My driver will pick you up and bring you here."

McKeever was dubious. "If it's a public place, why don't we meet somewhere that we both agree on?"

"Because I don't trust you. You'll tell your cop buddies and that'll be that."

"You don't trust me, but I'm supposed to trust you?"

"I don't care if you trust me or not. We're not getting married, we're just gonna talk. That's the deal. Take or leave it."

McKeever thought quickly. He had no idea who Susan Hayward was, nor whether she was a crackpot, a police informer, or just an ordinary criminal.

"You have a driver, you said?"

"Yeah. Like I said, you don't have to worry. I promise you'll be perfectly safe and you'll be home in time for dinner with Mrs. Medical Examiner."

What choice did he have? Golden wasn't returning his calls and those two bastards from IA were bullying him. For all McKeever knew, his was the next name on Sunstone's hit list. Maybe the enigmatic Susan Hayward's appearance was providential.

"I'll meet, provided you give me your word that I'll not be harmed."

"I can't speak for your good friends in the police department, but I promise that I have no intentions of hurting you. Like I said, I just want to talk and I can't talk to a dead man."

"Okay, call me back when you want to meet."

"I will." The call abruptly ended. The telephone receiver was slick with his perspiration as McKeever returned it to its base. His secretary saw his light wink off on her phone and poked her head in his office.

"Everything okay?"

"I really don't know," he said. "I guess so. Turns out, she didn't know anything about our John Doe."

"You were on the phone a long time."

McKeever smiled wanly. "She wanted to talk."

***

"You the police chief?" Golden already didn't like the tone of the female caller.

"This is Chief Robert Golden of the Phoenix Police Department. Who is this?" he barked. Susan

Hayward returned his telephone call three hours after he left it. He was idling at a red light in his city-issued Cadillac when his cell phone buzzed.

"I already told you who I am. Now I'm gonna tell you something else. Detective Ramses told me all about your little arrangement with him and all the rest of your merry band of cocksuckers."

The light switched to green and Golden punched the accelerator, rocketing through the intersection. He was driving west; the burning orb of the setting sun appeared to rest, exhausted, on the hood of his ATS Coupe, searing through the polarized lenses of his dark glasses.

"I don't know what you're talking about."

"No? That's funny because, before you killed him, Ramses told me the feds down at the US attorney's office know plenty. How come you're the fucking chief of police and you don't know anything? Explain that to me."

"Listen, I don't know who the fuck you think you are, but attempted extortion is a criminal offence, you piece of shit." Golden hoped he sounded intimidating.

"Who's talking about extortion? Don't get your panties in a wad, chief."

Golden flicked the air conditioner up another notch. "You think you're the first scumbag that's ever threatened me? Go fuck yourself, asswipe."

"Relax, chief, nobody's threatening anybody. We're just having a nice chat, that's all. If you don't feel like chatting, I'll just gather my marbles and head down to the US attorney. From what I hear, they're good listeners and don't get so worked up over shit."

She paused. "Then again, that's probably because they're not ass-deep in it."

Golden was trying to figure out the point of their conversation.

"So, why'd you call me?"

"I think you and I should sit down for a confab."

"About what?"

"I have something I think you'll wanna hear."

"What?"

"I don't want to spoil the surprise. I'll give you a hint, though. It's about Detective Ramses."

Goddamn it! It fucking figures.

"I don't give a crap about what you claim to have. I'll ask Detective Ramses about it when he gets back. Better yet, you can ask him."

"'Gets back'? From the grave? I don't see that happening. But if you're not interested, I completely understand. I'll quit wasting your time and run it past the US attorney."

"If you're so interested in my hearing it, why don't you just send it to me, like you did the DVD?" Golden wheeled the Cadillac into a restaurant parking lot and pulled into the shade on the east end of the building. Putting the transmission in 'Park,' he allowed the engine to idle while the air conditioning blasted over him.

Katrina was genuinely puzzled. "DVD? I didn't send you a DVD. It must have been one of your other admirers."

Now it was Golden's turn to be confused. "You didn't mail me a DVD about two weeks ago?"

"No."

Sonofabitch! Who the hell are all these people coming out of the woodwork? For all the chief knew, Susan Hayward was working for Mr. Julius, a plant intended to sabotage him. Sunstone was no stranger to such subterfuge.

"So, mail me whatever you have, anyway."

"No. I want to be there when you hear it."

"Then bring it to my office," Golden urged, already knowing how his suggestion would be received.

"I've got a better idea. You come to me. We'll have a little pow wow. Feel free to bring your gun, or whatever you want, but you'll be perfectly safe."

"Where are you?"

"I'll send a car for you."

"A car?" Maybe Susan Hayward wasn't the low-life trash that Golden imagined her to be. He was impressed that Ramses was apparently fucking a woman who could command a car to pick him up. "You mean a cab?"

"Did I say 'a cab'?"

Golden ignored the question. "When do you want to meet?"

"I'll call you. Don't be a smartass and run a trace on this number, because I'll use a different cell phone next time."

"So, I'm just supposed to wait around until you decide to call me again?"

"Pretty much. It'll only be a day or two. You gotta hot date, or something?"

"No, I'm just wondering how long your little game is going to last."

"Game? That's an interesting choice of words, coming from you, Chief." Katrina ended the call.

***

The dark maroon Lincoln Town Car pulled into the no parking/standing/idling zone in front of Phoenix Police Headquarters on Washington Street. Its tinted windows were nearly opaque, preventing Golden from seeing the interior. The uniformed driver who emerged from the vehicle to hold open the rear passenger's door was a young female.

Golden knew that his rendezvous with Susan Hayward was perilous. If she was a common blackmailer, he'd once again probably have to contact Mr. Julius, which he was loath to do. On the other hand, she may simply be bullshitting, or nothing more than a nickel-and-dime crook. Under the circumstances, it appeared the only way to determine how to deal with Susan Hayward was to indulge her demand for a personal meeting. The chief could then size her up and determine the best way of dealing with her, ideally without getting Sunstone involved. Even so, he was uneasy about getting into a vehicle en route to an undisclosed destination to meet an anonymous woman for an unknown purpose. As a precaution, Golden had earlier tabbed two Phoenix detectives to unobtrusively tail, in a nondescript car, whatever vehicle picked him up that evening, explaining that it was part of a confidential sting operation. They were instructed not to interfere or intervene in any way, merely to follow. The driver of the Town Car neither spoke nor establish eye contact with him.

Golden slowly approached the Lincoln. Looking across its roof, he could see the two detectives in a white Dodge parallel parked on the other side of Washington Street.   He bent and entered the Town Car.

Medical Examiner McKeever was already a passenger.

"For Christ's sake, what are you doing here?" the startled chief cried. He slid onto the seat and swung the heavy door shut.

"You got a call from her, too?" McKeever responded as the Lincoln pulled away from the curb and entered the stream of traffic.

"Susan Hayward?"

"Yeah."

"Well, I'm, here aren't I?" Golden sourly replied.

McKeever lowered his voice, though the driver seemed to pay no attention to them. "What did she tell you?"

"Hey, where are we going?" Golden asked the back of Carol's head. She didn't answer. He turned to glance out the vehicle's heavily-tinted rear window. The detectives' Dodge was nowhere to be seen among the cars behind them, but that was a good thing.

"What did she say to you?" McKeever repeated.

"Nothing, just that she wanted to see me."

"Do you know who she is?" whispered McKeever.

"Larry, I know exactly as much as you know. I got a call from a woman who said that she wanted to talk," the chief crossly hissed. "Beyond that, I have no idea."

"Do you know what she wants?"

Golden ignored him.

Silence prevailed in the Lincoln as they headed west on Washington Street.   At Interstate 10, the taciturn driver headed north then, after a couple of miles, exited the freeway east onto Van Buren Street.

They were now heading back toward downtown, albeit slightly north of police headquarters. Golden periodically looked behind them in an effort to identify the trailing Dodge, but was unable to spot it. The fact that the windows were tinted nearly black didn't help, although it kept the interior of vehicle marvelously cool. The Town Car's driver made no apparent effort to elude possible tails, so the detectives would have no difficulty following them, irrespective of their location in the stream of late afternoon traffic.

After a half-dozen additional turns, the Lincoln finally slowed to a stop before a decrepit structure on Lincoln Street. To the passengers in the rear seat, it looked like it was liable to collapse at any minute. It was impossible to ascertain whether it was a functioning business or simply an abandoned building.

"You're here," Carol stated. She didn't budge from her seat. The two men looked at one another before wordlessly grasping their respective door handles, opening their doors, and stepping out onto the cracked asphalt. The withering heat almost took their breath away.

Golden slammed his door shut and glanced around, looking for the white Dodge. It was nowhere to be seen, but that didn't surprise him; a nice, clean car in this shitty neighborhood would stick out like a turd in a punch bowl. The detectives had undoubtedly parked a block or more away, though close enough to keep an eye on developments. The Town Car pulled away, leaving the two men standing in front of the dilapidated building.

"Well, I guess this is it," McKeever nervously gulped.

"Yeah, I guess," the chief said. They approached its weathered door and Golden pulled it open.

EIGHTEEN

The interior of Katrina's was dark and cramped and stale. Standing at the threshold between the sunlit street and the dingy interior, Golden and McKeever found it impossible for their eyes to adapt to the contrast.

"C'mon in." Katrina's strangely pleasing voice drifted from the void. "How was the ride over? Nice car, huh?" The two remained silhouetted in the doorway. "C'mon, don't be bashful," she invited.

Goldman and McKeever stepped slightly farther into the room, letting the door swing shut behind them. In the half-light they were able to vaguely see a pool table in the center of the floor and, to their immediate right, an unattended bar with a few half-empty liquor bottles on a shelf behind it. They were unable to ascertain the precise location of their hostess, nor could they determine in the gloom whether there were any other people present.

"Back here," said Katrina. "Keep coming."

The two men stepped tentatively forward into the semi-darkness, Golden reassured by the weight of the Kahr 9mm pistol tucked in his waistband holster.

They skirted the pool table and, beyond it, the dim form of a corpulent creature sitting in a booth emerged from the murkiness.

"Susan Hayward?" asked Golden.

"You can call me 'Katrina,'" she said. "Sit down, gentlemen, though I use the term loosely."

Susan Hayward/Katrina initially appeared to be totally nude, but Golden concluded that she was wearing a flesh-toned negligee of some sort. He could tell that the hair piled on her massive head was bleach-blonde but, beyond that, could see little.

"Who else is here?" Golden asked.

"There's some guys back there," Katrina indicated by bobbing her head, "but they're regulars. Don't worry about them."

Golden looked where she indicated and discerned in the far corner a booth that seemed to be occupied by three men. Unable to see their faces, the men were hunched forward, engaged in murmured conversation. They appeared oblivious to the newcomers. Golden nodded and pointed to the booth, indicating that McKeever should slide in first. The coroner reluctantly complied.

The chief sat directly across from Katrina. "So why are we here?" he asked.

"Which one of you is which?"

"I'm Chief Golden and he's Dr. Lawrence McKeever," Golden told her.

"Hmmmmm...well, you're actually the one I wanted to see," Katrina revealed. "I wanted you to hear what kind of riffraff you've got working for you in the police department." She paused. "Wait a minute, *you* work for the department, too! I just brought the doc along so he could provide some details that I'm still a little fuzzy about."

"What the hell are you talking about?" Golden snapped.   "You're pretty ballsy, threatening to blackmail us, bringing us to this dump.   What's to keep me from just arresting you, here and now?"

"For Christ's sake, Bob, cut it out!"   McKeever blurted. "Let's hear what she has to say!"

"Shut the hell up," Golden told him. "I'm fed up with your being such a pussy." He glanced toward the other occupied booth but the men hadn't budged. He wasn't sure they even heard him.

Katrina appeared unruffled.

"You won't arrest me until you hear why I brought you here. After that, you can arrest me if you want." Golden raised his eyebrows expectantly, so she continued. "Detective Ramses used to come in here a lot. He was a tit-man and I've got great tits." She leaned back in order to display her ample bust beneath her negligee.

"So?"

"So, me and the detective got pretty tight. He used to tell me about all kinds of shit that he was involved in with the Phoenix PD: shakedowns, protection, extortion, even murder." Katrina hoped that Golden found plausible the yarn she was spinning.

"Bullshit. Neither Ramses, nor the Phoenix PD, is involved in any of that. You're a liar."

Katrina shrugged. "I'm just passing along what Ramses told me. Don't shoot the messenger."

"Then *he's* a liar," said Golden. He was beginning to feel slightly more at ease. If this fairy tale was the only reason this fat cunt brought them here, he clearly didn't have anything to worry about. She was just another piece-of-shit criminal trying to scam the system.

"Maybe," Katrina continued, "but he named a lot of names. Even yours."

"That's a fucking joke. *You're* a fucking joke!" Golden snorted. McKeever simply listened, though his heart was pounding and he feared he might faint.

"Well, I don't expect you to take my word for it," said Katrina. "Here, listen to the man himself."

She reached down a flabby arm and retrieved a tiny cassette recorder from the seat beside her. Plopping it on the table between them, Katrina clicked the 'play' button. The spindle began to slowly rotate and, moments later, a voice emerged.

"Here's what I know," said Ramses' voice, "Alto tipped me off that Dawson was gonna be at the depot. Alto's an informant and has a habit of vaporizing. The only way I'll hear from Alto is if I use a Ouija board. Like I said, both the arson and murder have got to do with me. My job was Rosedea's murder. We already established that. It ain't Rosedea whose head Dawson blew off months ago. Rosedea ain't been dead for months; he's been out drivin' an Escalade. I outta know. Ask Rosedea's family."

Katrina clicked the recorder off and returned it to the seat beside her.

"Ramses was pretty much in his cups when he recorded that," she said. "That's why it sounds kinda disjointed. But you get the idea. And that's just a sample; there's lots more on the tape. You scalawags have your fingers in a lot of pies."

The recording was culled from Pruitt's and Saturday's previous interviews with Ramses. They merely redacted and juxtaposed some of his statements, but it was indisputably Ramses' voice on the tape.

Golden's initial insouciance instantly disappeared. It was one thing for a fat bitch with zero credibility who ran a broken-down bar to make outlandish allegations against the Phoenix PD, but it was quite another for its own Chief of Detectives to make criminal admissions. Katrina's tape was catastrophic. It would absolutely prompt a legitimate investigation and, even if Golden didn't end up in prison, Sunstone would undoubtedly kill him because of his repeated blunders. Either way, he was fucked. He had to bury that tape.

"Give me that fucking tape, you fat cunt," Golden barked, rising to his feet.

"Jesus!" McKeever cried.

Golden yanked his pistol from its holster. He leaned toward Katrina and pointed it directly at her face. "I will fucking kill you," he said.

"Stop, stop!" McKeever shrieked. "Bob, are you crazy?"

"Fuck you, Larry! Sit down! I am not kidding you," he growled at Katrina, "give me the mother fucking tape."

She appeared unperturbed. "Sure, I got no problem with that. No need to get excited." She slowly retrieved the cassette recorder and placed it back on the table. Golden's pistol never wavered from her face. "See? Help yourself."

At that moment Saturday hurled himself into the chief, hurtling Golden's body into the pool table. His pistol clattered across the floor.

"Oh no!" howled McKeever. "Oh no!" He tried to duck beneath the booth but, because Katrina's bulk blocked his way, could only hunker down on the seat.

Golden fought savagely to free himself from Saturday's grip but Pruitt quickly joined his partner to subdue the chief. Jim hastened to Katrina's table, where she watched with interest as Golden thrashed about on the floor. McKeever continued to cower on the seat beside her, whimpering.

"You okay?" Jim anxiously asked her.

"I'm fabulous," she replied. "But I'm glad you ladies were paying attention."

NINETEEN

It all came out:　Golden, Ramses, McKeever, Rosey, Earl Welch, Councilman Garcia, Councilman Bulfinch, all of it.　McKeever was the first to talk, but when they rounded up Welch and Garcia, they promptly pitched their lot with the medical examiner. Golden refused to break, but the evidence against him was overwhelming and rendered his cooperation superfluous.　The chief, alone, had direct knowledge of Mr. Julius, Red, and Doc, and he wasn't talking.　If he did, he'd end up dead, even in prison. Sunstone's reach and influence remained unfettered, notwithstanding the present, regrettable bump in the road.

The indictments issued against the defendants were lengthy and included multiple counts of fraud, money laundering, racketeering, conspiracy, kidnapping, and murder. Attorney General Butler had a heyday, of course.　He immediately scheduled a press conference, where he broke the news of the sweeping bust and trumpeted the success of his task force. His election as governor was assured. Bickman just about puked.

"That must've pretty damned exciting!" Carol declared over her chicken salad sandwich at Jim's restaurant. "I was so nervous that I just about peed my pants, and all I did was drive 'em to Katrina's."

"I wish I'd been there," Harvey said. "It sounds like an episode from 'Mission Impossible.'"

"It was something," Jim acknowledged. "I ain't never done anything like that afore and don't wanna do it again. Me and Pruitt and Saturday sat in a booth across the room from 'em. We couldn't hear exactly what they was sayin', but we kept an eye on 'em. When Katrina played that tape that we doctored, damned if the police chief didn't jump to his feet and poke his gun in her face! I thought for sure he was gonna shoot her, right then and there!"

"Good thing those cops were quick on their feet," Harvey affirmed.

"How's Katrina doin'?" asked Carol.

"She doin' good," Jim said. "I don't think that, if the devil hisself showed up, Katrina would bat an eye. She wasn't scared or upset or nuthin'!"

"What happened after they arrested Golden? He must've been pretty pissed off," Carol remarked with remarkable understatement.

Jim laughed out loud, displaying his beautiful teeth. "He was mad, all right. When Saturday hauled him to his feet, he looked like five miles of bad road, his clothes was messed up, his face was bruised, and he looked like a pig sty. Lordy, it was something to see!" he exclaimed.

"So, what'd they do with him?"

"Pruitt got on his walkie-talkie and asked 'em to send a police car to Katrina's and, about two seconds later, one pulls up right in front! Turns out, it was parked just down the block 'cause the chief ordered it to follow him and keep an eye on things. So, the cops that was supposed to be protectin' him ended up cartin' him to jail!"

Harvey grinned. "Amazing. You were just like a secret agent, Jim."

"So, what do you think will happen now?" Carol quietly asked, after a moment.

Jim sipped his coffee. "I reckon a bunch of 'em will go to jail. Hope so, anyway."

"And what about the cop that shot Jerry? Will he go to jail, too?"

Jim gazed at her sorrowfully. "The cop that shot Jerry didn't mean to do it, Carol. He thought he was doin' the right thing because his bosses lied to him. They're the ones that really killed Jerry, and they're gonna go to jail for it. That cop knows he did wrong and will have to live with what he done for the rest of his life. It ain't right or fair, but it's all we got. The Lord knows what was in his heart, and so does Jerry." The old man grasped Carol's hand as tears welled up in his eyes.

"What are you gonna do, Jim, now that the excitement is over?" Harvey inquired, trying to lighten the mood.

"I guess I'll just keep makin' fried egg sandwiches for you, Harvey. I got nuthin' better to do, unless you found a better place to eat."

"Hell, no, I haven't!" he protested. "You know better than that. And if you want to stay at my place, bring your stuff and move in. I kinda like the idea of livin' with a celebrity."

Jim smiled. It was good to be home.

***

The only sounds in the room were Jim's shallow breathing and the soft beep of the electronic monitor at his bedside. Lying in the hospital, sleeping, he looked very old and frail. Four days of white beard covered his chin. Carol sat at Jim's bedside, holding his rough, calloused hand.

The stroke occurred two days after the defendants entered guilty pleas to multiple criminal charges. The only holdout was Golden, who insisted on going to trial, defiantly asserting his innocence and vowing that he would be vindicated. Harvey found Jim lying on the floor of the restaurant's kitchen when he stopped in for his customary lunch. At first, he thought Jim may have experienced a heart attack or had fallen and hit his head; it was only at the hospital that they learned he'd suffered a debilitating stroke.

Jim suddenly gasped in his sleep and his eyes flickered open. Unable to lift his head, Jim's eyes darted about the room wildly, fearfully.

"Hey, it's okay...I'm here," Carol softly comforted him, gently squeezing the old man's hand. She reached forward and lovingly stroked his cheek. "Can you hear me, Jim?"

The old man slowly turned his head toward her to focus on Carol's face. He parted his lips slightly in an effort to speak; the stroke contorted his mouth.

"Hi," he managed to whisper.

"Hi," she smiled, tears running down her cheeks. "You had a stroke, you're in the hospital."

Jim tried to smile, tried to nod, but couldn't.

"You're gonna be okay, Jim," Carol said, because she didn't know what else to say.

"I know," he acknowledged in a whisper.

"We finally got justice, Jim. The bastards pleaded guilty. Can you remember?"

Jim tried to shake his head. "There's no justice, Carol. There's just us." He struggled to smile at his unintentional pun, but his face was paralyzed by the stroke. Jim closed his eyes.

"I'm tired," he whispered. "Tired... I think I'll go see Lorraine now. Jerry, too." A slight shudder passed through his body and Jim slowly exhaled for the last time.

Carol pushed the nurse's call button, laid her head on the old man's shoulder, and wept.

The End

TERMS OF USE

This is a copyrighted work and WF Waldrip and his licensors reserve all rights in and to the work. Use of this work is subject to these terms. Except as permitted under the Copyright Act of 1976 and the right to store and retrieve one copy of the work, you may not decompile, disassemble, reverse engineer, reproduce, modify, create derivative works based upon, transmit, distribute, disseminate, sell, publish or sublicense the work or any part of it without WF Waldrip's prior consent. You may use the work for your own noncommercial and personal use; any other use of the work is strictly prohibited. Your right to use the work may be terminated if you fail to comply with these terms.

THE WORK IS PROVIDED "AS IS." WF WALDRIP AND ITS LICENSORS MAKE NO GUARANTEES OR WARRANTIES AS TO THE ACCURACY, ADEQUACY OR COMPLETENESS OF OR RESULTS TO BE OBTAINED FROM USING THE WORK, INCLUDING ANY INFORMATION THAT CAN BE ACCESSED THROUGH THE WORK VIA HYPERLINK OR OTHERWISE, AND EXPRESSLY DISCLAIM ANY WARRANTY, EXPRESS OR IMPLIED, INCLUDING BUT NOT LIMITED TO IMPLIED WARRANTIES OF MERCHANTABILITY OR FITNESS FOR A PARTICULAR PURPOSE.

WF Waldrip and his licensors do not warrant or guarantee that the functions contained in the work will meet your requirements or that its operation will be uninterrupted or error free. Neither WF Waldrip nor his licensors shall be liable to you or anyone else for any inaccuracy, error or omission, regardless of cause, in the work or for any damages resulting therefrom. WF Waldrip has no responsibility for the content of any information accessed through the work. Under no circumstances shall WF Waldrip and/or his licensors be liable for any indirect, incidental, special, punitive, consequential or similar damages that result from the use of or inability to use the work, even if any of them has been advised of the possibility of such damages. This limitation of liability shall apply to any claim or cause whatsoever whether such claim or cause arises in contract, tort or otherwise.

The author gratefully acknowledges the copyrighted or trademarked status and trademark owners of the following mentioned in this work of fiction: BMW, Buick, Bunn, Cadillac ATS, Cadillac Escalade, Chevrolet Caprice, Coke, Dairy Queen, Dancing With the Stars, Denny's, Diet Coke, Dockers, Dodge, eBay, Ford Crown Victoria, Glock, GM, Hilton, Interpol, Kahr, Lincoln Town Car, Man With No Name, Memorex, Mission Impossible, National Geographic, Nissan, Ouija, Oxford English Dictionary, Pepsi, Plexiglas, Plymouth, Pop Tarts, Ray Ban, Sam's Club, Southwest Airlines, Styrofoam, Sunny Delight, The Bachelorette, Walther PPK.

Also available from

WF Waldrip

⭐⭐⭐⭐⭐ **great novel!**

What a wonderful novel! The author drew very vivid pictures of the characters and events. What a riveting book! A fascinating read !

Published on June 3, 2014 by Vincent R. Mayr

Find more at www.amazon.com

Also available from

WF Waldrip

☆☆☆☆☆ **A must read,**
December 31, 2018
Format: Paperback

Great book! A fast read that kept me
interested through the very end. Highly recommend!!

Find more at www.amazon.com

Also available from

WF Waldrip

⭐⭐⭐⭐⭐ **Steven King can relax**
By Doug T. on March 14, 2018
Format: Paperback   Verified Purchase

Steven King can rest easy and retire knowing Wade Waldrip can carry the torch and scare the wits out of people.

Find more at www.amazon.com

ABOUT THE AUTHOR

WF WALDRIP is a widely traveled author,
and Arizona native.

His writing style is true to life,
bypassing the 'Politically Correct."

www.ingramcontent.com/pod-product-compliance
Lightning Source LLC
Chambersburg PA
CBHW062014170626
46813CB00001B/151